BABY, I'M HOWLING FOR YOU

Christine Warren

St. Martin's Paperbacks

NOTE: If you purchased this book without a cover you should be aware that this book is stolen property. It was reported as "unsold and destroyed" to the publisher, and neither the author nor the publisher has received any payment for this "stripped book."

This is a work of fiction. All of the characters, organizations, and events portrayed in this novel are either products of the author's imagination or are used fictitiously.

BABY, I'M HOWLING FOR YOU

Copyright © 2018 by Christine Warren.

All rights reserved.

For information address St. Martin's Press, 175 Fifth Avenue, New York, NY 10010.

ISBN: 978-1-250-12072-4

Our books may be purchased in bulk for promotional, educational, or business use. Please contact your local bookseller or the Macmillan Corporate and Premium Sales Department at 1-800-221-7945, ext. 5442, or by e-mail at MacmillanSpecialMarkets@macmillan.com.

Printed in the United States of America

St. Martin's Paperbacks edition / February 2018

St. Martin's Paperbacks are published by St. Martin's Press, 175 Fifth Avenue, New York, NY 10010.

10 9 8 7 6 5 4 3 2 1

Also by
Christine Warren

The Gargoyles series
Hard Breaker
Hard to Handle
Hard as a Rock
Stone Cold Lover
Heart of Stone

The Others series
Hungry Like a Wolf
Drive Me Wild
On the Prowl
Not Your Ordinary Faerie Tale
Black Magic Woman
Prince Charming Doesn't Live Here
Born to Be Wild
Big Bad Wolf
You're So Vein
One Bite with a Stranger
Walk on the Wild Side
Howl at the Moon
The Demon You Know
She's No Faerie Princess
Wolf at the Door

Anthologies
Huntress
No Rest for the Witches

Praise for *New York Times* bestselling author
CHRISTINE WARREN

The Gargoyles series

"Hot . . . a steamy success."
—*RT Book Reviews* (4 stars) on *Heart of Stone*

"Soars with fun, witty characters and nonstop action."
—*Publishers Weekly* on *Stone Cold Lover*

"Fiery, fierce, and fun."
—*Publishers Weekly* on *Hard as a Rock*

The Others series

"Sizzling sex and off-the-wall adventure."
—*RT Book Reviews* on *Drive Me Wild*

"An incredible, alluring world . . . Christine Warren continues to dazzle our senses with her books of the Others."
—*Single Titles*

"Warren has made a name for herself in the world of paranormal romance. She expertly mixes werewolves, vampires, and faeries to create another winning novel in The Others series."
—*RT Book Reviews* on *Not Your Ordinary Faerie Tale*

"Excitement, passion, mystery . . . characters who thoroughly captivate."
—*Romance Reviews Today*

"Warren packs in lots of action and sexy sizzle."
—*RT Book Reviews* on *Born to Be Wild*

"Warren takes readers for a wild ride."
—*Night Owl Romance*

"Five stars. This is an exciting, sexy book."
—*Affaire de Coeur* on *You're So Vein*

Chapter One

The valiant old Nissan ran out of gas thirteen miles short of her destination. Renny would ponder the irony of that number some other time. Right now, she needed to run, and run fast.

She jumped from the car the minute it stopped moving, abandoning the vehicle on the shoulder of the two-lane highway. Before she reached the tree line, she was already tearing off her shirt, ignoring the chilly bite of the pre-spring March air. She threw the garment aside and immediately reached for the button of her jeans. She continued to hop forward as she struggled out of the confining denim, but the minute that last restriction fell away, she shifted.

Fur replaced skin, arms became forelegs. Between desperate breaths, humanity slid away, and in the place of the panicked woman, a sleek red wolf began to weave through the trunks of the trees.

Her claws dug through the lingering patches of wet, heavy snow and soft leaf litter to the soil of the forest floor, flinging small clumps of mud into the air in her wake. She needed to put as much distance as she could between herself and her pursuers. She might not have seen them on her tail from the highway, but it wouldn't take much longer. They were the reason she hadn't been able to stop for gas for the last couple of hours. They'd already chased her across two state lines and more than five hundred miles, and that was just this time. Somehow, she couldn't picture them giving up now.

She didn't bother to think about what she'd left behind on the roadside. If the pack caught up to her, it wouldn't matter whether or not someone ransacked her car and stole all of her worldly possessions. She didn't think she'd need a good book or many changes of clothes in the afterlife.

If there was such a thing. Frankly, Renny wasn't all that anxious to find out.

Keeping her head down and her feet moving, she continued to track north and west from the roadside, calling up the map in her head to guide her in the right direction. The last road sign she'd seen had put the Snoqualmie Pass about twenty-five miles northwest by the highway. Heading directly north instead should put the town center of her destination somewhere in that thirteen-mile range, so she had to keep running. Just a little farther.

Alphaville, or die trying.

The town of Alpha, Washington, had shimmered like a mirage on her horizon for years now. As a pup, she'd heard stories—everyone heard stories—of the northwestern town founded and run by shifters as a haven for those of their kind with nowhere else to go. Wolves driven from their packs, bears with injuries and scars inflicted by careless hunters, lions who couldn't control their shifts, leopards who needed to change their spots—they all went to Alpha, and they all, eventually, got better.

Surely a town like that could provide a safe haven to one small wolf with a teensy-tiny little stalker problem. Right?

Please, Goddess, let her be right.

Renny's ears swiveled back and forth as she ran, their extra-large proportions helping to catch and funnel in the sounds of pursuit. And damn it, she thought she heard the first indications of it already. They'd found the car, and even if the muddy snow weren't perfect for holding tracks, they knew she would have fled into the forest. That was what wolves did, after all.

She poured on another burst of speed, paws barely seeming to skim the cold ground as she flew toward sanctuary. Or what she prayed was sanctuary, anyway. If she was wrong, she wouldn't live to regret it.

The first staccato bark confirmed her fears. One of her pursuers had picked up her scent trail and was alerting the others to the location. Now it was only a matter of time before they found her. All she could do was run and pray she made it to safety before they all caught up.

If just one came at her, she could handle it. In a fight between a lone wolf and a single coyote, the wolf almost always won, even a smaller and lighter red wolf like her. Which was why Geoffrey had sent five of them after her. No way could she beat those odds. Five trained male enforcers of any species against little ol' her? She'd need to be a polar bear to survive that.

Branches snapped behind her, urging Renny to move even faster. If the coyotes on her tail weren't worried about making noise, then they wouldn't bother choosing a clear path to follow her. They'd plow through anything to take the straightest line right to her. Clearly, her nemesis had instructed them not to mess around anymore.

A sharp yip of anticipation gave her a single instant of warning, and that will to survive made her dip her shoulder and twist into a sharp right turn. She dove into the underbrush, ignoring the clumps of snow that plopped onto her head and the way the thorns ripped through her thick fur to scrape at the skin beneath. She could warm up and lick her wounds later, when she was safe.

If she managed to save herself at all.

The unexpected maneuver may have gained her a few inches of distance between herself and the lead coyote, but that didn't last. She could feel the enforcers closing in again, harrying her as if she were some kind of prey animal, like a wounded deer on the way to becoming the pack's next meal.

The comparison fit way too close for comfort.

She tried to calculate how far she'd traveled in the last frantic minutes, but all she could do was guess. Running flat out, she could probably manage thirty-five miles an hour, but she couldn't keep it up for more than a few minutes. Already, burning muscles and oxygen-starved lungs begged her to drop down to something more reasonable. So where had her panicked flight left her in relation to shifter Shangri-la?

Not fricking close enough. If she was lucky, she'd covered eight of the thirteen miles between her and safety. Nine, if the Goddess happened to be looking out for her. It wasn't nearly enough.

Then something changed.

A new smell cut through the atmosphere of pine needles and wet soil, rocks and wildlife. Something heavier, muskier. Male. Wolfish. Alpha. The realization almost made her slide to a terrified halt.

Shit. She'd just stumbled into someone else's territory—another shifter's, by the scent of it—and that could be either good for her or very, very bad. A wolf shifter might take her side against a pack of coyote goons, or he might decide to kill her himself for trespassing on his territory. There was no way to tell.

Maybe now would be a good time to dedicate herself to serving the Goddess and a life of prayer?

She sent one up, hastily but earnestly begging the Moon and all Her Sisters for a miracle. Something, anything to get her out of the reach of the coyotes, who would drag her back to Sawmill, California, and her death at Geoffrey Hilliard's brutal hands.

Zigzagging through the underbrush, Renny spotted a pinpoint of light in the distance and made a beeline for it. Maybe the prayer had worked, and the light represented the town of Alpha, or at least its outskirts. Town meant people, and a town like Alpha meant people capable of holding off a small band of coyote enforcers long enough for her to beg for help.

It meant a spark of hope.

She called up the last of her reserves of strength and flew toward the light, but the attack came so fast, she didn't even have time to second-guess that whole prayer strategy. She'd gotten too busy bleeding.

She yelped as a set of fangs sliced into the back of her hind leg.

The pain jolted through her, but her attacker had

missed the big tendons, so at least she didn't fall or lose the use of her limb. That would have ended things fast. But Renny could keep moving, for the moment. So she did.

Stubborn, desperate determination welled up within her. Damn it, she had not lived this long, come this far, or run this hard to let herself be caught now. She refused.

With a frantic yip, she leapt forward toward the clear pool of moonlight she could see through the branches. The beckoning light reflected off a patch of snow dead ahead, just a few hundred yards away. If she could get there, this would be over. One way or another. She'd have reached safety or not, and in either event, she'd be out of options.

She broke out from a thicket of salal bushes, almost blinded by the glare of moonlight off the lingering puddles of white snow, but it didn't slow her down. She didn't need to see to know she had to keep moving.

Run or die.

Heart pounding, lungs burning, muscles screaming, Renny raced ahead, no chance to take a breath, no chance to scream, no chance to think. She just focused on that light as it flickered closer.

Almost there.

Almost—

He hit her from the side this time, a cannonball of momentum that knocked Renny clean off her feet and sent her skidding through the detritus of slush, twigs, and leaves covering the forest floor. The shock left her dazed, but she still recognized the stink of him. Bryce. Geoffrey's beta and one of his closest friends.

And almost as evil as the alpha coyote himself.

She scrambled for purchase, trying to halt her slide and get her feet back under her before the other four caught up to them. If she let them surround her, it was over. She had to keep them off her back.

Bryce snarled at her, lips curling back to expose fangs that dripped with anticipation. At least she knew he was anticipating her death, not her rape and *then* death, as Geoffrey would. Bryce wanted only her blood, and in the heat of the moment, she suddenly wondered whether he'd bother following his leader's orders. Tearing her throat out himself would bring the big coyote a lot more personal satisfaction than hauling her ass back south and watching while his alpha did the honors after a day or two at Geoffrey's mercy. Bryce had performed the hunt, now his beast would want the kill.

He positioned himself between her and the light she'd tried so desperately to reach. He held his head low and forward, his hackles raised as he stared her down with his malicious yellow gaze. He was waiting for her to move, knowing she was already injured, knowing that if he remained patient long enough, either she'd come at him and expose herself to a counterattack or his buddies would reach them. Five against one would see her dead or captured in the space of a heartbeat.

Renny didn't like either of those options.

Her ear flicked backward, catching the sound of the others gaining on them. She had seconds, if that, to find a way out of this. It wasn't as though she had much choice. The only way open to her was up.

She crouched down, mirroring the coyote's attack posture, but she didn't bother going for his throat. She knew that even if she managed to take him down, the others would be on her before he started bleeding. She wouldn't get out of this by fighting. She had to take a leap of faith, literally.

Powerful muscles coiled and released with a shocking force, launching Renny into the air and toward her enemy, but she hadn't aimed for him. She'd aimed for the space over his head, behind him, and she'd almost cleared Bryce's tail before he realized what she was doing. He jumped up, teeth flashing, and caught her in the side, slashing a deep, bloody furrow over her ribs.

She screamed, the sound emerging from her canine throat as a sort of high-pitched howling yelp, but she didn't bother to assess the damage. She just ran straight toward the light.

Behind her, Bryce gave a yip-howl of rage and frustration and leapt after her. She could practically feel his hot breath stirring the hairs at the tip of her tail, and that only made her run faster.

She'd broken through another stand of trees before she realized that the distant light she'd prayed was the outskirts of Alpha wasn't quite so distant, and it wasn't anything like her long-sought sanctuary. The light shone from a single spotlight mounted in the apex of the peaked roof of a lone, otherwise darkened cabin.

A cabin that smelled so strongly of wolf, she was surprised the siding hadn't sprouted fur.

Her heart barely had time to sink before a distinctive metallic rasp caught her attention. The sound was almost immediately followed by the sharp, echoing report of gunfire.

Bryce yowled, and suddenly Renny couldn't sense

him at her back. She chanced a look over her shoulder and saw the coyote spin on his heels, making a diving retreat into the cover of the trees. Drops of blood sprayed the snow and mud behind him.

In front of her, a tall figure stood on the porch of the cabin, almost hidden in shadows. The stock of a rifle remained braced on his shoulder, his head bent toward the barrel as he sighted for another shot.

Huh. After all these days of running and fearing her death might be just around the corner, Renny had never even considered the end might hit with the impact of a bullet. Who'd have thought?

Her paws stumbled over the uneven ground at the edge of the cabin's yard, and she felt her knees buckle. Her hind leg throbbed in time to her racing heartbeat, and the gash in her side felt like a burning stripe of fire. She could feel blood streaming from both wounds and thought it almost didn't matter if the man fired again. A bullet in the head sounded like the better choice when compared with bleeding to death in front of a stranger, and either was preferable to what Geoffrey planned to do to her.

That was her last (semi-)coherent thought.

She folded like a cheap card table, collapsing onto the wet ground with a low grunt. Her head bounced once before darkness claimed her, and in that last dizzy moment, she could have sworn she heard another wolf growling.

It sounded a lot as though he'd just muttered, "Shit."

Sitting alone in the light of the dying fire, Mick decided he made a damned pathetic sight. Here he sat, home alone on yet another Friday night, nursing a warming beer and trying to keep his mind clear of old, familiar memories. So far, he was failing miserably.

He swallowed more warm, bitter liquid and stared into the glowing coals in his living room hearth. Nights like these, when spring had begun to stir and his latest project was packed off to his publisher, sleep became sadly elusive, and he found himself right here on his battered sofa, trying not to think.

Actually, he could have slept if he'd tried, he admitted. He just didn't make the effort. Sleeping opened the door to dreaming, and lately every dream led back to the same place. His wolf seized control and steered them straight back to their dead mate. It wasn't what Mick would call restful.

Fuck. It had happened more than eight years ago, he reminded himself. You'd think he'd be over it, that he'd have done his mourning, let go of the past, and settled into his new life here in Alpha.

But you'd be wrong.

Maybe the eight years was the problem. Few wolves survived losing a mate as suddenly and traumatically as Mick had. Most followed the other half of themselves into the darkness and never had to endure the passing of time. He still didn't know why he hadn't, but after all these years, he wondered if his wolf was maybe coming unhinged from the loneliness.

He snorted, disgusted with himself. One more sleepless night and look at him—he was getting fucking maudlin. Maybe it wasn't loneliness at all, maybe he was just losing his damned mind.

A scream of canine pain hit him like a sucker punch to the back of his head.

Mick jumped to his feet, his hand already reaching

for his rifle before his mind could grasp what was bothering him. He'd lived out here in these woods long enough to have become used to the sounds they made at all hours of the day and night. He could tell a gust of wind from the rustle of the underbrush, the step of a buck deer from the footfalls of the rare moose calf.

He also knew which of the locals had the balls to run and hunt on his property in the middle of the night, and none of them had given him a heads-up about their presence. Which meant that somewhere outside his small house, he had some uninvited guests.

Cursing under his breath, Mick almost put down the rifle and flung open his door bare-handed. If the teenagers of Alpha were daring one another to play chase in his woods again, a bullet would probably be over-kill. Most of them were so scared of him, he wouldn't even have to raise his voice to send them scattering like frightened bunnies. Seeing a gun in his hand might make the little shits pass out, and then it could be hours before they got the hell off his property. Besides, that scream had indicated someone was injured. He couldn't shoot a wounded kid, no matter how much they'd pissed him off.

A distinctive bark-howl cut off that line of thinking and had his fingers tightening around the barrel of the weapon. He recognized that sound, as out of place as it was, and it had the hair on the back of his neck standing on end. That was a coyote calling his pack to the hunt. Last time he'd checked, they didn't have any coy-otes in Alpha, let alone a pack of them. So what the hell were they doing in his woods?

He shifted his grip on the rifle and checked through the front window before opening the door and stepping out onto his unlit front porch. The room behind him remained illuminated only by the fire, but something had triggered the motion sensors that activated the spotlight near the roof. It shone onto the hard-packed dirt of the drive, but the glow managed to extend a little way across the scattered islands of lingering snow toward the edge of the woods to his right.

Mick faced that way and peered into the darkness. At first, he couldn't see worth a damn, but his eyes adjusted quickly and his ears were already picking up the sounds of flight and pursuit through the dense northwestern forest. Two more short, sharp cries answered the first bark-howl, followed by a third and a fourth. Definitely a pack, or at least a hunting party. But what were they doing here, in Alpha, on his land?

And what the hell were they hunting?

He got his answer an instant later. A sleek, fur-covered form launched itself from the trees into the cleared area around the cabin. Reflex had the rifle to his shoulder, but instinct kept him from pulling the trigger.

The calls he'd already heard had him thinking coyote, and if the animal hadn't landed near enough to the edge of the light, he might have kept thinking it. But something about that shape bothered him.

It looked on the large size for a 'yote, maybe seventy or seventy-five pounds, and sturdy as much as lithe, too substantial for the average coyote. Its ears seemed out of proportion to its skull, too large for the breadth of it. Then the light caught its fur, and he could see the russet coloring around its ears and neck, a rusty shade that seemed to darken to near black along its spine.

That same rich red also decorated its flank near the site of a bloody tear in the muscle.

That was no coyote. It was a wolf, or a hybrid at best, half wolf and half coyote. He should recognize one when he saw it. Instinct had him drawing in a breath, and the scent cleared up his confusion. His yard had been invaded by another wolf shifter, a red wolf, he realized, and she was badly injured.

His supposition was confirmed when another shape crashed into the yard, this one lighter and leaner, looking almost delicate when he compared it with the wounded shape. This one was pure coyote shaped, and the dark, wet stains around its muzzle identified it as the cause of the female wolf's injuries.

He squeezed the trigger almost before the reality finished registering and felt the rifle's stock nudge back into his shoulder. The bullet grazed the side of the coyote's shoulder, making it yelp in pain and surprise. Its head swung around, yellow gaze fixing on him for an instant before it turned tail and dove back into the cover of the trees.

Mick waited for a minute to see if any of the others in the hunting party felt like trying their luck to get to the she-wolf. Driven by the instinct to kill or mate, a regular coyote might press its luck, but a shifter would think twice. When no other animals appeared, he slowly lowered his gun and stepped down into the yard.

The female was unconscious, but her sides still heaved as if she'd been running a marathon. The sharp aroma of blood hit him first, and he knew from the way it almost overwhelmed her natural scent that she was losing a dangerous amount of it.

He also knew from one more deep inhalation that he'd been correct in identifying her species. She was more than a rare red wolf; she was a red wolf shifter, and she was in serious trouble.

"Shit."

He muttered the word even as he crouched down beside her, setting his rifle near his feet within easy grabbing distance. A swift rake of his gaze took in her condition—good muscle tone, healthy size, but clearly exhausted—as well as the extent of her wounds. In addition to the gash he'd noticed on her rear leg, he could see blood saturating the cream-colored fur of her belly where her side pressed against the ground.

He rolled her gently over and muttered an even stronger curse. The wound on her flank had looked ragged and bloody, but the damage to her side made it seem like a love bite.

Fangs had torn deep under her fur and opened a laceration almost as long as his forearm. It extended from just behind her shoulder, across her rib cage, and nearly to her groin. The ugly slash had been ripped open by her exertions and it continued to bleed heavily under the layer of mud and debris that now clung to the surface. Shifter or not, it looked deep enough to need stitches.

Damn it, he'd have to make a phone call.

But first things first.

He scooped the limp wolf into his arms, catching his rifle in his fingers as he rose. She flopped in his hold like a sack of grain, but he'd hauled heavier burdens on one shoulder, so the weight didn't bother him. What bothered him was her stillness and the way she didn't even twitch when he lifted her.

It took just a minute or two to carry her into the cabin and kick the door closed behind them. After depositing her on his sofa, he returned immediately to bolt the door and engage the security system he'd installed the first day he'd moved in. If those coyotes decided to try for her again, Mick wanted some advanced warning.

Secured inside, he strode into the hall to grab a stack of clean towels from the closet. On the way, he snagged his cell phone from the coffee table and dialed a familiar number.

"What?"

Mick ignored the annoyed tone of the greeting, filled his arms with terry cloth, and returned to the sofa. "I need you out at my place. Now."

Zeke Buchanan muttered something foul under his breath. "It's fucking three o'clock in the morning, asshole, and I'm not on duty. Call the office."

"I've got an injured shifter in my living room, and I just shot the coyote who was trying to kill her. Only grazed him, but it sounded like he had friends, and I don't know how determined they might be. Get out here. And send an ambulance."

He didn't bother to listen while Zeke swore again. The snap and rustle of fabric and the squeak of mattress springs told him what he needed to know. The sheriff's deputy would be here as soon as he got some pants on. In the meantime, Mick needed to stop the she-wolf on his sofa from bleeding to death until help arrived.

His knees hit the floor, his hands reaching to press a folded towel to the more severe of her wounds, when the air around her wavered and fell out of focus. While he blinked, the figure of a wolf blurred and shifted, leaving a petite, naked, and badly injured woman passed out in his living room.

A very attractive naked woman.

Shit.

He told himself to avert his eyes, but damned if the damage hadn't already been done. His man and wolf had already both sat up and taken notice. He could almost feel the twitch of a whiskered black nose in the back of his head as the beast pushed itself forward to take in her scent.

She smelled amazing. Under the sweet coppery note of her blood, he could detect notes of citrus and green leaves and something deeper and spicier that simply reminded him of home. He hadn't smelled anything like it in more than eight years, not since—

He cut that speculation off at the knees—not boarding *that* train of thought, thanks—and made himself focus on assessing the female's wounds.

Her change of shape had jump-started her shifter ability to heal quickly, but it would take more than one trip from fur to skin to close a wound as serious as the one on her side. The ragged gash now covered a swath of milky skin from just to the side of a pretty, pink-tipped breast, all along her torso to the crease between her hip and thigh on the right-hand side.

Dirt still clung to the torn and bloody flesh, which Mick almost found a relief. It helped pull his attention away from all the uninjured bits he could see and focus it where it needed to be—on helping her, not ogling her.

Gritting his teeth and fixing his gaze on the injury,

Mick pressed a towel hard against her ribs with one hand and used the other to tuck more towels under her opposite hip where he'd seen the less serious laceration. Her weight should provide the necessary pressure to stop the bleeding on that side, but he had to lean into the deeper wound. Thank fuck she remained unconscious, because if she'd been awake, she'd probably have been screaming from the pain.

He lost track of time while he knelt there applying pressure and waiting for help to arrive. Even if Zeke floored it all the way from town, it was at least a ten-minute drive out to Mick's place, which left way too much time for him to get a good, long look at his uninvited guest.

It made him feel like a pervert, staring at her while she remained completely out of it, but he couldn't help himself. Something about her drew his gaze like a magnet, and he really wished his subconscious weren't so anxious to needle him about what it was.

Her wolf looked like Beth.

A corner of his mind gave thanks that she had shifted back to her skin, because it cut the resemblance considerably, but when he'd first seen her burst out of the forest, he'd thought for one wild, insane second that his mate had come back from the dead. It had nearly stopped his heart.

The two animals had the same delicate build, the same pointed muzzles, the same creamy coloring on their chests. Beth had been a little taller, a little more muscular, but she'd been mistaken for a red wolf more than a few times in her shifted life. She hadn't been just a hybrid—half gray wolf like him, half coyote like her father—but her looks in her furred form bore a strong resemblance to the woman who had almost died tonight in his front yard.

That was an image he had never wanted to see again—a woman bloody and broken, torn apart, and left for him to find. He'd left that nightmare behind him, buried it in California before he'd moved north and settled here in Alpha. Not even the devil himself had the power to drag him back to the town where he'd been born. Not on the coldest day in hell.

A pounding fist shook his front door in the frame, jerking Mick back to the present. His wolf sprang to attention, ready to tear out the throats of any coyote who tried to get inside his home. It took a second for him to realize that it had been long enough for Zeke to have arrived. He opened his mouth to call for his friend to come in, then remembered how he'd double-locked the door as a precaution. He'd have to go open it himself.

A quick check at the underside of the towel revealed way too much red soaked into the cotton, but the active bleeding appeared to have slowed to a trickle. At least it looked safe enough for Mick to step away for the seconds it took to disarm the alarm system and flip a couple of locks.

Zeke pushed inside almost before Mick released the dead bolt, and the aggressive move ripped a snarl from his wolf before he managed to get hold of himself. He'd known who was on the other side of the door from both the knock and the smell, but the night's events had riled up his beast, and the wolf didn't like another male forcing his way into its den, even if he'd been invited.

Mick smacked the animal down and stepped back to let the other man enter. "C'mon in."

Zeke grunted and moved aside to reveal a second, much smaller form standing behind him. Molly Buchanan smiled and waved with one hand. In the other, she carried a large plastic case like her brother's favorite tackle box, only this one was bright yellow and had a big red cross emblazoned on the lid.

"Hey, Mick," she chirped, bouncing on her toes as if it weren't the middle of the night and she hadn't been dragged from her bed minutes ago to come racing out into the woods. "You called for the cavalry?"

Mick supposed that, as an EMT, racing places in the middle of the night wasn't so odd an experience for Molly. He waved her inside. She might not be in an ambulance, but she rode in one most other nights. She'd be able to help the she-wolf.

Molly stepped inside while her brother laid a hand on Mick's shoulder and squeezed.

"Okay," Zeke grumbled. "Why don't you tell me exactly what the hell is going on? Injured shifters? Coyotes? And you shot one of them? What the fuck, Mick?"

"Yeah, Mick. What the fuck?"

The third figure to appear in his front door caused the greatest surprise. John Jaeger had dropped by Mick's house on precisely two previous occasions. The first had been a thinly veiled evaluation when he'd first arrived in town. As mayor of Alpha, Jaeger took his duty to protect and manage his town seriously. To have a new, lone wolf move in but refuse all attempts from the locals to integrate him into their community had raised an alarm for the mountain lion shifter. He had wanted to ensure that Mick didn't intend to make trouble.

The second visit had been harder to anticipate but infinitely more entertaining. Jaeger had dropped by to return a pair of boxer briefs he had found in his truck bed after the woman he'd been seeing had borrowed the vehicle to "move some furniture." The only thing that had gotten moved were the bodies in the bed of the pickup when she'd invited Mick out for a moonlit picnic. The boxers came with an offer to let Mick keep the woman, too, but as it turned out, neither he nor the mayor had much keeping in mind for the woman in question. They had all gone their separate ways, and the two men had never spoken of the incident again.

"Jaeger." The growl rumbled up in Mick's throat before he could stop it. Adrenaline still rode him enough that his beast was expressing its displeasure at both the man's unexpected appearance in his territory and the deputy's belligerent manner. "What are you doing here?"

The man lifted an eyebrow and jerked a thumb toward the woods behind him. "Zeke told me you had some trouble out here tonight. Something about injured strangers, coyotes, and bullets. I came to make sure it wasn't the kind of ruckus that called for shovels."

"Not yet."

Molly cleared her throat loudly. "Um, not to inconvenience anyone, but I heard someone was bleeding around here. Would any of you big, strong men like to point me in that direction before the patient runs out of the red stuff? You know, if it's no trouble."

The lioness might be a head shorter than the smallest male in the room, but such an insignificant detail

never had done much to hinder that smart mouth of
hers. Mick gritted his teeth and swallowed another
rumble of displeasure. His wolf seemed ready to go on
a tear.

Of shifters' throats.

"She's in here." He turned on his heel and led Molly
and the others into the living room.

The lioness strode to the sofa and crouched in the
same spot where Mick had been kneeling. In seconds,
she had her fingers on the woman's pulse and her kit
open on the floor beside her. She nodded to herself,
then snapped on a pair of bright blue gloves before she
briskly and competently began to examine the unconscious woman's side.

"Her temp's a little low, but it's cold out tonight, so
I imagine that will come up on its own. That last snow-
fall just won't go away, will it? The wounds look messy
and painful, but not life-threatening," Molly proclaimed, poking gingerly at the lacerated tissue. "Not
for a shifter, anyway. I can clean it up and bandage it,
but it should heal on its own."

Mick scowled. "No stitches?"

"You know stitches just piss shifters off. They itch
like crazy, and they pull at all sorts of weird angles
when we try to shift. Bandages are better."

She didn't bother to look up, just reached for a bottle
of clear liquid and a handful of gauze. She began ir-
rigating the wound, washing away the mud and debris
that had contaminated it when the wolf collapsed. Her
calm manner and sure movements seemed to calm
Mick's wolf, and he felt himself take his first deep
breath in what felt like hours. It had probably been less
than twenty minutes.

Jaeger shifted his weight and stepped forward, peering over Mick's shoulder at the injured woman. "Who is she?"

Mick shrugged one shoulder, the movement still short and tense. "No idea. She just showed up in the yard, bleeding like a butcher's hog, and keeled over. Didn't stop to exchange pleasantries."

"And at what point did you find yourself shooting at strange coyotes?"

"When one of them came after her with her blood on his jaw and a few friends at his back."

The mayor looked grim. "You sure you hit him?"

"I saw blood in the snow, and it wasn't all hers. He yelped, too. I figure I at least grazed him."

"It was a male?"

"The one I saw was. I didn't see any others, but I could hear them coming through the woods. They must have backed off when they heard the gunshot."

Zeke didn't look up from the small pad where he'd been jotting down notes. "They were definitely shifters, not regular coyotes?"

"Like I said, I only saw the one, but I got a look at his eyes, and I got a whiff of him. He was Other, which means his buddies probably were, too."

Jaeger agreed. "Most likely. We've got our share of coyotes in this state, but not many in the area around Alpha. They know they can't compete with the bigger predators we have roaming these woods, so they tend to give us a pretty wide berth."

"Right." Zeke snapped his notebook shut and shoved it into a pocket. "I'm going to take a look around outside while Molly bandages up the victim. I'll need to ask her a hell of a lot of questions, but they can wait till she's conscious."

"You'll get better answers that way," Jaeger said, mouth curving.

The lion shifter shot the mayor the bird on his way out the front door. The other man just chuckled, then turned back to Mick. "So." He rocked back on his heels and hooked his thumbs into the front pockets of his jeans. "It's three thirty in the morning, you have an unconscious and wounded female on your sofa, an EMT patching her up, a deputy nosing around your property, and a mayor in your living room who'd be willing to consider performing several illegal acts for a good hit of caffeine. Ideas?"

Mick rolled his eyes. "I'll make coffee."

He spun around and stalked toward the kitchen, Jaeger hot on his heels. What else was there to do? Molly was treating the she-wolf, Zeke was playing cop, and his wolf had no intention of letting him sleep anytime soon. Not with that intriguingly scented female currently passed out in his living room.

Might as well drink a pot of coffee. He'd take it black, like his mood at having all these uninvited guests in his den. So much for his wolf feeling lonely.

Chapter Two

Renny couldn't decide what woke her. Was it the burning pain in her side, the throbbing pain in her thigh, or the dull ache in her head? Or maybe it was the sound of voices drifting quietly to her from someplace nearby. Whatever had done it, she wished it would go fuck itself. She'd rather stay asleep.

"I think she's coming around." A female voice, unfamiliar but nonthreatening, sounded as though it had come from a couple of feet above and behind her. That confused her. She had the feeling she'd been expecting to wake to the sound of male voices, and unfriendly ones at that.

Where was she?

Memories came flooding back. Being chased. Driving. Running out of gas. Fleeing through an unfamiliar forest.

Mud and snow.

Bryce.

Pain.

Gunfire.

She jerked into full consciousness, and the instinctive tightening of her muscles made her gasp at the sudden rush of pain. Damn it, everything hurt.

She opened her eyes and found herself blinking up at four strange faces. Three large men loomed above her, while a woman hovered a few feet below them. It took a second for her fuzzy brain to put together the fact that she was lying on someone's sofa with three male shifters staring down at her and a female perched on the edge of a coffee table at her left. Instinct made her wary, but she had to admit it beat waking up to find herself surrounded by Bryce and his Merry Morons.

She tried to shift herself a bit more upright but winced and quickly abandoned the idea. Instead, she tried a tentative smile. "Um, hi?"

"Hey there." The woman leaned forward, her smile casual, utterly genuine, and naturally kind. "Welcome back to the land of the living. How are you feeling?"

Renny focused on her. Compared with the wall of males ringing them, the woman looked tiny. It was hard to tell while she was sitting, but she likely fell somewhere around dead average in height, maybe five four, and built with the kind of softly curved muscles common to cheerleaders and college softball players. The woman had dark blondish hair with a few intriguing shades of red and brown streaking through it. She looked normal and safe and genuinely concerned about Renny's condition.

"I'm good. I mean, I'm sore," Renny corrected herself, "and I feel like I got rolled around inside a cement truck full of rusty nails for a few hours, but I'm fine. I'll *be* fine."

One hand instinctively went to her side where a

wound continued to ache and burn. She might have worried about it more if she hadn't noticed just then that she seemed to be stark naked and covered by nothing more than a cotton blanket. She flushed and drew it a little higher around her shoulders. Shifters might not have a lot of hang-ups about nudity, but there was getting naked for a few seconds before and after changing shapes, and then there was lying naked on an unfamiliar sofa in front of three strange men.

The woman, who smelled feline to Renny, noticed the movement and grinned, but she didn't comment. Instead, she said, "You *will* be fine. I promise. I'm an EMT, and I gave you a check before I bandaged you up. You're suffering from some signs of exhaustion—the unconsciousness being one of them—and those wounds are going to take a few days to completely heal, but I don't think there will be any permanent damage. Just take it easy for a day or two, and you should be back to normal before you know it."

Renny resisted commenting that "normal" would take a bit more work for her than for the average wolf about town. "Thanks. I really am grateful for the help. I owe you one."

The woman shook her head. "Just doing my job, ma'am."

"Renny. Renny Landry." Deciding that waving would upset her blanket coverage, she just waggled her fingers above the hem in an abbreviated greeting. "And even so, I do owe you." She glanced around at the other figures in the room until her gaze hit on the only one who looked vaguely familiar. "And you. You're the one who drove off Bryce and the others. Thank you. You saved my life."

The man standing at the far end of the sofa had his legs braced wide and his broad shoulders back. Put him in an eye patch and a billowing shirt and she'd have said the man carried himself like a pirate. He had his large hands cupped around a heavy mug of what smelled like coffee and held the drink low against a belly that looked intriguingly firm and sculpted.

Overall, he exuded an attitude so confident and masculine that Renny wondered if it had to shave by the end of the day. Everything about this man screamed alpha to her, and his scent clearly identified him as the wolf who lived in this house.

He had dark hair cut close around the sides but left a little longer on top. Dark sideburns framed blade-sharp cheekbones and only emphasized the dark stubble covering his chin. Either he *did* have to shave twice a day, or he hadn't bothered with a razor in at least a week.

His skin had a dusky quality she associated with time outdoors. Not sunbathing or barbecuing, but living and working in the open air. Either that, or the Goddess had just blessed him with a complexion like golden honey.

His eyes looked dark, but she couldn't quite make out the color across the distance separating them. Or maybe she was just distracted by all the other colors he sported. Despite the chill she could feel around the edges of her blanket, the wolf wore a shirt with no arms, revealing the two full-sleeve tattoos decorating him from shoulders to wrists.

Elaborate, intricate, and boldly beautiful, the shades of red and green and blue and purple twined across the sleek, strong muscles of an athlete. The body art and the chiseled build gave him the look of a rock star or a biker. Definitely the kind of man who could hold his own in a fight. The scar cutting across his forehead and bisecting his left eyebrow didn't exactly hurt that impression, either.

He watched her with those dark eyes, his expression blank but his gaze intense, until Renny wanted to squirm. She realized she'd been staring for at least a minute or two and felt heat surge into her cheeks.

"Um, anyway, I'm grateful." She stumbled over the words and cursed her own tongue for working against her. When the wolf said nothing, she glanced nervously to the other two men in the room.

The one to the wolf's left stood a little over six feet tall and held himself with the kind of lazy, coiled tension of a cat shifter. A few sniffs made her think he might be a mountain lion in his other shape. It would make sense with the tawny gold of his skin and the black-streaked sandy shade of his hair. His eyes looked like the dark green of tree moss, and his chiseled features bore the lines of a man who smiled often. He wasn't smiling now, though. He watched Renny with a carefully neutral expression and a feline intensity.

Standing between the mountain lion and the other woman in the room, the largest of the males didn't bother keeping his expression neutral. He stared down at Renny with open curiosity edging toward suspicion. The dark navy of his sheriff's uniform might explain that, and the striking resemblance between his features and the EMT's added weight to the idea that this man was a cop to his bones—protective and inclined toward caution around strangers.

Probably especially around strangers who'd been hunted by other shifters.

He had short hair in an interesting mix of shades from ashy blond to copper gold to chocolaty brown all tumbled together. He looked like the kind of man who cut it to keep it under control, but the strategy failed him. It stood up in tousled disarray, as if he'd been running his fingers through it, or as if he'd rolled out of bed without so much as looking near a comb. It softened the impression of a granite jaw and furrowed brow. Well, maybe a little. His scent told her she could subtract the mountain from his shifter identity. This was a lion-lion, if she'd ever smelled one.

"I'm Molly Buchanan," the female said, shooting the male beside her a pointed glance. "And we were glad to help. Do you mind me asking what happened, though? Mick said you were chased onto his property by coyotes."

Renny stole a glance at the wolf, whose expression didn't change. He continued to brood in her general direction. "Yeah, it's kind of a long story."

"Like Molly said, you'll need a couple of days to heal." The mountain lion gave her a look that expressed both humor and insistence. He'd get the story from her one way or another, but he was willing to be entertained by it. Or so Renny hoped. "My name's John Jaeger, by the way. You can consider me all ears."

The lion scowled at his compatriot and turned a stern face to Renny. "What the mayor means, is that you were attacked within the jurisdiction of the town, so we need to know if there's any continuing threat from the folks who did this to you."

Renny felt her pulse jump. "The mayor? Of where?"

"Alpha, Washington."

"Oh, wow," she breathed. "I can't believe I made it."

"Made it?" The deputy stiffened at her words. "You mean you were heading to Alpha when you were attacked?"

Renny clutched her blanket and shifted into more of a seated position, wincing when the movement pulled at her wounds. "I was headed to town when my car ran out of gas. I knew the coyotes were following me, so I took off into the woods hoping to lose them. I hoped I was still going in the right direction on foot, but I couldn't be a hundred percent certain. And I was a little preoccupied."

"Why were they following you?" he demanded in a harsh tone.

"Zeke, quit it," Molly scolded. "Does it matter why? They chased her through the woods and seriously injured her. Can you think of a reason why she'd deserve something like that?"

"Maybe she committed some kind of crime against their pack," the lion grumbled, but he looked uncomfortable as he said it. Most shifter communities had their own form of justice, and hunting parties did occasionally pursue fugitives who tried to escape it. But several coyotes against a lone female wolf didn't paint a very pretty picture.

"Maybe you're an idiot," Molly shot back. "Forgive my brother, Renny. Sometimes I think he wears that uniform a little too tight."

Renny appreciated the lioness's reassurance, but she understood where the man was coming from. "No, it's okay. He's with law enforcement, so he's responsible for people's safety around here. The mayor, too. They have a right to ask if I'm a danger to their community." She looked both men in the eyes. "I'm not, though. I promise. The coyotes who attacked me were working for someone else. Their alpha. He's . . . well, he's been . . . following me."

"Following you? Following you where?"

Renny laughed. It had become a habit, because if she didn't laugh, she'd have to scream, and that scared people. "Everywhere. To work. From work. To and from the store, the doctor's office, the post office, friends' houses. Everywhere. I quit my job, I left town. Hell, I left the state, and he just sent his pals after me."

Molly frowned. "That's not being followed, Renny; that's being stalked."

Mick had to grab his wolf by the scruff to keep it from jumping straight out of his skin. It wanted to feel some coyote throat under its teeth, and it wanted to start now. The she-wolf had a *stalker*?

Fuck. That.

He heard a click and looked down to see his own claws tapping the side of his coffee mug. He set it down before he cracked it and willed his human nails back.

"Whoa." Zeke held up a hand. "That's a serious accusation, Moll. You might not want to put words into Ms. Landry's mouth."

The she-wolf shook her head. "She isn't. I've used the term myself. It fits."

"Women are usually stalked by men they've had relationships with in the past. Is this guy an ex of yours?"

Mick's wolf rumbled its displeasure.

"Absolutely not." Her mouth firmed as she said it,

her eyes flashing. "I never wanted anything to do with him, but right from the beginning, he refused to take no for an answer."

"Hey, guys, hang on a minute, would you?" Molly pushed to her feet and still had to look up to glare at the men. "You're questioning Renny like she's suspected of something while she's sitting here wounded, naked, and probably in desperate need of some Advil and a glass of water. Can you maybe give her a break and, I don't know, a T-shirt or something, before you make with the Inquisition routine?"

Immediately—and predictably—three pairs of male eyes focused all their attention on the woman in question. Since Mick's were one of them, he understood the instinctive response to the possibility of spotting something yummy, but his wolf failed to sympathize. It suggested he shift and let it eat the eyeballs of the other men before they got a peek.

He channeled the urge into motion. "I'll get her something to wear."

The others continued their discussion as he stalked down the short hall to his bedroom. Thanks to his shifter hearing, he didn't even need to strain to keep track of their words.

"That's a start, anyway. And you." From the way she emphasized the pronoun, the lioness could only be referring to her brother. "Go get her some water. I've got meds in my kit. There's no reason she should be naked or in pain while you guys break out the rubber hoses."

"But, Molly, we figured the interrogation light would keep her warm," Jaeger teased. "And the waterboarding would wash the rest of that blood and dirt right off her."

"Very funny, Mr. Mayor, but I notice you seemed perfectly happy to let my brother give Renny the third degree."

"He was doing his job."

Jaeger's words overlapped with the softer tones of the she-wolf, and Mick's wolf did not like the way their tones blended or the soft chuckle they shared when they realized they'd responded in unison. He grabbed a long-sleeved shirt from his closet and started back to the living room before they could get any cozier. Then he thought better of it and turned back to add a comfortable old T-shirt, a pair of sweatpants with a drawstring waist, and his thickest socks to the pile of fabric.

Layers. Layers would keep her (*covered*) warm.

He returned to the other room to find the wolf accepting some tablets and a drink from Molly's hands.

"Here." He thrust the clothing toward her. "You can change in the bathroom. First door on the right."

She looked up, and for the first time he got a good look at her eyes. They were wide and soft and the color of green tea, a pale shade with almost tawny undertones. Beth's eyes had been brown, like sweet milk chocolate.

Molly intercepted the clothing and stepped protectively toward the injured woman. "Come on. I'll help you up. You just hang on to the blanket. I'll give you some privacy, but I'll be right outside the door if you need me, okay?"

Mick's wolf huffed a reluctant approval in his head.

It would prefer to be the one picking their mate up off the sofa, but at least it wasn't one of the males trying to touch her—

Shit.

He winced and smacked the animal back. They didn't have a mate. Not anymore. Beth was dead.

"I'm sure I'll be fine," Renny protested as she leaned on the other woman and made her slow, stiff way toward the bathroom.

"And I'm sure that I'm the EMT here. You're injured, and you were unconscious for almost an hour. I don't take chances with my patients."

When the door closed behind her, sealing Renny in the bathroom alone, Zeke turned toward the others and kept his voice low. "If what she says is true, I doubt tonight will be the end of it. Stalkers don't give up easily, especially not ones willing to follow their victims across state lines and involve proxies in the stalking behavior. That's some serious shit."

"Agreed." Jaeger angled his body slightly away from the deputy, the move subtle but deliberate. It didn't take more than a glance back at Molly's crossed arms and fierce scowl in her brother's direction to explain it. Or for Mick to follow the mayor's example out of the direct line of fire between the siblings.

"Then you realize that by coming here, that girl has brought her problems right onto our doorstep," Zeke said. He wore a grim look, the one Mick called his cop face. "If she stays in Alpha, they could spill over onto our residents."

Jaeger didn't look much happier than Zeke, but he shrugged. "And what's the alternative? We get her gas tank filled up and send her on her way? Tell ourselves it's not our problem? I can't do that, and I doubt you could, either."

"What if someone else gets hurt?"

"Then we have twice as many reasons to make it clear to some coyotes that just because Alpha takes in shifters with problems doesn't mean that assholes get a free pass," Jaeger said. "I'm not going to turn the girl away."

Zeke frowned. "I'm not saying we shove her out the door with our boots on her ass. I'm just saying we need to know more about her situation before we commit ourselves to getting in any deeper."

"Zee, we're in. Deal with it."

Mick's wolf agreed, both with protecting the female and with kicking coyote ass. It thought the mayor had the right idea.

The click of the door opening drew his attention, and he watched as Renny emerged from the bathroom with the blanket draped over her arm and the rest of her fully covered. He experienced a surge of satisfaction at seeing her in his clothing, as huge as it was on her. The sight made his possessive wolf nearly purr like a house cat. It wanted to get closer to see if she smelled like them now, if the lingering scent of their clean laundry would be enough to mark her as theirs.

Fuck. Not ours. She's not *ours,* he snarled.

His wolf ignored him.

She padded back toward the living room, her sock-clad feet silent on the wooden floors. "Thank you again," she said, laying the blanket down over the arm of the sofa. "I have a feeling I'm going to keep saying that a lot tonight, but I mean it every time."

Mick managed a curt nod while his wolf kept trying

to sniff her. It wasn't even being discreet about it, the fucker.

"You're very welcome," Jaeger said, giving him an odd look, but stepping naturally into the role of gracious host. "Why don't you sit down, Ms. Landry. You've been through a lot tonight. And, I suspect, for well before that."

Renny sank down onto the edge of the sofa and rubbed her hands over her face. It looked pale and bruised, but clean, as if she'd washed up before she dressed. She'd also done something to tie her disheveled hair back from her face, and when she turned her head to look around the room he thought he saw a strand of unwaxed dental floss wrapped around the auburn strands.

"Yes, about that." She placed her palms flat against her knees and licked her lips as if she were nervous. "I realized while I was getting dressed that I probably haven't made much sense to anyone since I woke up, so I figured that in addition to my thanks, I owe all of you an explanation. It's a long and not very pretty story, but I'll try to stick to the *CliffsNotes* version."

Molly returned with another glass of water and set it on the coffee table in front of the she-wolf. "Only if you want, Renny. I still think you need more rest."

"No, you guys have helped a stranger who showed up at your door with someone trying to kill her. You could have just let the coyotes have me. Like the deputy said, I could have deserved to have them hunting me. You had no way of knowing. But if I plan to stick around, you all need to know what's going on. What kind of trouble I might be causing."

Her voice grew stronger as she spoke, as if she'd

begun to calm and relax into more the kind of person she was when she wasn't running for her life or waking up with serious injuries. After a sip of water, she continued.

"So, here's the gist of it. About two years ago, I took a job at a small public library in Northern California. I grew up farther south, but this was a chance to run a library all by myself. At my age, it seemed like such an amazing opportunity."

Jaeger looked bemused. "You mean, you're a librarian?"

She nodded. "I have my master's degree in library and information sciences, but I'm young. I'm twenty-six, and I've only been out of school for a couple of years. I thought I'd be a junior reference librarian for at least another two or three years, and not running my own facility for at least a decade, so I jumped at this chance."

Mick tried to blame his wolf for the images that flashed in his head as he listened to her story. Unfortunately, he didn't think he could pin the fantasies about horn-rimmed glasses and tight gray skirts solely on the animal. That came straight from the human side of his brain.

"What I didn't know was that the reason the town needed a librarian so desperately was because the last one had been killed during a coyote takeover of the town." She grimaced. "Apparently, the wolf pack that had controlled the area for decades imploded a few years ago, leaving a shifter power vacuum in town. For a while, that made it appeal to a variety of Others who prefer not to have strong pack control. But eventually, the coyotes moved in and took over. That made some of the locals pretty unhappy, and a war broke out. The former librarian—an ocelot, I think—was one of the casualties. This all happened before I got there, though, and the coyotes were careful to keep all that buried until I had already settled into the job."

"Oh, shit," Molly said. "Everything wasn't quite as peaceful as it seemed, was it?"

Renny snorted. "Not by a long shot. The coyotes kept everything looking pretty on the surface, but I found out fast that the alpha ruled through fear and violence. Anyone who stood against him mysteriously disappeared, and sometimes their families, as well. It was like he'd set up this weird little psycho kingdom where everything and everyone belonged to him, and no one was allowed to protest." She rubbed her hands against the thighs of her borrowed sweatpants and chewed on her bottom lip. "I certainly wasn't allowed to turn him down when he decided to ask me out."

Mick felt his lip curl in a snarl and tightened the muscles around his mouth. His wolf had to stop acting like White Fang every time anyone so much as hinted at Renny being with another male. It was getting ridiculous.

"Anyway, I didn't take it seriously at first, but the longer I was there, the more I learned about the town, the more nervous it made me that he wasn't giving up on trying to make me date him. I had realized by then that telling him off might backfire, so I tried just brushing him off, pretending I didn't know what he was getting at, but that just made him escalate. That's when the stalking started. At that point, I knew I had to just get away, so I quit my job and left town. I didn't even have anything else lined up. I just had to get out of there."

She paused again for more water. Molly, now seated beside her on the sofa, leaned closer to pat her shoulder. "Of course you did. You'd have been crazy to stay."

"Well, leaving made *him* crazy," Renny said, her mouth turning down as she related the story. "He actually followed me to the next town I went to. Just showed up at my door, out of the blue, like I'd never left. Like I'd never said no. That just plain scared me, so I ran."

She plucked at the fabric of the shirt she wore, the hem pooling in her lap because it was so big on her.

"That was two months ago. Every time I changed my location, either he found me or his buddies did. Once he sent them after me, I knew things had changed. He wasn't acting like just a guy who was interested in me anymore; it was as if we had actually been in a relationship that he expected us to continue. Like I was his long-term partner, and we'd just had a fight, or something. It got really weird."

Molly shuddered. "Creepy."

"Very. A couple of times, his goons almost got me, and it became clear he had ordered them to bring me back to him, no matter what. I managed to escape and run again, but they found me about a week ago near Eugene, Oregon. I've been trying to stay ahead of them ever since."

The men had remained quiet while Renny told her story, just listening while she explained herself. Or at least, Mick assumed that's what the other two had been doing. *He* had been trying to keep himself from interrupting to demand a name, location, and recent photo of this dead coyote walking, while his wolf had been trying to break free of his control and get started on the hunt already. Somehow he didn't think she needed to witness any more physical violence tonight.

Zeke remained standing, but Jaeger had taken a seat in Mick's favorite armchair. He looked like a judge hearing arguments or a feudal lord hearing petitions, his expression focused and serious as he listened.

"You mentioned earlier that you were headed to Alpha when your car ran out of gas," the mayor said. "What made you decide to come here?"

She sighed. "Their newest tactic. Lately, every place I stop in seems to suffer from an outbreak of antishifter sentiment as soon as I get there. The first couple of times, I figured it was just a symptom of the current climate."

"Sure." Molly nodded. "We've all seen on the news how human-nationalists have been getting bolder over the past year or two."

"Yeah, but that's mostly in big cities or superconservative areas of the country. Not in liberal areas like the Pacific Northwest. And not as soon as I settle into a place."

Jaeger steepled his fingers under his chin. "You think your stalker has been stirring up human radicals just to target you?"

"I'd be skeptical, too, but he basically admitted it the last time I spoke to him."

"You *talk* to him?" Zeke sounded incredulous.

"Not voluntarily, but he finds ways to find my phone number, or if he gets really frustrated, he'll join the others in the hunt for a few days. And the last time, he said I should just realize that there's no place I can hide from him, that I'll never be safe among humans, and no Lupine pack will ever accept me if I don't put down roots with them. Which I can't do with him always after me."

Mick knew she was right about the last part. Wolf shifter packs could be insular, suspicious little clans, loath to accept outsiders. Lone females usually fared better than males at gaining acceptance into unrelated packs, but most had to go through phases of testing before becoming members. If Renny had been on the run, never really able to settle in any one place, she wouldn't have had a chance to earn the trust of a pack. That meant she'd be unwelcome in pack territory.

Shunned by other wolf shifters and faced with a climate of hostility from humans, she must have felt like she literally had nowhere to go.

"He had me backed into a corner," Renny said. "And that's when I thought of Alpha." She looked straight at the mayor. "Every shifter knows about this place. It's like our version of a bedtime story—the place where different species of shifters live together in a single territory, without packs or prides, and look out for each other. We're safe if the anti-Other sentiment continues to build, because shifters founded the town and still run it. And any shifter is welcome, as long as they obey the law. Alpha doesn't turn shifters away, even the ones with issues."

She shifted her gaze in turn to each of the people in the room, her expression earnest. "I'm tired of running. I want to build a life, but I can't do it around humans. Not only is it not safe for me, but it wouldn't be safe for them. The coyotes could decide to hurt them, either to get to me or in an effort to turn them against me. And this is the only place where other shifters would welcome a stranger with my kind of baggage."

Mick's wolf wanted to welcome her in a graphic way. Then as soon as it had that taken care of, he wanted to hunt down the bastard stalker who had been making her miserable and end him in as bloody and violent a way as he could think of.

Neither Jaeger nor Zeke responded right away. They exchanged meaningful glances, seeming to communicate silently until Molly gave an exasperated huff.

"Oh, give it a rest, you two," she grumped. "You know she's being perfectly honest with you. Nothing about her story smelled like a lie, and we all know that situations like hers might not be the reason Alpha was founded, but it's still a damn compelling argument for coming here. We *do* take care of our own, and we *are* more capable than any other town out there of defending ourselves if any of the threats to Renny spill over. Give her a break already, and tell her how we're going to deal with this."

"Now, hold on a minute," Renny protested, her eyes widening. "I'm not asking anyone else to 'deal with' my problems for me. This is my mess and my responsibility. All I'm looking for is a place where he can't drive me away and where there are authorities who can handle a shifter if I need to call for help. That's it. Frankly, I'm hoping that once he realizes where I've gone, he'll finally understand that I'm not worth the trouble he'd cause by continuing to harass me."

"I wouldn't hold my breath," Zeke grumbled. With his arms crossed over his chest and his cop face on, he looked like he could stop a whole pack of coyotes. He just didn't look like he wanted to. "Stalkers who become this obsessive rarely just give up and go away. Either they get what they're after, or they go to jail. End of story."

Molly's foot darted out, landing a solid kick to her brother's shin. "Shut up, you jerk. Way to go with being welcoming and reassuring."

"Hey, I'm just being honest." The deputy held up his hands. "It won't help anyone if we don't look at the situation clearly. If Ms. Landry stays in town, her stalker will show up here eventually. We all need to be prepared for that."

"Renny," the she-wolf insisted. "And I will be staying, unless you tell me I need to leave."

"No." The growl escaped Mick's throat before he could stop it. Jaeger's knowing look made him want to unleash another one. He cleared his throat with a cough. "No one can run forever. No one should have to. If she's decided to make a stand here, she's got every right to do it."

Plus, his wolf whined, if she left, they'd just have to chase after her. They wouldn't survive losing another mate.

Not. Our. Mate.

The wolf ignored him. Again.

"She does," Jaeger said, putting an end to the debate. He rose from his chair and offered Renny a smile. "Welcome to Alpha, Ms. Landry."

"Renny."

"Renny," he conceded. "You'll find out fast enough that we're not some kind of fairy-tale paradise. Some of us can be real assholes, given the chance, but we do guard each other's backs." He rubbed his hands together in a brisk, businesslike gesture. "Now, let's get practical for a second. It's going to be dawn in another hour or so, but it seems like a cruel thing to wake up the owner of the B and B at this point to get you checked in. We don't have a motel in town, but I assume you'll need to rent a room until you find a place to stay?"

Renny winced, then nodded. "I don't have a lot of cash left, though, so I need to find a job fast. I'm willing to wait tables or babysit or anything in the short term, but eventually, I'll need to find something more stable."

Jaeger grinned. "I have a feeling that won't be a problem, but we can talk about that in the morning. In the meantime, I'm sure Mick won't mind if you spend a few more hours on his sofa. Right, Mick?"

"Oh, I couldn't—"

"Fine," Mick grunted, even as his wolf gave a happy yodel. It loved the idea of keeping the female around as long as possible. In fact, it would be happiest if she moved off the sofa and spent the remainder of the night in their bed, where he could touch and smell her. "In the morning, I'll take her out to get her car and lead her into town."

"Tomorrow's one of my days off, so I can meet her at the gas station and show her around," Molly volunteered, looking excited at the prospect. "I'll take her by Mrs. Wilczek's so she can check into a room, and then we'll check around town to see if anyone's hiring right now."

"Bring her by my office," Jaeger suggested. "I might have a line on something more suitable than waiting tables or manning a cash register."

The look of hope that dawned over Renny's face made Mick's wolf both happy and angry—happy that the female appeared to be relaxing and starting to believe she had found a safe place to rest, and angry that she'd been through so much before she got here.

"Wow. Thank you all," she said, her eyes brightening with tears. She blinked to dispel them and offered the room an unsteady smile. "Really. There aren't enough words to tell you how grateful I am, to all of you. This almost doesn't seem real."

Jaeger covered his mouth and yawned hugely. "I find most things don't at four thirty in the morning, so I suggest we break up this party and all get some sleep. Molly, I'll see you and Renny in the morning. *Late* morning," he said meaningfully. "Zeke, I know you said you didn't find any sign that the coyotes had stuck around after Mick drove them off, but I'd feel better if you took one last look around before you went home."

Zeke nodded and headed for the door. His sister paused to give Renny a hug before she picked up her kit to follow. "I'll meet you at the garage around ten? That should give you time for a couple hours' sleep before Mick takes you back to your car with a can of gas."

The she-wolf returned the embrace with a kind of visible relief that made Mick wonder how long it had been since she'd experienced a gesture of real warmth. He'd bet it had been way too long.

"Great. Meeting adjourned." Jaeger clapped his hand on Mick's shoulder, then turned to leave. "I'll see you all tomorrow. Well, later today, anyway."

There was a brief whirlwind of noise and motion as Mick's guests all made their way out of the house and into their cars. Then there was a heavy silence as he realized that he and the she-wolf were suddenly alone. Together.

He watched as she shifted her weight and nervously clasped her hands in front of her. Her fingers twisted together as she offered him a tentative smile. "Um, thank you again. Really. I owe you my life. If you hadn't—"

Mick cut her off. He didn't want more of her gratitude, and his wolf disliked hearing her sound so submissive. It didn't suit her. He had the feeling that under normal circumstances, her wolf would give him a hell of a fight, if he managed to get her pissed at him.

"Don't worry about it," he said, glancing behind her at the blanket still draped over the arm of the sofa. He knew that after being wrapped around her naked body, it would carry her scent strongly. Maybe he should be a gentleman and offer her his bed so that he could spend the night stretched out under it on the sofa, wallowing in her unique, intoxicating fragrance. . . .

His wolf panted at the thought, which meant it was a bad idea. He turned abruptly for the linen closet. "Let me get you a pillow and a couple more blankets. It still gets cold at night."

He felt her eyes on him all the way across the room. It did get cold at night, but the way he was feeling, that was a good thing. Blankets would keep his guest cozy, but he could do with a naked roll in a snowbank. Too bad it was already late in the season and the few raggedy puddles of snow were rapidly melting.

Mick wondered if he'd last through a prolonged spring thaw without losing his damned mind. His wolf wondered why he cared. They'd claim the female before long, anyway, no cooldown necessary.

Not.

Our.

Mate.

He used the words like a bludgeon over his wolf's head, but the beast didn't even flinch. It just gave him the mental equivalent of a knowing look before settling down to wait him out. The wolf knew that even the human could fight his own instincts for only so long. It could afford to be patient.

Especially considering the value of the prize.

Chapter Three

As exhausted as she was, Renny gave up on the idea of sleeping after an hour. Her body might be worn out, but her mind wouldn't rest. She lay in the darkened living room and stared up at the ceiling while her thoughts continued to race through her mind like fleeing prey. Ninety percent of them featured a tall, tattooed wolf with eyes like the midnight sky.

Stupid hormones.

They had gone into overdrive the moment she'd set eyes on Mick, the mysterious wolf man. When she'd gone into the bathroom and slipped into the clothes he had lent her, her idiot glands had struck up their own version of the "Hallelujah Chorus." Her wolf took one whiff of his scent clinging to the garments and informed her they had found their mate.

Her human side wanted to laugh. Oh, there was nothing funny about it. It just figured that with her luck, Renny would find herself destined to mate the man who saved her life, then seemed to instantly regret it.

The whole time she had been explaining her story to the mayor and the deputy, Mick had stared at her as though she had a contagious disease. Normally, she might have taken his focused attention as a sign of his interest in her, but he paired it with such strong go-away vibes that she had quickly decided he was just trying to figure out the best way to get rid of her as fast as possible. He spoke to her only when he had no choice, he did everything he could to avoid getting close to her, and he'd beaten land speed records getting away from her as soon as they'd been left alone.

It didn't indicate much of a mutual attraction.

Her wolf whined inside her head. The male confused them. He smelled like a mate, warm and musky and intoxicating, but he didn't act like a mate. Not the way she'd always imagined her mate would act when she finally met him.

Most shifters thought about that moment. The idea of true mates, destined to be together, lived in the collective consciousness of all of them, but wolves took the idea especially seriously. After all, their animal sides mated for life without the pesky habit of falling out of love that humans seemed to manage on a regular basis. To find a mate and know you'd never want anyone else was a powerful lure.

All the stories said that the moment a wolf met its mate, it knew. Certainty struck like a bolt of lightning sent from the Goddess. One sniff was all it took. A blind wolf could pick its mate out of a room full of other shifters just by their scent, and that instant attraction always went both ways.

Or so they said. It made Renny wonder if anyone had ever bothered to explain the process to Mick, because he certainly hadn't reacted to her like he never wanted to be apart from her. More like he couldn't wait to get away from her. If she'd had a lower sense of self-esteem, his behavior might have given her a complex.

Instead, it gave her a puzzle to solve. Why would the wolf she recognized immediately as her mate act as if he wanted nothing to do with her? He couldn't deny their connection; it just wasn't possible to repudiate a true mating. At most, she supposed a really determined shifter could attempt to ignore it, but why would anyone want to? Who didn't want to be with their perfect partner for the rest of their lives?

Mick, the lone wolf, she realized, frowning when it occurred to her that she had never learned his full name. John Jaeger, the mayor, and Molly Buchanan had introduced themselves to her, and Zeke Buchanan had been clearly identified as Molly's older brother, but no one had bothered to give her Mick's full name. The wolf hadn't volunteered the information, and in the habit of friends of long acquaintance, it obviously hadn't dawned on anyone to address Mick by anything but his familiar nickname.

At least, Renny assumed it was a nickname. Wasn't Mick short for Michael? Did parents actually give it as a full first name? Not that she had room to talk. Her parents *had* given her a nickname as a first name, her great-grandmother's nickname. Reine-Yves Goudreau, a wolf from a French-speaking village in Quebec, Canada, had been dubbed "Renny" by her English-speaking neighbors after she married an American and relocated to the United States. Her grandson's wife had so loved the sound of her nickname, and admired her life story so much, that she'd used it as her daughter's proper name. For all Renny knew, maybe Mick actually was Mick's full first name.

It made her squirm a little to realize that she'd known the man less than a few hours, spoken no more than a handful of words to him, and still would have bared her throat and let him mark her if he so much as sniffed in her direction. For all that she shared her heart and mind with a wolf, Renny had grown up in a human-dominated world. She'd even lived mostly outside of a pack structure, given how few red wolf shifters like her still existed.

To her, most of the relationships she'd seen modeled had been between humans or between mixed-species couples, and humans never had the same mating instincts as shifters. A shifter might recognize a human as her true mate, but a human never felt the corresponding match. Oh, they could fall in love with a shifter and commit to spending their lives together, but for a human there always remained the option to walk away if things went wrong. For the shifter, the bond could never be broken. If her mate left, a shifter would pine over the loss for the rest of her life.

In fact, many shifters never survived the loss of a mate. The death or departure of the one person to whom a shifter was irrevocably bound caused an emotional trauma that sapped away her life. All true mates lived with that risk, but fiercely monogamous species like wolves took it harder than most. Renny could count on one hand the number of lupines she had met who had outlived their mates, and most of them hadn't done so for long.

Could that be the shadow she saw lurking in Mick's dark eyes? Could he possibly have had and lost a mate sometime in his past? She thought about his appearance and guessed he must be in his mid-thirties, which was certainly old enough to have mated and lost, especially if his mate had died from some sort of unexpected trauma. Shifters rarely died of diseases, and certainly not as young as a mate of his must have been when he lost her.

If she'd guessed right, maybe this might be a good time to reevaluate that instinct about Mick being her mate. Maybe she didn't find the man all that fascinating after all. Her life didn't need any more complications, and nothing would be more complicated than trying to mate with a man who'd already lost the other half of his soul.

Her wolf snarled. It could care less about complications. It *knew* the alpha wolf was their mate, and it had no intention of turning aside because the male had been mated before. If the other female was out of the picture, then the path to their mating led straight ahead.

It might be rocky as all hell, strewn with pitfalls, and salted with potentially painful traps, but it led straight ahead.

She shifted a little on the sofa cushions. Her wolf operated on pure instinct, but Renny had the reasoning skills to know a bad bet when she saw one. Too bad her inner bitch couldn't give a rat's ass for the concepts of reason and logic. It saw its mate, and it would have him. End of story.

Sighing, Renny finally closed her eyes. Contemplating the effort it would take to win over a reluctant, trauma-scarred mate might just be enough to put her to sleep. Just thinking about it left her exhausted.

Renny blinked awake, surprised that she'd ever fallen asleep. Who knew the prospect of a doomed romance could work better than a sleeping pill?

She pushed herself into a sitting position, taking the movement slowly and assessing her body's reaction as she did. Her side still ached, but the wound in her leg had progressed from painful to itchy, which was a good sign. It meant at least that the injury had healed enough to go from a serious weakness to more of a nuisance. Maybe the day was looking up.

Looking around, she immediately felt the emptiness of the space that surrounded her. Mick's scent lingered everywhere, but in the way that said he lived here, not in the way that indicated he'd occupied the space in the last few hours.

She strained to listen to the rest of the house but heard nothing beyond the hum of the appliances and the sound of the wind stirring outside. Was she alone?

Renny got to her feet and took a second to neatly fold the blankets she'd used through the night. Her mother's lectures about being a good houseguest still stuck with her, even after all these years.

A sudden wave of bittersweet nostalgia had her fussing with the stack of linens, aligning the edges of the covers with the corners of the pillow on which she'd piled them. Her parents had died when Renny was a freshman in college, killed in a car accident with a tractor-trailer. It had been almost eight years, and she still missed them every day.

She pushed the thought aside with effort and stepped around the coffee table to check whether she was really alone. Somehow, she had expected to find Mick waiting for her when she woke up, anxious to hurry her out of his hair and back to her car. Judging by the weak light filtering into the room, though, it couldn't be all that far past dawn, and the male wolf was nowhere to be found.

Weird. That meant either that Mick trusted her enough to leave her alone in his home with no fear that she meant any harm to him or his belongings; or that he wanted to get away from her so badly that he was willing to take the risk that she would rob him blind or set his house on fire while he was gone. Somehow, she wasn't willing to bet on the answer behind door number one.

Still, she checked the other rooms just make sure. It wasn't a big house, just three modestly sized bedrooms, a single bath, kitchen, living, and dining rooms. It took maybe five minutes to search from top to bottom, and at least two of those were spent talking herself out of nosing around in the man's drawers and cabinets. By the time she finished, she knew for certain that Mick was gone. The message sank in immediately.

He didn't want to be near her. Renny dismissed the pang that caused in her heart and raised her chin. Well, that was just fine. She could take care of herself, after all. She didn't need a man to rescue her, and she didn't want to be a burden on anyone. She could handle her life just fine on her own.

Resolved, she yanked open the front door, shed her borrowed, too-big clothes that smelled of reluctant, confrontation-avoidant wolf, and shifted into her fur.

The stretch of muscle stung where she'd been injured, but once she settled into her other shape, she could feel how much she'd already healed. She could handle the trip back to her car.

If she could grab her wallet and a change of clothes, she could make her own way to the garage and arrange to get a ride out with some gas. That way she'd be out of Mick's hair with no further inconvenience to him.

Head low to pick up her own trail from the night before, Renny set off into the woods at a trot. As she'd told the others the night before, she didn't expect anyone to solve her problems for her. She could take care of herself just fine.

If Mick had thought he could run Renny Landry out of his system, he'd been sadly mistaken. After two hours of tossing and turning in his suddenly empty-feeling bed, he had given up trying to sleep and snuck out of his own bedroom window like a teenager breaking curfew.

He told himself it was so he didn't wake his guest, who had already been through enough, but he knew better. It was because he was a coward and an animal, too afraid that if he went out to the living room and saw the sweet little female sleeping in his clothes, he wouldn't be able to resist touching her. Just to see if her skin really felt as soft and silky as it looked.

Goddess, he was such a jackass. He really ought to shift into something with hooves.

He returned home in his fur, shifted so he could climb back in the open bedroom window, and found himself instinctively scenting the air. He wanted to know if the she-wolf had woken yet or if she remained asleep in his living room. Either way, he had no intention of setting eyes on her again until he put on some fucking pants.

Getting his jeans zipped and his shirt buttoned took just enough time that he hoped the leash he'd put on his wolf would hold for a while. All he needed was enough control to get Renny to her car with the can of gas he kept in the garage for emergencies. He'd give her enough fuel to get herself back to town and send her on her way. Then, with any luck, he'd go back to his regularly scheduled life of drawing and writing the graphic novels that had kept him somewhere in the vicinity of sane after Beth's death.

Too bad he hadn't shared his plan with the she-wolf. When he finally opened his bedroom door and stepped out into the house, one sniff told him she was gone. Why didn't that fill him with relief?

His wolf supplied the unhelpful image of the female lying in her own blood the way he'd seen her last night. It insisted that their mate—*Not. Our. Mate.*—was in danger and might be falling beneath another coyote attack right this minute. Any attempt to reason with it fell on deaf ears.

Mick had expected as much. His stubborn beast had a habit of ignoring him when it didn't like his human logic. What surprised him was the way his usually rational mind seemed ready to back up the wolf.

She could be in danger, the traitorous voice whispered. *And you did take tacit responsibility for her safety last night when you allowed her to stay here instead of sending her off in the custody of the sheriff's department or the mayor. Do you really want to have to explain things to them if she's out there getting hurt on your watch?*

He tried to convince himself that if she'd left on her own, he had no right to haul her back. She was an adult and free to come and go as she pleased. Besides, how was he supposed to know where she might have run off to? What could have been so important to her that she'd risk her safety if the coyotes chasing her had lingered in the area?

Try all her worldly possessions. Didn't she tell you all last night that she threw everything she owned in her car when she ran from her stalker? Don't you think she might want to make sure no one had stolen them from her, or even stolen her car, after she abandoned it on the side of the road?

Mick cursed and stalked into the kitchen to grab his keys. Goddamned she-wolf was nothing but trouble, he told himself as he stomped out of the house and climbed into his truck. If he got out to the highway and found her waiting by her car like the blonde in a bad horror movie, he might just let his wolf bite her. But he'd be aiming a hell of a lot lower than her shoulder. She needed a fang to the ass if she was willing to put herself in danger for the sake of a carful of clothes and knickknacks.

Hell, he might even be so mad he forgot to sneak in a taste while he had her skin between his teeth.

Renny stared at the trail of bright fabric strewn across the asphalt and felt her hands clench into fists. Clearly, someone else had circled back to her abandoned vehicle first, and they'd decided to leave her a message. She could smell it from the tree line.

All four of the small SUV's doors hung open, the one beside the driver's seat hanging drunkenly from the top hinge. The bottom had been ripped from its mooring. Judging by the lack of any artificial light from the interior, Bryce and his buddies had done this hours ago, more than long enough to drain the vehicle's battery dead.

Then again, the open hood and tangle of wires, as well as the clearly out-of-place bits of metal scattered about indicated someone had played with the engine, too. The boys hadn't wanted to take a chance that a simple jump start might have her on her way.

Of course, crippling her car hadn't been enough for the coyotes. The strong scent of urine wafted up both from the clothes they had tossed willy-nilly onto the highway and from the upholstery of her poor little Nissan. Shattered glass and splinters of wood marked the place where her few framed photos had been smashed on the hard pavement. From what she could tell, almost nothing she owned had survived the night unscathed.

Teeth clenched and shoulders tight, she climbed stiffly over the metal barrier separating the woods from the shoulder of the forest highway. She should have expected something like this, she told herself. She knew how vicious and vindictive Geoffrey and his minions could be when they failed to get what they wanted. Destroying her stuff likely struck them as inconsequential in comparison with what they had planned for her. They probably expected her to be grateful they had torn up only her clothes rather than her body.

She wasn't, though. No, Renny didn't feel so much

as a scrap of gratitude. What she felt was a nearly over-whelming blaze of pure, unadulterated fury.

Mother. Fucking. ASSHOLES.

Reaching out, she snatched the remains of a chewed-up shoe from the car's passenger seat and flung it with all her might at an unsuspecting cedar tree. A chunk of bark flew off at the impact, startling an innocent squirrel into panicked retreat.

It didn't make her feel any better.

It also didn't clean up the mess, repair her clothes, stitch up her slashed upholstery, or reveal the location of the purse she had left on the front seat. When she noticed the bag's absence, Renny froze.

Immediately, she raced to the rear of the car, finding the back hatch open and the cargo area as empty as she expected. Everything had been dumped onto the ground, soiled, and ruined. Even her box of precious books had been tossed aside and marked with the tell-tale, arcing horizontal stain of a male dog that had lifted its leg to leave a message.

Message frickin' received.

What really mattered to her, though, wasn't the stuff they'd pulled out of the car's open rear hatch, or even the empty depths of the hidden cargo compart-ment they'd found beneath the floor of the trunk. It was the fact that they hadn't looked any further than that.

Carefully, Renny reached into the car and fiddled around with the molded plastic bottom of the small storage area. A couple of tugs pulled it free, and she quickly set it aside. She sent up a brief prayer when she reached into the unfinished space beneath, holding her breath until her fingers closed around a small, mostly flat object. It was safe.

"Just what the hell were you thinking?"

The harsh demand startled Renny so badly, she lost her balance and tumbled off the small SUV's rear bumper. Her ass landed on the pavement, but her fingers still clutched her hidden treasure. The one thing Geoffrey's minions hadn't managed to find and destroy. The one thing she'd been smart enough to secret away.

Her emergency kit.

It wasn't much, really, but for someone who'd been forced into a life on the run, it meant everything to Renny. It contained the keys to building herself a new life.

The purse she'd left in plain sight in the front of the car had been a decoy. Oh, it functioned well enough and held a wallet with a couple of credit cards, a respectable amount of cash, and a copy of her driver's license. It also carried her cell phone, which she really would miss, some tampons, crumpled receipts, lip balm, and all the other miscellaneous junk that usually wound up making its way into a woman's purse. But it was all for show.

The things she really couldn't afford to lose, Renny had stuffed into a slim folder, barely thicker than a checkbook, and concealed under the "hidden" cargo compartment in the floor of the trunk. She'd hoped none of Geoffrey's goons would bother to tear up the shell, and for once, the Goddess had been looking out for her.

Too bad She hadn't bothered to warn Renny about the big, bad wolf who had snuck up on her while she retrieved her valuables. It might have saved her a bruised tailbone.

"What the hell do you think you're doing?"

Renny blinked, surprised by the vehemence of that growled question. "Um, I came to get my stuff back." Duh.

Mick glared down at her, not bothering to help her up off the ground. "I said I'd bring you out here in the morning. It's not even eight o'clock. The garage won't open till nine. You couldn't wait another hour?"

"I've already put you to enough trouble. When I woke up, you were gone, so I figured I could take care of this myself and save you the aggravation."

"How's it look like that worked out?"

His thunderous scowl, straining jaw muscles, and clenched fists pointed to a less than successful outcome. Renny knew that facing an alpha wolf's rage should have her trembling in her skin, but her instincts voiced no warning of danger. In fact, her wolf preened under such focused attention from its mate.

Renny wanted to smack it. "Look—"

Somewhere nearby, a cell phone rang. Her cell phone.

Mick's head shot up, and he looked around the mess of the ransacked car. "What the hell is that?"

Renny didn't bother to answer. She was already crawling into the open hatch and following the digital trilling to the space under the driver's seat. She reached beneath the upholstery and fumbled around until her fingers closed on a familiar, slim rectangle. It must have fallen from her purse during the festival of destruction.

She twisted back up to a sitting position and peered down at the display. She barely caught a glimpse before her vision was cut off by the impact of flying fabric.

She snatched at the obstruction with her free hand and found herself with a fistful of flannel. Mick had thrown his shirt at her face.

He also used the momentary distraction to lean into the cargo area and grab the phone from her hand. He accepted the call before she had time to protest.

"Who's this?" he snarled into the device. He kept his eyes on Renny and made a gesture to indicate he expected her to put on the shirt.

Crap. In the anger over what the coyotes had done to her things, she'd completely forgotten that she was sitting on the side of the road bare-assed naked. She shrugged into the oversize garment.

Her acute hearing and his close proximity allowed Renny to hear both sides of the conversation. She heard the long pause before a voice replied, "Where's Renny?"

Geoffrey's voice had her belly clenching and her hands hurrying to fasten the buttons on Mick's shirt. Instinct drove her to cover herself, even though the coyote couldn't see her. Her beast couldn't stand the idea of being vulnerable around even the sound of her stalker.

"I asked first, asshole."

"You sound familiar." Renny could picture the coyote's yellow eyes narrowing, his sharp features drawing in as he frowned. "Tell me your name and where to find Renny Landry, and I'll tell you who I am."

"Fuck you."

She heard Geoffrey growling over the cellular connection. "You don't know who you're dealing with, asshole. I know Renny's last location, and I *will* find her again. It's just a matter of time. And when I find her, I'll find you, too."

Mick snorted. "Remind my knees to start shaking. I'm going to assume you're the limp-dick coyote who's been stalking Renny all the way from California. Well, I have a message for you: She's safe now. You can't get to her, so be a good little dog-boy and leave her alone. Do that, and you won't have to get hurt."

Renny winced. The overt disdain in the wolf's voice told everyone what he thought of Geoffrey's threats, and he didn't sound impressed. Instead, he sounded dismissive and intimidating—two things guaranteed to enflame the coyote's fury.

"I don't know who the fuck you think you are," Geoffrey hissed, sounding so enraged that she could picture his face turning red, the veins popping out on his throat and forehead. "But I'm only going to say this once. The wolf bitch belongs to me, and no one stands between Geoffrey Hilliard and what's his. If you do, you'll die."

Because she was watching so intently, Renny saw the moment when Mick's expression changed. She saw his nostrils flare and his pupils expand and knew even before he spoke that Geoffrey had said something surprising and infuriating to the wolf.

"Geoff fucking Hilliard." Mick snorted and gave a chuckle that had absolutely nothing to do with humor. "Never thought I'd hear from you again. How's that cut on your throat doing? I bet that left a scar."

Renny felt her eyes widen. Did the alpha wolf know the coyote? How? Why? How the fuck could the world possibly be that small?

"Michael Kennedy Garry." Geoffrey's voice had gone soft and full of astonishment. "After all these years. And here I'd hoped you were dead. You were the sort to find trouble wherever you went, after all. The folks around here still talk about you, you know. About how you destroyed your pack and left the bystanders out to dry."

"I'm no Garry," the wolf growled. "I left that name dead next to my grandfather, and I'll piss on it the same way I pissed on him. Don't use it again."

A laugh vibrated through the phone, menacing but somehow unnatural, as if stress as much as amusement had set it off. "You never could get past your daddy issues, Michael. Or your granddaddy issues. I see that hasn't changed."

"Neither has my ability to kick your ass, Geoff. Or have you forgotten the last time you tried to challenge me?"

Holy shit. Geoffrey Hilliard and Mick Kennedy Whoever-he-was knew each other. By the sound of it, they knew each other well.

Renny's head spun as her mind raced through the scraps of information she could tease out of the conversation so far. Obviously, the two men had met and done so often enough or closely enough to not just know each other's names, but for Geoffrey to know details about Mick's family history. And Mick knew Geoffrey at least well enough to have physically fought with and defeated him in the past. When? Where? How?

What the fuck?

And had the wolf really just implied that he'd killed his own grandfather?

Geoffrey snarled, "Things have changed in the last

eight years, Michael. I don't think you'd have such an easy time of it now. I'm not a scrawny college kid anymore."

"And I'm not worried about upsetting your sister."

"Elizabeth was already dead."

"Not to me."

More growling. "Dead is dead, wolf."

"As I'd be happy to demonstrate for you." Mick blinked and focused on Renny again. Something in his face told her that for the past few minutes, he hadn't really been seeing her. He'd been somewhere else inside his head. Now his eyes narrowed. "Stay away from Renny Landry, Geoff, or I'll come after you again. Only this time, I won't be grieving for my mate, and I won't be holding back."

His thumb shifted over the phone screen and ended the call. Renny watched him warily.

When he said nothing, she cleared her throat. "So." She searched for something to say that wouldn't get her throat ripped out. "You know Geoffrey Hilliard, huh? What a coincidence."

Mick slid her cell phone into the pocket of his jeans and turned his back on her. "If you can find anything worth saving, grab it now. We're leaving."

"Hey, wait a second!"

Renny had bitten her tongue through the entire phone conversation, but now she wanted answers. How was it possible that she had collapsed onto the property of a man who knew her stalker? Talk about "of all the gin joints."

Mick ignored her, and she frowned. She scrambled from the SUV, reached out, and grabbed his arm before he could walk away. "Mick, wait—"

She didn't get out another word.

The moment her hand touched his skin, he went off like a nuclear warhead. At least, she felt as if she'd been hit by one. The wolf reversed their grips, seizing her by the wrist she'd held out to him and jerking her toward him. She crashed into his body and felt the impact as if his muscles had turned to concrete. He was hard all over.

All over.

His mouth slammed down on hers, all heat and hunger and barely controlled fury. She wasn't entirely sure what he was mad at, whether it was she or Geoffrey who had earned his wrath, but when the taste of him sank into her, she no longer cared.

Coffee and pine and thick, powerful musk combined on her tongue. The flavor was so rich, it made her head spin. Seriously. If he hadn't had her wrapped up against him by then, she would have toppled over. Her legs went weak and threatened to buckle, and still he kissed her as though he wanted to devour her whole.

For the first few seconds, shock kept her frozen. She couldn't do anything but let him kiss her. Not that she suffered from it, of course. In the back of her mind, her wolf had thrown back its head, howled for joy, and promptly thrown itself over to wriggle around on its back like a golden retriever begging for belly rubs. Their mate was kissing them!

Then the initial surprise wore off, and Renny did the only thing she possibly could. She grabbed on and kissed him back with every ounce of passion in her soul. If this turned out to be a momentary aberration, and he went back to trying to ignore her existence the way he had the night before, she intended to enjoy every single toe-curling second of it while it lasted.

Judging by the way her belly clenched, her insides melted, and her pussy dampened, her body was totally on board. As far as it was concerned, she could just lie down on the asphalt and let her mate have her. Road rash and passing vehicles be damned. This was the kiss she'd been waiting for all her life.

If any last thread of doubt had existed in her about whether Mick was really her mate, the kiss burned it up like the fuse on a stick of dynamite. He feasted on her mouth, his tongue mating with hers like he wanted to taste every inch of her from the inside out. The feeling was mutual. She felt herself drowning in the essence of him, and her body began to ache with the need to feel him inside her, above her, behind her, touching her everywhere, in every way, all at once.

Fuck reality. She would defy the laws of physics if she had to, but Renny needed him. Now.

And then he yanked himself away from her as violently as he'd pulled her to him. One minute she was drowning in pleasure, and the next she was just drowning. Or at least, that's what it felt like, because at some point during that kiss, she had forgotten how to breathe.

She stood there, mouth open, lungs straining, and Mick just clenched his jaw and turned away. "Let's go."

Go?

A voice inside Renny's head laughed a little. No, scratch that. It giggled a bit hysterically. She couldn't feel her arms or legs, couldn't get oxygen to her brain, and he wanted her to master the art of independent locomotion? Was he high?

He was not, she realized, as sanity slowly began to leak back into her body. Her lungs expanded in a gasp, and she staggered for a second before she could catch herself. She'd been the one who'd gotten high, and it turned out that the alpha wolf was her drug of choice.

She looked down and around in a daze. Where was she again? Oh, yeah. On the side of the highway, naked except for another borrowed shirt that smelled of her mate, watching the male walk away from her as though she had plague, leprosy, fleas, and a raging case of shingles, all at the same time.

If he kept this up, she was going to develop a complex.

His words finally penetrated the haze of lust he'd created in her mind, and she stumbled forward a few steps. Get her things and go with him, he'd demanded. Her "things" lay in shredded, stinking piles all over the pavement. Her emergency kit, hidden from the coyotes, was all that had survived, and she'd already recovered that.

Well, the kit and her phone. The one Mick had spoken to Geoffrey on and then shoved into his own pocket. When she looked at the wolf stalking away from her, she felt pretty certain now wasn't the time to ask for it back.

She followed Mick to the beefy pickup truck he'd parked a few yards in front of her abandoned vehicle. She couldn't believe she hadn't heard him drive up earlier, let alone stalk toward her across the gravel-strewn pavement. *Way to be on your guard, Ren.*

Mick said not a word to her, just slid behind the wheel of the truck and waited while she climbed into the passenger seat. He maintained the silence even as he put the machine in gear and pulled out onto the empty highway.

They drove for what felt like forever in a tense, tangible silence. Tangible as in if she'd been more musically inclined, she was pretty sure she could play "Chopsticks" on it. And probably display her favorite photos, all of Liberace's candelabra, and some small, tasteful statuary.

She waited for him to say something, anything, for several minutes before she realized it wasn't going to happen. The man who had barely spoken to her last night and done so only to yell at her this morning was back in control. He seemed happy to pretend she didn't even exist, let alone that she was sitting less than two feet away from him wearing nothing but his shirt.

Talk about committing to your strategy. The man hadn't just wedded his, she felt pretty sure he'd worked it somehow into his tattoos.

It didn't take a genius to figure out from his scent, his silence, and his body language that if Renny tried to initiate a conversation about that kiss, she'd find herself out of luck. Or possibly under the tires of his truck. His "Don't Go There" signs were flashing in bold, bright neon. Still, she had to do something or the silence was going to smash her into the pavement like something out of a *Road Runner* cartoon.

She searched for a safe topic, decided after another glance at his face that there wasn't one, and settled on just asking the questions she figured she most deserved the answers to. Like, who was he that he managed to have some hidden backstory with Geoffrey Hilliard?

"So, if your last name isn't Garry, what is it?" she finally asked.

For a minute she thought he wouldn't answer. His gaze remained fixed on the road, his fingers curled around the steering wheel. He might have looked at ease if she hadn't seen the way his knuckles stood out a stark white against his tanned hands.

"Fischer," he grunted.

"Mick Fischer, not Michael Kennedy Garry." She digested that and felt a spark ignite in her memory. Something about that name, or rather those two names together, meant something to her. Something significant.

When the spark flared into a bonfire, she almost slid onto the floorboards. Wolves. California.

Garry.

Fischer.

Elizabeth Hilliard.

Dead grandfather.

The facts served as kindling for a sudden conflagration of realization. All at once, the mysterious alpha wolf who had saved her life and rocked her world became a lot less mysterious and everything fell into place.

Mick Fischer was Michael Garry, the grandson and heir to the pack alpha of the Sawmill, California, wolf pack. He was the one that the people in the town she had moved to just a few years ago still whispered about, after checking to make sure no one could hear.

The Garrys had led the Sawmill Pack for generations, the most recent being a senior wolf named Abraham Garry. The alpha had a reputation for stable, efficient rule achieved through tyranny and corruption. When his son had mated against his will and then died shortly after childbirth killed Patrick Garry's mate, the old man had taken his grandson in and raised him as his heir, but not as a beloved family member. The younger wolf was blamed for his father's death and expected to walk the straight-and-narrow path from which his father had strayed.

Yeah, that apparently hadn't happened.

Another generation of Garry wolves had mated against Abraham's wishes. Eight years ago, Michael Garry's half-wolf, half-coyote mate had been murdered. When he'd found out that the grandfather who had raised him from infancy had ordered the kill, Michael had torn the entire pack apart. He had hunted down and killed the enforcers who had taken his wife's life, slaughtered the pack's beta and corrupt hierarchy, and then ripped out his grandfather's throat for commanding it.

And after it all, he had turned his back on the tattered remains of his pack and walked away. He had disappeared from Sawmill eight years ago, and no one there had seen or heard from him since.

The power vacuum he left in his wake was what had allowed Geoffrey Hilliard to claim the abandoned wolf territory. As the half brother of the alpha-heir's mate, he had the nearest thing to a hereditary claim to the leadership of the small lumber town's shifter community. He had stepped into that opening and then started a war when the locals objected. When the dust settled, he emerged as alpha and Sawmill had become a coyote town.

And then they had advertised for a librarian.

And Renny had answered.

Small world?

She closed her eyes and let her head drop back against her seat.

Try small chance at survival.

Renny had just realized that her destined mate was a man who had lost his own beloved wife and killed those responsible for her death. And if that weren't enough, he also turned out to be the ex-brother-in-law of the coyote who wanted to rape her and kill her. And, unless she missed her guess, kill her newly discovered mate as well.

To top it off, she'd brought all of it down on the town she'd always dreamed of as her perfect sanctuary.

Fuck. Her. Life.

Chapter Four

Mick clutched the steering wheel in a white-knuckled grip and tried to think up as many words as possible to summarize what had just happened. Debacle, disaster, fuckup, mistake, snafu, and (his personal favorite) cluster fuck. Epic cluster fuck. Any one of them would do to describe the monumentally wrong decision he had made in kissing Renny Landry.

Hot. Erotic. Delicious. Arousing. Mine, his wolf countered.

Mick seriously considered what effect on his human half it would have if he just had the Goddess-damned animal neutered. The vet claimed it was just a simple snip.

"Your mate was Geoffrey's sister."

Her quiet voice stroked over him like an electric current, making all the hairs on his neck stand on end. She spoke softly, but not hesitantly. Respectful, but not afraid. His wolf liked that.

"Half sister," he bit out. Beth hadn't always made the distinction, but Mick had. Did. They might have shared their coyote father, but Beth had taken after her mother in all the ways that mattered. She'd inherited her humor and compassion and gentle strength from her wolf side.

"I'm sorry for your loss."

The simple statement rang with sincerity and clenched around his heart like a fist. He was sorry, too, even after all these years. Beth had been part of him, and her loss had left him with an empty, aching hole inside. One his wolf thought this woman could fill.

Mick didn't know if he wanted her to.

And what did that make him? a voice in his head demanded. Was he trying to martyr himself to the loss? He had expected to die soon after he'd taken his vengeance on Abraham Garry, had thought that the need to avenge Beth's murder had been the other reason he hadn't followed her immediately into the darkness. But eight years later, time kept passing and Mick kept breathing. He'd never been able to figure out why.

Her, his wolf insisted.

He suppressed a snort. As if the wolf could have known they had another mate out there somewhere and had just been waiting for her to come along. Yeah, right. No one could have expected that to happen, because wolves didn't mate a second time. It just didn't happen.

He could feel Renny's eyes on him. She had turned a little in her seat, her shoulders pressed against the passenger door as she watched him. Tension stretched between them, some his, some hers. He could almost feel her chewing on something, some thought she wanted to voice, but she couldn't quite get the right grip on it, so she kept turning it over and over in her mind.

When he couldn't take it anymore, he snapped, "Go ahead. Ask."

"Why didn't you stay?"

The question surprised him. He'd expected the one he usually got, if people managed to dig up the story of his past. Most of them immediately wanted to know the gory details. Had his grandfather really ordered his wife's death? Had Mick really torn out the old man's throat and howled in triumph? Had he killed seven of the alpha's enforcers just to get to him? Had he fought like the crazed monster the anti-Other organizations tried to say wolf shifters really were?

This woman asked none of that. Instead, she wanted to know why he hadn't taken over the pack and the territory that he'd won in battle.

"Why the hell would I?" he asked gruffly as he tried to hold back the tide of memories. "That place had nothing for me but pain and bad memories. I killed Abraham because he was an evil, corrupt, vicious old fuck. He had my mate murdered because he was a bigot who couldn't stand the idea that his great-grandkids might not be pure wolf. It was never a challenge for his position. I didn't want his pack. The whole thing was rotten, just like him."

Renny thought back on the people of Sawmill, the ones who had lived in fear under the ruthless tyranny of Geoffrey Hilliard's rule. They hadn't seemed inherently rotten to her. They'd been regular people, some good, some bad, and some just too scared to do anything but follow along where their alpha led them.

"If that's true, I can promise you they're being punished," she finally said. "Living under the coyote pack hasn't been easy for them."

"Good."

The word was spoken calmly, evenly, and without emotion. It made Renny frown. If he'd sounded pleased at the thought of others suffering, she thought she might have felt sick. She had no desire to mate with a man who could take pleasure in others' pain. She also wouldn't have liked it if he sounded bitter, because that would mean he was still living in the past, that he couldn't let go of the things he'd lost. A mating between them couldn't survive that.

But she didn't know what to make of the flat, matter-of-fact tone he'd used. It could mean anything. How was she supposed to interpret the emotions behind a statement that sounded so lacking in emotion?

How was she supposed to know what he was feeling?

Her wolf whined and began pacing.

Renny faced forward and stared out the windshield. If she'd needed any proof that this mating was doomed from the start, she supposed she had it now. Any man who could close himself off to his feelings about what had to be the most painful experience of his life couldn't possibly open himself up to the intimacy of a true mate bond. Every word he spoke, every action he'd taken since they'd met, told Renny that Mick Fischer didn't want to mate with her. She would need to accept that and move on.

Her wolf filled her head with images of the kiss, replaying the sensations in her mind until her thighs clenched and she had to work to calm her breathing.

She felt herself dampen and prayed the man beside her wouldn't need to take a deep breath. There was no way he'd miss the scent of her arousal in such a confined space. How humiliating.

Renny beat back the memories. Okay, so there'd been one action to demonstrate he at least felt a similar instinctive animal attraction to her as she did to him. But one kiss and an expression of lust did not a mating make. Did she really want to spend the rest of her life with a man who wanted her but resented the fact that he did?

No, thank you.

So, where did that leave her? At the moment, in a truck with a man who didn't want her, in a new place surrounded by people she didn't know. That counted as normal for her after the past few months. She'd learned that the key to going on was just to go, to do what needed to be done without angsting over it. Renny could take care of herself, so that was exactly what she'd do, and if the wolf who was meant to be her mate refused to acknowledge their connection, so be it. She'd live.

Hell, give her a little time and a decent chance to build a new life for herself, and she'd damned well thrive. Just see if she didn't.

"I get that," she said, finally filling the silence that had enveloped the truck's cab. "And I guess that means I owe you an apology for bringing this all back into your life. Of course, I didn't mean to, since I didn't know you or that you would be living here in Alpha when I headed this way, but still. I didn't intend to involve you in my business, or to dig up your past. If you'll just drop me off at the garage, I'll take things from here. You can step back again, and I'll do my best to keep the coyotes away from you."

She felt the weight of his gaze on her and turned to find him staring at her as if she'd lost her mind. Anger mingled with disbelief in his expression. "Are you fucking kidding me?"

"I beg your pardon?"

Mick snorted and looked back at the road. "Sweetheart, you're going straight to the proper authorities so we can report Hilliard's latest threats and arrange protection for you. Then you're going to stay where we put you while we hunt down the enforcers who came after you last night and eliminate them as a threat."

Renny listened, shocked by the matter-of-fact recitation and kind of offended. Even her wolf bristled at the implication that not only were they expected to obey a decree without so much as having been asked their opinion, but she would have no active role in dealing with her own problems.

That wasn't why she'd run to Alpha. She'd needed a safe place to regroup, and Others around her who could defend themselves against shape-shifters so she wouldn't have to wallow in the guilt of putting humans at risk. She hadn't been some kind of damsel in distress looking for big, strong men to protect her. Screw that.

"Um, not so much." She straightened her spine. See? She really did have one. "I'm grateful for the way you stepped in last night and dealt with Bryce and the others while I was injured, but I don't need bodyguards. I especially don't need to involve the entire sheriff's department in my problems. They already have a job to do. I can deal with Geoffrey."

Mick took a corner faster than was strictly necessary, sending her shoulder thumping against the truck door. "How?" he demanded. "So far, your idea of dealing seems to have consisted of running away and hoping no one noticed."

Anger flooded her. "Hey, you haven't been in my shoes, buddy, so—"

"You're right, I haven't, but I've dealt with bullies before, ones way more dangerous than Hilliard, and I know the only way to stop one is to confront him. Zeke and the others can make sure you're safe while I do."

"Why should you bother?" she shot back with a glare. "You've gone out of your way so far to make me feel like nothing more than a nuisance to you, so why the hell would you suddenly care about my problems enough to solve them for me? I'd think you would leap at the opportunity I'm giving you to walk away and not look back."

A muscle jumped in his jaw, and his fingers tightened on the steering wheel until it creaked in protest. If he didn't let up, the thing was going to bend under the pressure like something out of an *Incredible Hulk* comic.

Renny wasn't even sure what she wanted him to say. Which answer would she rather hear? That he was a cold, remote bastard who didn't care if a subordinate wolf in his territory got kidnapped, raped, and killed by any rogue who happened along? Or that he knew she was his mate, and that gave him both the right and the responsibility to keep her safe?

Okay, so her wolf cast a vote for door number two, but this wasn't a democracy. Renny's human mind ran the show, not her animal instincts, and it said that both options cast her in the role of victim, and she was damned sick of playing the part. She made a noise of disgust. "You know what? Forget I said anything. About anything. Let's just get to town, and then you can do what you need to do, and I can do what I need to do." Hopefully, on opposite ends of Main Street.

As if on cue, Mick braked and drew the truck to a stop in an angled spot at the curb. Renny blinked and looked around. A discreet wooden sign in the yard of a sprawling Victorian mansion proclaimed that the building housed the offices of the City of Alpha, Washington (population 17,860). A quick glance at the surrounding area showed a bustling, tree-lined downtown area that boasted a mix of historic and newer buildings housing mostly businesses and professional offices. Apparently, they'd already gotten to town.

The realization knocked some of the wind from Renny's sails. It looked like she'd need to start making good on her speeches right away.

She took a deep breath and reached for the door handle. "Well, I guess this is it, then." She mustered a smile and wondered vaguely if it looked half as fake as it felt. "Thanks for your help. Really. I appreciate it. I'll . . . um, I'll see you around."

Fingers shot out and closed around her wrist like an iron manacle, preventing her from going anywhere. Surprised, she shot her gaze to Mick's face. She couldn't read his expression, or at least, it made no sense to her. He looked angry and impatient and . . .

Possessive?

"Oh, you'll be seeing lots of me, sweetheart," he growled, the tone rough and silky at the same time. "In fact, you'll be seeing so much of me, you'll forget to stop when you close your eyes at night. Geoffrey Hilliard isn't going to lay one fucking finger on you, and I intend to be the one who makes sure of it."

It felt as though a war council had convened in John Jaeger's pleasant, light-filled office. In reality, it was just a small group of men—the mayor, the deputy, and the mercurial alpha wolf—and one lone woman. A woman who was about to start picking the men off, one by stubborn, chauvinistic one.

"No." She repeated the word for the nine-gizillionth time in the last ten minutes and got the same reaction she'd received with every other utterance— stony stares, crossed arms, and blatantly intimidating postures. Seriously, they looked like a trio of actors trying to outdo one another on an audition for *Bad Cop, Worse Cop*. If it weren't her life they were trying to run, Renny would have laughed.

Instead, she just wanted to scream. And ask the nice secretary downstairs who'd lent her some yoga pants if she happened to have a cattle prod on hand as well.

"Ms. Landry," Jaeger began again, using what she had already identified as his conciliatory politician's voice, "it's for your own protection."

"I told you to call me Renny, and I told you to drop the bullshit." She stood facing the men, glad she'd refused to sit in the chair she'd been offered. Half a dozen times. Even when she was on her feet, they towered over her. If she'd been sitting, she'd have felt like an ant at a giant's family reunion. "It's not your job to protect me. None of you. I may have brought my issues with me to Alpha, but I always planned to deal with them on my own."

"You can't," Zeke said bluntly. "You're one woman against an obsessed man and his five closest buddies. You're also a victim of stalking, which is a crime. As a deputy in the Alpha Sheriff's Department, it literally *is* my job to protect you, and my boss expects me to do my job."

She glared at him. "Then I'll just have to explain to your boss."

"My boss just left on a two-week vacation."

Renny gritted her teeth. "Okay, how about *his* boss?"

"That would be me," Jaeger said, the touch of smug in his voice making her want to knee him in the junk. If only she had longer legs. "The sheriff is technically an employee of the city, so as mayor, he reports to me. And I say it's the best arrangement for everyone."

"And it really doesn't matter how I feel about it?"

"Sure, it matters, but it doesn't outweigh the risk of you living on your own while this coyote is still out to get you." Jaeger shrugged. "In a perfect world, you'd be safe *and* happy, but at the moment, I'm willing to settle for you just being safe."

Mick's nod snapped like a judge's gavel. "You'll stay with me at least until we round up Hilliard's minions. Once Zeke has them in custody, we can reassess if Hilliard himself is a genuine threat, or if he'll come to his senses and leave you alone once he can see you're protected."

By which point, Renny would have already lost her mind from the stress of living under guard with a mate who didn't want her and who reacted to the most amazing kiss of her life by shoving her away and then pretending that it had never happened.

Yippee.

She shook her head and prayed for strength. "There's got to be another option. I'm not an idiot, and I realize that living alone would be riskier for me than sharing a place with someone else, but I don't want to feel like some kind of prisoner. I came here to start a new life, and I won't put that on hold just to make you more comfortable. I'll find someplace else to stay, somewhere with a roommate or something."

"You can stay with me."

Renny turned at the sound of a new voice. Molly Buchanan stood in the doorway of the mayor's office with her hand still on the knob. She glanced from face to face, taking in the expressions of the whole group before she raised her eyebrow and strode into the room to stand beside Renny.

"My apartment has two bedrooms, and I like Renny," the blond woman said, daring the men to argue with her. "I'd be happy to have her stay with me until she gets on her feet. I'm sure once she finds a job and gets comfortable in town, she'll want her own place, but for now, I've got the room. It'll be fun. We can give each other facials and talk about boys all night."

Molly winked at her, and Renny felt a wave of relief. "That would be—"

"Out of the question," Zeke snapped, glaring at his sister. "This isn't about Renny being new in town. It's about the fact that she has a dangerous stalker—or half a dozen of them, if you count Hilliard's little brute squad. She needs to stay someplace where she'll be protected, not having slumber parties. And you don't need to put yourself at risk if she gets attacked again."

When Molly grinned at her brother, the expression looked sharp, as did the fangs that Renny could see had appeared in her mouth. "Fuck you, Ezekial. The day I can't take care of myself is the day I let you tell me who I can date. I can handle a few coyotes, and when she's not injured and on the run, I'm sure Renny can, too. We'll protect each other, and you boys won't need to worry your handsome little heads over us."

"Molly, you live in a converted house with three other apartments." Zeke tried a different argument, but Renny could hear the tension behind his reasonable tone of voice. "Do you really want to put your neighbors at risk if the coyotes attack?"

"At risk?" Molly snorted. "My neighbors are one of your co-workers at the sheriff's department and his panther mate, a pair of cantankerous badger shifters, and Mrs. Pendergast, whose wooden ruler has tanned more hides in the back room of her little candy store than an entire convent full of Catholic nuns. My neighbors can take care of themselves, Zeke, and you know it."

Renny hadn't failed to notice that Mick had remained silent during the argument, his gaze fixed on her and his customary scowl fixed on his face. He didn't look any happier about the prospect of having her for a roommate than she was, but he'd been the one to suggest she stay at his house. Why? Did he like seeing her suffer?

"Besides," Molly continued, "all those people just make it harder for someone to sneak up on us. Mick lives out in the woods. His place would be a whole lot easier to get to without attracting notice, and it would take help a lot longer to reach it if something bad did happen. I live two blocks from your office, which is filled with law enforcement–trained shifters. Most of the deputies could hear something happen at my place before I could even dial 911."

Jaeger pursed his lips and nodded. "She does have a point there."

Zeke skewered the other man with a glare. "Two young women living alone are still more vulnerable than a woman living with an alpha shifter experienced in combat."

"And anyone living surrounded by nosy, sharp-sensed shifters is *less* vulnerable than someone living out in the woods," Molly snapped back, hands on her hips. "Or haven't you ever seen a horror movie? Hell, haven't you ever read one of his books?" She stabbed a finger in Mick's direction but continued to direct her anger at her brother.

It took Renny a second to understand the reference. Mick wrote books? He was a writer? Wow, that was so not the profession she would have guessed for him, but she supposed male underwear model would have been too out of character. Still, he looked more like a tattoo artist than a glasses-wearing, metaphor-molding wordsmith. His own ink proclaimed his appreciation of art, and she could imagine his hands holding a needle and coloring the story of pain and beauty into someone's flesh.

Color.

Art.

Books.

Mick Fischer.

Mick Kennedy Fischer.

Renny felt her eyes practically bug out of her head.

Holy shit, was he M. K. Fischer, the graphic novelist? Was that what Molly was referring to?

Her mental card catalog flipped to the entry for the most renowned master of a genre that had been dismissed as "comic book stuff" twenty years ago. M. K. Fischer was widely regarded as the most influential writer of graphic novels in the world, and unlike most in the genre, he did both the art and storytelling for his work, combining his own words with a sharp-edged, gritty style of drawing that had garnered praise and awards from around the globe. His current and most famous series, *Hounds of Hell,* had set sales records with its breathtaking art and brutal story lines about a group of vigilante werewolves who dispensed justice to the rogues and bad seeds of the shifter world.

Others appreciated the quality of the drawing and the creativity of the storytelling. To them, reading *Hounds of Hell* was like a human reading a *Superman* comic—it let them vicariously experience larger-than-life versions of themselves doing the things their own laws and customs kept them from doing. At the same time, humans saw the series as a safe way to peek into the hidden world of the lupine shifters. It fed their thirst for violence and played into their long-held beliefs about werewolves as monsters, while at the same time it conveyed the message that shifters used their incredible strength and speed only against one another, and only when one of their kind had gone rogue or broken the laws of their people.

Everyone had read *Hounds of Hell,* and *everyone* knew, or thought they knew, about its famously private and reclusive creator. He was practically a household name.

Holy shit. M. K. Fischer was destined to be her mate. Her. Renny Landry. Ordinary, everyday librarian, whose one claim to fame consisted of having caught the attention of a coyote with obsessive delusions. How was that even possible?

While her head still spun with the revelation, brother and sister continued to argue over the relative safety of city versus country living. It took Jaeger stepping between them to temporarily silence them both.

"Maybe we should ask Renny what she thinks. After all, she's the one who will have to live with the decision. No pun intended." He looked at her and made a gesture of encouragement. "Well? Do you have a preference for roommates?"

It took a minute to wrestle her wolf into submission so that it couldn't cast its vote by pouncing on top of Mick in full view of the others. Reason, she reminded herself. She would be ruled by reason, not by her raging hormones.

She considered the possibility of living with Molly Buchanan. Sure, they'd only met the day before, but Renny liked the lioness shifter. She was smart and competent and funny, and she'd treated Renny with nothing but generosity and kindness. From the first, Renny had felt comfortable around the other woman, and in fact, she'd already entertained a couple of stray hopes that they could end up being good friends.

So, what did she think of the idea? It countered all the men's objections to her living alone, because she wouldn't be. She'd have someone else to keep an eye out for Geoffrey's minions, someone capable of defending herself against a coyote shifter, but she wouldn't have to spend every single day surrounded by the sight and scent of a mate who rejected her at every turn. It was perfect. It might actually keep her sane.

Zeke continued to scowl at his sister, a look seconded by Mick, but Renny ignored them. This was her life up in the air, and she was tired of not having one. It was time she started to live the way she meant to go on, and that did not include pining after a mate who didn't want her.

She lifted her hand to her cheek and smiled. "I think my skin has been feeling a little dry and rough lately. . . ."

Molly laughed. "I have just the thing. Honey and yogurt. You'll thank me later."

Chapter Five

Renny set a single cardboard box, about the size of a case of copier paper, down on the floor of her new and starkly bare bedroom. She hadn't needed to carry it up a bunch of stairs—since Molly's apartment occupied the bottom quarter of an old Victorian house just a few blocks from Alpha's main street—but she still felt the need to catch her breath. It wasn't every day a girl learned that all she had left in the world was a folder of cash and identifying personal documents, a single pair of jeans, one pair of battered hiking boots, and an even more battered copy of the *Poems of Robert Frost*. Everything else was toast.

Well, that wasn't precisely true, although Renny had briefly contemplated setting the remains of her car and her life on fire rather than taking the time to clean it up. Instead, she'd loaded the debris into plastic trash bags, which were currently on the way to the town's small waste-processing center. Molly had helped with the cleanup, and her angry chatter about what she'd do to Geoffrey's minions if she ever got her hands on them had gone a long way toward cheering Renny up during the sweaty, stinky task.

The car had been totaled and towed back to Alpha's lone garage for scrap. As Molly had observed, all the windows had been broken, and the hood had either been beaten in with a baseball bat or jumped on like a trampoline by five coyotes in a killing rage. The upholstery was shredded, along with most of her clothes, and all of it stank of wild canine urine. It had really pissed Molly off that the bastards had marked the *inside* of the poor Nissan, and somehow that made it easier for Renny to let go of her own anger.

Without the other woman's company, it would have taken her a lot longer to shake off the impulse to wallow in boohoos for the rest of the day. Self-pity wouldn't accomplish anything, and she already had a lot to do. She had to build a new life for herself, here in Alphaville.

"I know it's kind of small, but it's all yours. I just painted it a few weeks ago, and I never got around to moving any furniture or anything back in. It's almost like I knew you were coming."

Renny turned to find Molly standing in the open doorway, wearing her trademark smile and jingling a set of keys in one hand.

"I asked the landlord to drop off another set of keys for you. The solid one is for the front and back dead bolts, and the one with the cutouts is for the storage room in the basement." She shrugged, looking sheepish. "You might not need it right away, but you never know what might come up."

Renny smiled. Already, the lioness had done so much for her, bending over backward to make Renny feel welcome. She couldn't begin to express her appreciation.

"It's amazing," she said, squeezing Molly's hand and smiling at her with sincere warmth. "*You* have been amazing, Molly. I already owe you so much, I'll be turning over my firstborn child just to make a dent in my debt."

Molly wrinkled her nose. "Um, no thanks. I don't do diapers. Keep the kid, just fill me in on how things went with you and Mick last night." She wriggled her eyebrows suggestively.

Renny tried to laugh it off. "What things? We pretty much went straight to bed." Catching herself and Molly's wide grin, she hurried to clarify while her cheeks flushed. "I mean, he went to bed, and I slept on the sofa. Sort of. That is, I didn't get that much sleep. Too much to think about. And I already told you what happened this morning."

Molly grimaced in sympathy. "Yeah. Sorry. I'm not trying to make light of your situation, especially not after seeing what those assholes did to your car. It's just that in all the time I've known Mick, I've never seen him react to anyone the way he does to you."

Renny tried not to squirm. Part of her wanted to change the subject, since the only reactions she'd gotten from the alpha wolf had told her just two things: one, that the attraction between them was mutual; and two, that he'd rather chew off his own paw than give in to those feelings.

Unfortunately, the other part of her—specifically the furry part—wanted nothing more than to pump Molly for every scrap of information they could get on their destined mate. She might know his backstory, but she wanted the details. She also wanted to know who he was *now,* not who he'd been before he'd lost his first mate and turned his back on a lifetime of memories.

"How long has it been?" The question popped out without her permission. She might not be the cat shifter in the room, but her wolf was apparently as curious as one, at least when it came to their mate. "Since you met Mick, I mean?"

The blonde didn't appear the least bit surprised by the question. "Gah, it's been . . . what? Ten years now? Almost that, anyway. My family is one of the ones that settled in Alpha early, so Zeke and I actually grew up here, unlike at least half the town. Most people move here once they're adults, like you did, though I admit"—she smiled—"most don't do it with quite your dramatic flair."

Renny made a face. "Yeah, that's me. I love it that my life has become a bad soap opera."

Molly immediately stepped forward and gave her a hug. "I'm sorry, sweetie. You've been through a lot, especially the last couple of days. You don't need me digging for gossip when you've lost everything you brought from California."

"It's not like I had a lot with me anyway. You can only fit so much into the back seat of a 2007 Nissan."

Molly frowned. "Still, if I ever get my hands on one of those coyotes, I'm going to introduce them to a vet student friend of mine. She needs to practice her neuter surgery."

The blonde's expression of evil delight made Renny laugh. "Wow, remind me not to get on your bad side."

"Impossible. Didn't you know? You're my new bestie, and as such, I refuse to allow you to live in an empty wasteland." Molly glared at the bare carpet and empty walls of the bedroom as if they should be ashamed of themselves. As if they *could* be ashamed of themselves. "Which is why I'm not being a nice, considerate roommate and giving you your privacy. We need a plan so we can deal with the basics."

Renny blinked. "The basics?"

Molly planted a hand on her hip and gave Renny a dubious look. "Sweetie, I know that minimalism is all kinds of in right now, but even you can admit that this is ridiculous." She gestured around them. "You can't live like this. You need furniture, curtains, posters, bedding. We have to set you up. I mean, I've got the kitchen covered, dishes and silverware, things like that, and you can worry about putting your own stamp on the common spaces later, but for now, you've got to at least make this room livable for yourself."

"Molly, I've been on the run for months, living out of my car and cheap motels." She rolled her eyes. "You'd be surprised at what I consider 'livable' these days. Hell, the carpet looks cleaner and softer than some of the beds I've slept in lately. I'll be fine."

"Don't be stupid. My mother would skin me if I let you sleep on the floor. You at least need a bed. Come on. I can help you pick one out."

Renny laughed and grabbed Molly even as she headed for the door. "Hold on a minute. I don't think shopping for furniture is in my immediate future. I've got other priorities. Alpha has a hardware store, right? I can pick up a cheap air mattress for tonight and worry about the rest of it later. How about we work on the plan first, and shop later?"

"I'm not suggesting we hit the mall and empty your

bank account," Molly said. "Who wants to drive all the way to Redmond?"

"Who has a bank account?" Renny countered. "Running from a stalker, remember? I closed all my accounts to make it harder for Geoffrey to track me. I've been living off cash and off the books as much as possible. Which is why planning all this out is going to be so important. I need to prioritize so that my money holds out until I can find a job."

"Well, that's not going to take long." Molly's eyes twinkled. "Marjory Caples has been planning her own retirement party for the past five years."

"Who is Marjory Caples, and why does her retirement affect my employment status?"

"Because she runs the Alpha Public Library, and she's been complaining about the problem of finding a replacement who meets all the job requirements set by the city council, *and* who is willing to live in a small town in Washington State. Apparently, there aren't as many non-urbanite librarian shifters out there as you might think."

Renny's head had begun to spin. She had spent all of her time in recent months living under a constant weight of stress, waiting for the next thing to go wrong, for the next time that Geoffrey or his enforcers found her. She'd forgotten what it felt like to hope that good things might be on her horizon, and yet coming to Alpha seemed to have opened up more possibilities to her than she had even let herself dream.

Calm down, a voice inside her said sourly. *Remember that the special corollary to Murphy's Law is called Landry's Law, and it states that after anything that can go wrong has, the solution to fixing it all will never be as easy as it first appears.*

She shook her head. "Just because I have a degree in library science is no reason to think the city council would automatically offer me the job, no matter how badly Mrs. Caples wants to retire. They'd need to interview me, see my résumé, review my qualifications, check my references. That could take weeks. Or even longer. And I've already agreed to live in your apartment when I don't know how I'm going to pay you rent."

Molly reached across the space separating them and bonked her on the head with an open hand. Renny jerked instinctively, then gaped at her new friend. "Hey! What was that for?"

"Did you hear me say anything about charging you rent? Or about anyone owing anything to anyone else?" the blonde demanded, scowling. "No, you did not, because I never would have been such an idiot. Friends help each other out, Renny, and they don't worry about keeping score."

"But—"

Molly spared her a warning glance. "Don't make me bonk you again, young lady, because I will. And then I'll be mad, because I've been working hard at curbing my violent tendencies. After growing up with a big brother like Zeke, they've become somewhat overdeveloped. I, of course, blame him."

Feeling a little as if she'd just been run over by a steamroller of openhearted generosity, Renny blew out a resigned breath and forced herself to relax. If Molly was willing to use physical force to make her accept the help she was offered, perhaps she should just sur-render to the inevitable. From what she could tell, its name was Molly Buchanan.

"Okay," she muttered. "But I *will* pay you back, pal. Whether you like it or not."

Mick had always known Fate was a bitch, but he hadn't guessed She still had a taste for his tired ass, not after all these years. He also wouldn't have predicted that She'd have turned his own friend against him. And the mayor. And what seemed like every damned person in Alpha and undoubtedly included everyone who had met Renny Landry. It felt like a fricking conspiracy.

He slid into a booth at Al's Diner that put his back up against a wall. Literally and figuratively. Zeke and Jaeger had ended their meeting in the mayor's office with a not-so-subtle invitation to breakfast at the popu-lar eatery and had somehow herded him out of the one building and into the other without giving him so much as a sliver of room to protest.

Which was part of the reason he found himself glaring at men he normally considered his friends while they cheerfully ignored him and thanked the young waitress who had come to fill their mugs with strong, dark coffee. The two of them chatted with her as though they didn't have a care in the world, while Mick tried to think up an excuse that would let him escape their subtle plan to kidnap him and force him to eat bacon.

Sure, he liked bacon just fine. Loved it, in fact. What wolf didn't? But he knew both the other men well enough to realize that they hadn't dragged him to the diner just for the pleasure of his company and crisp, smoked meat. They wanted to *talk* to him. The bastards.

The last thing Mick wanted was a discussion, especially one about a certain red-haired she-wolf. He'd much rather be at home, at his drawing board, working.

Hell, he'd rather be getting an un-anesthetized lobotomy with a grapefruit spoon. If someone offered one to him right now, he couldn't guarantee he'd refuse.

Zeke leaned back in his seat and eyed him over the rim of his coffee mug. "You gonna sit here and pout through our whole breakfast? 'Cause that just might kill my appetite."

"Men don't pout," Mick shot back, ignoring the smirk that decorated the face of his so-called friends. "We brood. But I'm not doing either."

"Suuure," Jaeger drawled. "Your lip's just hanging down to your knees because your team lost their chance at the playoffs last night. I get it."

Mick curled a lip but refused to answer. What was the point in arguing? Stubborn jerks would think whatever they wanted anyway. They always did.

Zeke smirked at him, then looked at Jaeger. "So, do you believe our friend here when he says he really didn't even take a nibble last night?"

The mayor quirked an eyebrow. "I don't know, Zee. That pretty little female spent all night in his house throwing off pheromones thick enough to paint the walls with, and he's trying to tell us he didn't even lay a fang on her?"

Mick glared across the table at them. "She was fucking injured, assholes. I'm a wolf, not a dog."

"You're a guy, and the two of you were shooting sparks off each other the whole time we were there," Zeke countered. "I'm still shocked the damn curtains didn't catch on fire."

"You're imagining shit."

"Yeah, my olfactory imagination has a mind of its own." Zeke rolled his eyes. "Dude, I can smell attraction when it's right in front of me, especially when it's pouring off both sides of the equation. She was just as into you as you were into her."

"No one was 'into' anyone." He took a slug of coffee, but honestly, there wasn't enough caffeine in the world to help him handle this shit. "Don't you two have official duties you should be dutying, or something?"

Jaeger shrugged. "I don't know about Zeke, but I'm officially pointing out what an asshat you're being."

That earned the mayor a full-on snarl. "What?"

"You heard me," Jaeger said. He had that look on his face that said he was just as alpha as the wolf across from him, and Mick had better brace himself for some hard truth. "You've got your head wearing a very posterior look right now. The woman tried running from her problems, and that clearly didn't work. She needs help, and she's landed in Alpha, so we're the ones who are going to have to give it. Since she's a wolf, like you, but clearly not alpha like you are, she'll need protection and she'll need the feeling of a pack. You're our resident alpha wolf, so what are you going to do? Step up, or leave her twisting in the wind?"

"There aren't any packs in Alpha," Mick grumbled. "The town is its own pack."

Zeke made a rude noise. "Save it for the Chamber of Commerce, dude. You want us to be blunt here?

We've known you for nearly ten years now, and in that time, I've seen you hook up with a few women and avoid anything that hinted at a relationship like the plague. But I have never seen you react to any female the way you did to that little she-wolf. That tells me something."

"What? To mind your own damned business? Because that's what I'm going to tell you."

Jaeger added his voice to bolster Zeke's argument. "It tells everyone that it's time you stopped mourning the mate you couldn't save and start working to protect your new one."

Oh, no, he thought. If the she-wolf and her delicious lips hadn't been enough to make him admit he'd found a new mate, then Larry and Curly over here sure as hell weren't going to manage it.

He bared fang at the two of them. "Wolves mate once in their lives. I had mine. She's gone. That's it. I'm done."

"Bullshit," Jaeger said. "Wolves mate *for* life. There's a difference."

"I shouldn't have even survived Beth's murder. Most wolves don't. Taking a second mate is a one-in-a-million thing, and I ain't that special."

Zeke raised an eyebrow. "Really? Bestselling graphic novelist in history? Local celebrity? Survivor of a damned blood war in your own pack? You ain't special? Thanks for the clarification. I must have been getting you confused with another Michael Kennedy Fischer I know."

"Screw you."

"Thanks, but I think I'll leave that to our newest resident."

Jaeger nodded, his expression so falsely innocent that he looked like a demon whose homemade halo had spontaneously combusted. "We can't let our forbidden passions interfere with a true mate bond. Our sordid affair will have to end." He sighed and fluttered his eyelashes. "At least we'll have our memories."

Mick swallowed the urge to rip out the throats of his friends. He might regret it later.

Possibly.

"I hate you guys."

Zeke grinned from ear to ear. "Aw, we love you, too, Rover."

"But not like Renny will," Jaeger said, nodding. "You know, with all the nekkid and stuff."

Mick closed his eyes and let his skull thump against the wall at his back. "Why the fuck didn't I just stay in California?"

Five hours after letting her new roommate drag her out of their apartment, Renny couldn't remember when she'd ever acquired so many things in such a short span of time in all her life. Not even on her best Christmas morning. In fact, she couldn't imagine *anyone* had ever gotten this much stuff in just a few short hours. This must have set some kind of new record.

Molly stuffed the last of the bulging bags of clothing into the back of her truck with a satisfied grin. "This was a total success."

Renny ran her hand over the end of the wooden headboard that managed to peek out from behind all the fabric and imagined reassembling the old-fashioned tester bed it belonged to. Okay, reassembling and repairing, since the frame had seen better days. But then she imagined stretching out across it for her first good night's sleep in months and her smile couldn't be repressed. "Absolutely. I can't believe she just gave us the bed frame. And the mattress. She wouldn't even take twenty bucks for it."

Her friend snorted. "That's because Cathy Reynolds is not an idiot. If she'd taken any money, she would have to explain to her husband why she had sold their old bed after he had specifically told her she was *not* allowed to buy the brand-new bedroom set she saw at the store in Redmond. Bill hates spending money, not matter how easily he can afford to and no matter how past time it's gotten. But now, Cathy can paint him the heartwarming picture of a selfless act done to benefit a young woman in need. This bed represents the first step on your journey to a new life. Twenty bucks wouldn't even represent the fine they'd have to pay when the neighbors reported their fight for violating the local noise ordinances."

"That's brilliant," Renny allowed. "And slightly terrifying."

"So is Cathy. Or hadn't you noticed?"

She tried to recall the woman's face, but frankly she had met so many people over the last few hours that they all kind of blended together into one amorphous blob of friendly welcome and unexpected generosity. By the end of their excursion to the four corners of Alpha (and, if Renny had guessed right, ninety percent of the points in between), the women had managed to buy, scrounge, borrow, or liberate (from curbs and such, no felonies involved) a new start's worth of clothing, home furnishings, and decorations.

Okay, so Renny's bedroom would still probably

look a bit Spartan compared with the cheerful clutter in the rest of the apartment, but as Molly had said, minimalism was in. And besides, Renny didn't need much.

Though you wouldn't guess that by looking at the packed cargo area of the burly SUV. Molly's behemoth of a vehicle made her poor, totaled little Nissan look like a Smart car.

She stepped back and bit her lip. "Do you think I went overboard? This is an awful lot of stuff. . . ."

"Bite your tongue," Molly said, closing the rear hatch with a solid thunk. "It only looks like a lot because it's all crammed into the back of one car. You barely got the necessities today. You need someplace to sleep, right? And these bags from the consignment store are absolutely required. Or did you want to start a movement to turn Alpha into a nudist colony?"

When she heard it put like that, Renny tried to relax. Honestly, when she thought about it, she really hadn't spent much money for what she'd acquired. Molly knew all the best bargains in town, from the Newcomers Committee, to the secondhand shop, to the homes of the local residents with junk they were holding on to until the summer garage sale season. And all of them had been happy to help Renny supply herself for a new life in Alpha.

Just a few hundred dollars had netted her a treasure trove of goodies. She had a free bed and an end table–cum-nightstand for the bedroom, as well as a pair of lamps to go with them. An army of plastic and wooden hangers of all shapes and sizes would fill her closet, and she had bags of jeans, tops, and like-new clothing suitable for work that she'd unearthed from a variety of new and used shops and outlets. Honestly, she owned more now after one shopping trip with Molly than she had before the coyotes had destroyed her car.

Her only big splurge had been the fifty dollars she had gladly handed over for a delicate old vanity table and stool she had found in the back of the same store where Molly had bought a vintage glass vase. The swivel-mounted oval mirror needed to be re-silvered at some point, and some wood glue would probably make a big difference in the way the legs of both the table and the stool tended to wobble when they took any weight. The white paint had chipped badly, but underneath, Renny had spotted grains of antique elm. Her fingers itched for a can of stripper and a putty knife. When she was finished, she felt sure the set would be a showstopper. And it was hers. For her new home.

Emotion welled up and threatened to spill out her tear ducts. She really didn't have to run anymore. Her life could finally start again. The only fly in her ointment remained a stubborn alpha wolf with a chip on his shoulder and a justifiable fear of commitment.

One thing at a time, girl, her inner voice reminded her. *Remember: baby steps. Look what you've managed to grab hold of in less than twenty-four hours. If you can manage all this, that male doesn't stand a marshmallow's chance in a campfire.*

Just wait and see.

Molly bumped her shoulder and smiled. "Come on, roomie. Let's haul our treasure home and start getting you settled in. I can't wait to see how that little tapestry looks against my expert paint job."

"Me either."

Renny was still grinning, still wrestling with her first experience with optimism in more months than she cared to count, when the fingers closed in her hair and jerked her backward.

Shit.

Chapter Six

"Fucking coyote scum."

Mick grunted in agreement. After breakfast, he had brought Zeke back to the site of Renny's trashed vehicle, or as Zeke called it in his official deputy voice, the crime scene.

"They leave her anything?"

"She had a handful of papers when I found her here, but that's about it."

Zeke curled a lip and kicked a chewed and stained tennis shoe across the pavement. "Fuckers."

"Agreed. Now can you do your job and gather evidence? Or whatever the hell you're going to do. I still say we should just track the bastards down and gut them. Have done with it."

"Haven't ruled that out, but first things first." Zeke reached into his cruiser and grabbed a digital camera. "Jaeger wants this on the record. Renny's new in town, so people might wonder about her story. They won't after they see this."

Mick stifled a snarl and paced out of the way while

the deputy moved carefully around the car and its scattered contents, documenting the scene. Personally, he could care less what the citizens of Alpha thought about his mate and her story. Anyone who wanted to challenge her would have to go through him first.

Shit. Now his friends had him *thinking* of the little she-wolf as his mate. He needed to slam on the brakes before he actually found himself biting and claiming her. They already had enough to worry about.

First, as far as he was concerned, was where to find the hunting party that had pursued Renny north from California and attacked her on his land the night before. Presumably, they were the same thugs who had destroyed her car and her belongings. No one had seen them since he'd chased them off, but the wreckage in front of him provided sufficient evidence that they hadn't left the area. And that meant they could still be a threat to his mate.

Double shit. To *Renny. Ren-ny, not mate.* Stubborn wolf.

While Zeke played by his department rule book, Mick used the time to get a leg up on the predatory coyotes who were about to become his prey. He moved around the shoulder of the road in a tightening spiral pattern, using his nose to gather up and analyze the scent of each member of the hunting party. The cool mud did a good job of holding on to the distinct odors.

He counted five of them, which lined up with what Renny had told them about Geoffrey's pals. The strongest scent was easy to place, since he'd gotten a good whiff of it the night before. It belonged to the coyote he'd shot, the one who had ripped open Renny's flank and side. Bryce, she had called the bastard. He'd be the first to die.

"Dude, you're getting fuzzy." Mick looked up to find his friend watching him with an expression of mingled concern and amusement. "Remember, we are on a public highway that humans use, even if it is in the middle of Bumblefuck. You need to get a grip."

Mick fought back his aggressive response and took a deep breath. Zeke was right. He had to get better control.

Things were different from the way they'd been when he was a pup. Humans knew about the existence of shifters these days, but the Others still tried to keep from rubbing the mundane species' noses in the evidence. Shifting in public was frowned upon, while shifting into a wereform—the half-human and half-beast shape of human horror movies—was absolutely forbidden anywhere humans could see. Plus, shifting required getting naked, and humans had all sorts of laws about that.

"I take it you got their scents?" Zeke asked. "Then let's get moving. I've got enough evidence here to charge them with destruction of property, harassment, and menacing. Oh, and littering. If we can round them up, I can haul them into town and keep them at least overnight. Maybe we can put the fear of the Goddess into them."

Mick would settle for fear of himself.

The men stripped, stored their clothing inside their vehicles, and locked up before shifting just inside the cover of the trees. Then, shoulder to shoulder (or maybe shoulder to armpit), wolf and lion set off along the coyotes' scent trail.

Mick led the way, his canine nose more attuned to following specific scents. Zeke could draw air in over his Jacobson's organ and taste odors on the breeze, but Mick could follow the minute traces of it left on the ground and vegetation the coyotes had passed. Five of them had traveled this way, the slightly fresher quality indicating it had been on their way back from trashing the car. Hopefully, that meant it would take him to where they had decided to hole up overnight. With luck, they might even still be there.

When they reached the trailhead, Zeke shifted back first. "Look at this. Fuckers camp like frat boys." He picked up a discarded beer can and crushed it in his fingers. "What kind of shifter treats the woods like this?"

Mick took in the litter that marked the temporary campsite with disgust. Most shifters fell just short of "hippie" on the scale of environmental consciousness. Their connection to nature bred into them a respect for the earth's remaining wild places that humans just couldn't match.

He spent a few minutes nosing around the area, drawing in much more concentrated doses of the five coyote scents. He sorted them in his head.

Bryce—or, as Mick liked to think of him, the Dead Man—smelled musty, like something that had begun to mildew and decay. The coppery overlay of blood confirmed that Mick's shot last night had at least grazed the coyote, but there wasn't enough of the odor to indicate a serious wound. He would heal quickly, but the bitterness underlying his signature scent made Mick want to curl his lip and sneeze to clear it from his nostrils.

Coyote number two, the one with the next strongest scent profile, bore an edge of something chemical under his natural odor. Mick had detected it before, but most often in humans. It was the scent of an addict, the coyote's drug of choice leaving a permanent stain that marked his skin and everything he touched.

Three and four had similar base notes, indicating a close blood relationship. Brothers, or cousins, maybe. Three smelled a little more of a sickly sweetness that made Mick's hackles rise, but he couldn't put his paw on the cause. He just knew it made him uneasy, and it made the thought of three getting anywhere near his mate inspire him to violent thoughts. Four was less sweet and much earthier, but not like the scent of clean soil. More like mushrooms and skittering insects, earthy but not entirely wholesome.

Number five seemed to leave behind traces of metal and motor oil, like someone who worked with cars on a regular basis—a mechanic. The one most likely responsible for the damaged engine of Renny's car. Mick's opinion waffled on him. Five had contributed to his mate's distress but also provided a reason why she couldn't leave his territory very easily. The coyote thug had essentially helped force the mates together. Maybe his death would be quicker than the others.

Mick's human mind struggled for control, but in his fur, his wolf's instincts held more sway over their thoughts and actions. The man inside him might still be fighting against acknowledging the she-wolf as his mate, but for the wolf outside, it was a done deal. All that was left was the biting.

"So?" Zeke's voice had him looking up from the tangle of odors to catch the other man's smirk. "You going to lead the way to where Timmy fell down the well, or what?"

He snarled, but the deputy didn't look scared. Maybe because they both knew a lone lion could kick a lone wolf's ass in a fair fight.

That just meant Mick would have to cheat.

Zeke chuckled. "Bite me later, pal. I want to round up these fools before they decide to take another shot at your woman. It will save a lot of paperwork if I don't have to fill out death reports on them."

Mick growled but turned his attention back to the business at hand. Now they knew the coyotes had roughed it the night before and camped out in the woods between the highway and his place, but they needed to know where the five of them had gone since then. A slow pass around the perimeter of the rough clearing told him the other trail away from this site led back toward Alpha.

An uneasy feeling prickled his skin. He'd assumed that the coyotes would be doing everything they could to stay under the town's radar for the simple reason that witnesses naturally made a kidnapping more difficult. Logically, the coyotes should want to get hold of Renny somewhere out of the way, where no one would know she'd gone missing until they had time to get far enough away to thwart any pursuit. But what if the hunting party wasn't using logic? What if their orders to bring Renny back to Geoffrey made them ignore the dangers of a public attack?

He set off along the trail at a lope, not even bothering to glance back when he heard Zeke cursing. The man could shift and follow him, or he could run naked and barefoot all the way back to Alpha. Mick didn't care. He just needed to find the fucking coyotes before they found Renny.

Renny's first thought was a curse, but her second came out of her mouth in a scream. "Molly, run!"

Immediately, her head snapped back, her captor attempting to haul her away from the truck by the hair. Damn, that hurt! The pain jump-started her instinctive fight response, and she reached up and around to grab the attacker's wrist. Fingernails turned to claws as she dug hard into skin, trying to loosen his grip.

Her eyes teared at the stinging pain in her scalp, but she could still see that Molly hadn't listened. Instead of running, the blonde had bared a set of impressive fangs and hissed out a challenge.

"Back off, cat," a voice snarled. "I only want the wolf bitch. Stay out of the way, and I won't have to hurt you, too."

"Fuck you."

Molly sprang forward, sailing toward Renny's shoulder, clearly aiming to knock her captor on his ass and free her friend from his grip. Unfortunately, she hadn't spotted the second coyote lurking nearby. Or the third, who'd been crouching down between the parked cars in the lot. Both of them leapt at her, one from behind, one from the side. The one on the left succeeded in intercepting her momentum, forcing it away from Renny and her attacker and slamming Molly into the trunk of a sedan on the opposite side of the aisle.

The lioness shifted into her fur in midair and roared when feline flesh met hard fiberglass. The material dented beneath her weight, but Molly seemed more concerned with striking back at the coyote who'd hit her than assessing the damage to a stranger's vehicle. Go figure.

The hand in Renny's hair twisted, dragging her head along with it and stretching her neck to an awkward angle. It pissed her off, but it also pointed her nose in the right direction to get a whiff of who had grabbed her. The sharp, chemical sting of ammonia assaulted her, and she growled.

"Jordan."

"Ding, ding, ding." The tweaker laughed, sounding almost more like a hyena than a coyote. Then again, after years of recreational meth use, he was probably about as crazy as a hyena. "Say my name, bitch. Especially make sure you say it to Geoff, so he knows who finally brought you back to him."

She didn't waste her breath on a witty retort. She just held it to avoid the man's stench and let her wolf out of its cage.

Renny had always thought shifting while fully dressed was life's most miserable experience. Unlike in the movies, clothing didn't magically disappear or tear away like tissue paper. It tended to tighten and tangle and generally make a person wish she'd stripped before getting furry. But now was not the time for nit-picking; it was the time for survival.

Shifting while someone had a death grip on her hair turned out to be even worse, but that was probably because the clothes she wore at the moment didn't actually fit all that well, consisting as they did of Mick's shirt and a pair of too-big yoga pants borrowed from Jaeger's secretary. The garments pretty much slid away, but she guessed she might have a bald patch on the back of her canine scalp. A handful of her fur remained caught in Jordan's fist when the rest of her twisted free. What mattered, though, was that the shorter strands and heavier muscle she shifted into allowed her to squirm until her teeth grazed his forearm, opening a gash and forcing him to drop her.

Renny fell to the asphalt with a grunt, but she got her feet back under her in the space of a heartbeat. That was long enough to glance in Molly's direction and make sure that her friend hadn't been taken down by the pair of coyotes that continued to harass her. The pair was using pack hit-and-run tactics to keep the lioness busy. One would dart in from the side to strike and then dance out of the way while the other attacked from a different angle to distract and confuse. It was a tactic the Molinas had perfected over the years. Tommy and Will were first cousins and had grown up playing and hunting together. Their routine was smooth and effective.

It was also leaving Renny on her own against Jordan. One-on-one, they were evenly matched. Renny's wolf might be an overall bigger species than the coyote, but Jordan was a large male and the gender difference pretty much evened out that discrepancy. She thought she might be quicker, but if he'd been using, he might be on the hyperactive dopamine high of the drug, giving him faster reaction times and increased strength to go along with his feelings of invincibility. Plus, she was still dealing with the stiffness and weakness caused by Bryce's attack. In all, the playing field between them was probably level.

Unless, of course, he'd brought more reinforcements than just Tommy and Will. She thought Bryce had been injured last night. She'd smelled his blood after

Mick had fired on him, but she didn't know how badly
he'd been hurt. He might be healed enough to come
after her, and he still had the last member of his hit
squad, Eric, to back him up. For all she knew, the last
two coyotes were lurking just out of sight, ready to
charge in and turn the odds against Renny and Molly.

The way things were going, that would be just her
luck.

Jordan squealed at the tear of her fangs, reaching
out with his good hand to strike the side of her head,
even as his injured arm fell to his side. The blow was
sloppy and badly executed, but it still managed to catch
the side of her skull hard enough to make her ears ring
for a second.

She shook her head to clear it. Once the buzzing
faded, she could hear the yowling, yipping sounds of
battle being waged between Molly and the Molina
cousins behind her, but one sound cut through the din
with a sharp echo—the sound of a revolver being
cocked.

Rather than shifting and taking her on in head-to-
head combat, Jordan had chosen the easy way out. As
usual. He'd pulled the gun from beneath his jacket and
leveled the barrel in Renny's direction. His eyes glit-
tered with manic glee, and his pockmarked cheeks
were drawn into a rictus. His shoulders trembled as
if he were laughing to himself. It creeped Renny the
hell out.

She froze, half crouched on the pavement, claws
digging into the surface in preparation to launch herself at the coyote. Maybe that wasn't such a good idea.
She was fast, but Jordan was high, and he might be
able to pull that trigger before she managed to get past

his guard and tear his throat out. Did she want to take the risk? After all, he and his gang were under orders to bring her back to Geoffrey alive, but trying to predict the behavior of an addict was like trying to forecast next month's weather—you could maybe get close in places, but never quite close enough.

"I don't wanna kill you, Renny." He paused, giggling. "Well, actually, I don't give a shit one way or another about killing you, but it would piss Geoff off something fierce. He's got plans for you." He leered, as if Renny didn't already know all about Geoff's plans. He'd described them to her more than once. Graphically. "He said to bring you back in one piece. But he didn't mention that the piece couldn't have any holes in it, now did he?"

She heard a whisper of movement and spun just as a blur of motion came soaring over the top of Molly's SUV. For a second, Renny's heart stopped, and she thought Bryce and Eric had arrived to back up their friends, but then Jordan hit the pavement and the hot smell of blood hit her nostrils.

Not the coyotes, a wolf.

Her wolf.

Mick couldn't see through the crimson haze of rage that clouded his vision, but he didn't need to. He'd assessed the situation in the parking lot of the second-hand store with one glance from fifty yards away. It was as though Renny acted as a magnet for his gaze; not even the parked cars surrounding her had been enough to keep him from recognizing that his mate was in danger.

The coyote, however, never saw him coming.

He hit the bastard center mass from behind, taking the shortest route to him, which happened to be over the roof of Molly's truck. The coyote—a user, by the smell of him—lost his breath in a startled grunt and went stumbling off to the side, the gun he'd been pointing at Renny swinging wide and discharging into the tire of a vehicle in the next row.

The smell of gunpowder and oil nearly obscured the scent of shock and fear. Good. Fucker *should* be afraid of him.

The two-legged shifter maintained his form and caught himself, apparently deciding the gun gave him more of an advantage in this situation than teeth and claws. He was probably right, but Mick could give a shit about being shot. He'd survive anything short of a direct hit to the heart or the brain, and he was willing to bet the tweaker's hands were shaking too hard to aim that accurately.

"Step away from the bitch, wolf. I already owe you for the bullet you put in Bryce. Two's just as easy as one."

Mick simply bared his teeth and stared the coyote down. He kept his eyes on the man, circling to put himself between the gun and his mate's body. Like he'd already decided, he'd take the bullet if he had to.

At least he didn't have to divide his attention. Zeke had tailed him like a shadow from the moment he'd first caught Renny's scent overlapping the trail left by the coyotes. He'd been following their scent closer and closer to town and getting more uneasy with every step they traveled. When he'd traced the group to a retail area, all of his senses had gone on high alert. Zeke had told him that Molly planned to talk Renny into going shopping with her, to replace some of the belongings destroyed by the hunting party.

It had been too much of a coincidence for his comfort. Mick had circled around behind the strip mall on the edge of town, nearly going feral when he caught Renny's scent mingling with that of the coyotes. He'd made a beeline for the source of the odors and found the skinny, high-as-a-kite ball of mange pointing a gun at his mate.

He had fucking lost it, but it looked like Zeke had kept his head. The deputy had roared at the sight of his sister in her shifted form being harassed by the two coyotes, but he'd maintained enough control to nod to Mick before he went after Molly's attackers. Mick knew Zeke would handle the pair and keep them from helping the one Mick was going to kill.

Now.

To hell with the gun. Mick sprang forward, and as he had suspected, the coyote was too strung out to shoot him. Reflex may have made his finger tighten on the trigger, but the second bullet went even wider than the first, and this time when Mick hit him, he took him down. The gun flew out of the addict's hand and skittered across the parking lot, leaving him unarmed and defenseless with two hundred pounds of wolf standing on his chest.

Mick shoved his muzzle right into the fallen man's face and bared his teeth. He wanted this little prick to see death coming before it ripped his throat out.

Zeke's voice stopped him an instant before he struck. "Back off, buddy. I'll take it from here."

His head whipped around, and he snarled at the deputy. Zeke had resumed his human form, and the coyotes who'd been attacking his sister appeared to have fled. They were nowhere to be seen. Not surprising, considering the chances two medium-sized canines had against a pair of fully grown lions. If they'd stuck around, the Buchanans would have turned them into catnip. As far as Mick was concerned, the asshole under his own claws looked a lot like a nice, juicy Snausage to him.

"Mick." Zeke stepped forward, his expression grim. "Let him go. He's under arrest for assault and attempted kidnapping, in addition to all the other charges he and his buddies racked up last night. Let me take him to the sheriff's office. He might be able to give us some information about where to find his pals."

"Fuck you," the coyote spat, and Mick opened his jaw for the kill.

Behind him, Renny let out a whimper.

His bloodlust didn't disappear, but it sank under the much more urgent need to check on his mate. He had to make sure she wasn't hurt, and to do that, he needed hands.

He shifted quickly and went to her side, running his fingers over her and checking for injuries. He paid particularly close attention to the semihealed wounds on her ribs and leg, but it didn't look as if she'd reopened the lacerations. Still, she'd made a noise of distress. What was wrong?

"Um, excuse me, but you are stark-ass naked right now, which is traumatic enough for me to deal with. Did you just pull a pair of handcuffs out of your ass, too?"

Molly's question had his mate huffing out a sound that could have been a laugh, if Renny had been in her human form. Relief washed over him.

"Of course not." Zeke's calm reply was punctuated by the metallic click of the locks engaging. "I stashed a pair in your truck the last time I borrowed it."

"But you've never borrowed my truck while you were on duty. The last time I loaned it to you was when you wanted to help Jessie Vargas haul away some—" Molly's voice cut off abruptly, followed by gagging noises. "Oh, ew! Gross! Ick! Blech! Yuck! That is *not* something I need to know about my brother. Argh! Get me some brain bleach."

Under his hand, Mick felt a flood of warm energy as soft fur gave way to smooth skin. This time, he couldn't mistake her laugh. Renny giggled like a loon.

"Oh, my Goddess, Molly, if you could see your face right now? You look like you just got your mouth washed out with soap."

"I wish. I'd shove it in my ear next, and hope it got someplace really useful!"

The giggles turned into belly laughs, and Renny leaned against him for support.

Mick felt something snap inside him. Without thought, without hesitation, and sure as hell without a plan in mind, he let fangs fill his mouth for an instant and then sank them deep into the curve of his mate's shoulder.

She was his, and he staked his claim with primitive satisfaction.

He marked her.

Renny cried out, not from the pain of Mick's claiming bite, but from the realization that the most momentous act of her life had just happened in the parking lot aisle of a used-clothing store. Her shout ended with a note of disbelief and anger.

"What the fuck?" she demanded.

"Uh-oh," she heard Molly chant gleefully. "I think someone's in trooooouuuuble. . . ."

Not just in the parking lot of a used-clothing store, but in front of a damned audience! The jerk!

She punched him in the chest, hard. "I can't frickin' believe you, you asshole! What the hell were you just thinking?"

"Dude, he's naked," Zeke said under his breath. "I think what he's thinking is pretty hard to miss at the moment."

Molly made a sound of agreement. The added note of appreciation had Renny growling a warning at her new friend.

The woman's eyes went wide and she stepped back behind her brother. "Yeah, so, Zeke, why don't you give our little friend here a ride back to town, huh? And I'll . . . I'll just . . . go. Away."

"Don't bother," Mick snarled, scooping Renny into his arms and surging to his feet. "My mate and I are leaving."

Without another word, he tossed her into Molly's car, snagged the lioness's keys, and sped out of the parking lot, leaving his friends naked and carless behind him.

Renny stared at his intense, strained expression and swallowed hard. Huh. It looked like she was getting kidnapped after all.

Chapter Seven

Within a matter of minutes, Renny found herself back in Mick Kennedy's isolated house in the woods, but this time, she didn't get anywhere near his sofa. He hauled her from the purloined vehicle straight through to his bedroom and tossed her down onto the mattress so hard she bounced.

Given that she was still naked from her shift, the resulting movements drew a hot look of appreciation. In fact, for a second, she thought he might scoop her up and throw her again, just to watch her breasts jiggle.

He prowled toward her, unhindered by the need to stop and strip. Being a shifter did have its advantages in the romance department, it seemed.

Renny watched while instincts and emotions twined inside her until they had her knotted up tight. Lust, of course, colored everything. How could it not when her mate had brought her to his bed and now crouched over her like a living god carved in muscle and sinew? His golden skin seemed to glisten with the light sheen of perspiration caused by arousal. It made the rich, brilliant color of the ink decorating his arms almost too intense to look at, but she had to touch.

Her fingers moved without her guidance, settling on the hot skin covering his biceps and tracing the curve of a deadly claw drawn in black and shades of gray and stained with crimson.

"Did you draw these?" she heard herself ask.

"No. I only draw on paper." His voice sounded tight and deep and so rough she could barely make out the words. Maybe words weren't what they needed right now.

She dragged her gaze from the collage of tattoos and met his, dark and intense. His blue eyes looked nearly black, even in the afternoon light that still filtered through the curtains. The pupils had all but swallowed the irises, and he looked as if he wanted to swallow her just the same way.

Well, maybe he looked like he'd pause for a little taste.

The thought barely registered before his head dipped and she felt the wet heat of his tongue press against the side of her throat. He licked a trail from collarbone to jawline, an agonizing journey that seemed to take days to complete. Everything in her softened and tightened, tensing and melting simultaneously. She felt the pooling dampness between her legs and the clawing fist of hunger below her belly.

"I thought I wasn't your mate," she gasped, struggling to hold on to the sanity he was slowly ripping away. "Thought you didn't want me."

He gripped her hips on either side, fingers digging in hard enough to bruise. She didn't care. All she could feel was that he was touching her. Her mate was touching her.

"Never said I didn't want you." He scraped his teeth across the base of her throat, the edges catching on the tendons at either side and making her shiver in reaction.

"You haven't acted like you want me." Her voice shook as Mick closed the slight gap between their bodies, settling his weight on top of her like a living blanket. A hot, hard, aroused living blanket.

"No?" He nuzzled the tender spot behind her ear, and a whimper escaped her. "How about now?"

A big, rough hand pushed between her legs and cupped her heat.

"Oh, fuck," Renny gasped.

"Good idea," he all but purred.

He dragged her under a tide of relentless need. His fingers probed and stroked, sliding through her wetness and dragging across nerve endings that seemed directly connected to the dopamine receptors in her brain. If this felt anything like the sensations using drugs gave Jordan, it was no wonder the coyote was an addict. She thought she could get hooked as well. In fact, she might already be.

Her arms rose to wrap around his shoulders, drawing him closer to her. At first, the move felt awkward, hesitant. He'd spent so much of the time that they'd known each other pushing her away that part of her couldn't believe that now he was letting her touch him. Now, he was pinning her to the softness of his bed and using his knee to spread her thighs until his hips could rest in the cradle of hers.

His fingers continued to tease her, and the hand

acted as a barrier that prevented her from feeling his erection where she most wanted it. Instead, it pressed against her hip, hot and hard, while he dragged a callused thumb in slow circles around her clit.

Goddess, he was killing her.

"Mick, please." She lifted her hips into his touch, begging for more. She felt hollow and aching inside, could feel her muscles clenching around nothing, and she moaned.

"Shh," he murmured against her skin, stringing kisses down her breastbone, nudging the soft underside of her breasts, and making her nipples tighten into hard little points of need. "Smell so good."

His tongue swept out and curled around her nipple in a caress she would swear went straight to her core. She bucked against his fingers and dug her nails into his back.

Mick.

She wasn't sure if she'd spoken his name, wasn't sure if she could still speak. She'd become a creature of sensation, her body nothing but the experience of his hands on her, his skin pressed close, his weight bearing her down. Goddess, was this what it was supposed to be like? Having a mate? Didn't it scare people? Because she was terrified.

She was terrified of being overwhelmed, and even more terrified that he might stop. He'd gone from being something she wanted to something she needed, like air or water. She had to have him or her wolf would go mad.

The bitch had finally stopped fighting her. It had gone silent, as if drugged by the scent and touch of their mate. This was what it had wanted all along, so it didn't need to drive the human self forward. As long as they stayed close, the wolf was content.

But Renny needed to get even closer.

She shifted to wrap her legs around him and lost her ability to breathe when the movement forced his touch harder against her. Two fingertips slid to her entrance and pressed. She lifted into him, trying to take him inside, but he eased back until she felt like screaming.

What was the matter with him? He'd already marked her, bitten her shoulder and left the imprint of his fangs on her skin, and he'd done it in front of the Goddess and everyone. Then he'd practically dragged her back to his bed, breaking land speed records on the way. She'd really thought he'd quit wasting time, but now he seemed determined to move at a glacial pace.

A glacial pace *before* the onset of global warming.

Renny rocked against him, her body seeking to urge him faster, closer, deeper, more. His response was a nip to the curve of her breast that only made her more desperate. Two could play that game.

She slid a hand up along his spine, letting her nails scrape the skin until he shuddered against her. Encouraged, she tangled her fingers in his hair and tried to pull him back up where she could taste him, but the alpha dug in his heels. He reached up and captured her hand, pinning it to the mattress at her hip, then repeating the pattern on the other side.

Eyes glittering, he lifted his head to stare down at her, his lips curved wickedly. "Not done yet, little red," he purred, just before he pressed that mouth against her sex.

She jerked as though she'd been struck by lightning. Hell, she wouldn't have been surprised if she glowed from the inside out like something from a cartoon, an X-ray image of herself lit up by the feel of his tongue parting her folds and tasting her.

Her head swam, the room seeming to tilt and spin as he pressed pleasure on her, touching and teasing and devouring her. She struggled against his hands and hoped like hell she wouldn't get away. She didn't want to go anywhere, didn't want him to ever stop, but she couldn't just lie there when the pleasure grew and grew until it became so intense, it felt like a living thing inside her, struggling to get out.

He dragged from her a climax she never saw coming. One second, she felt like every breath just twisted her tighter on the rack of desire, and the next, the tension inside her snapped. She flew apart like the casing on a firework, exploding in a burst of hot, wild energy. Her ears rang with a high, clear note, and it took a minute before she realized it came from her own mouth, that she had cried out, helpless against the power of it.

She blinked against a brilliant darkness, trying to figure out if her eyes were closed or she'd just gone blind from synaptic overload. Then it didn't matter, because before the echo of her voice had faded away, she was shouting again, overcome by the burning stretch and incredible ecstasy of her mate plunging inside her.

Mick shifted and drove himself inside her with primal urgency. With his mouth on her, she'd felt untethered and adrift, held in place only by his hands gripping her wrists and his lips and teeth and tongue driving her into mindlessness. Now, he loomed over her, blocking out the rest of reality until she felt pinned down and

overwhelmed, unable to feel or see or smell anything
but her mate.

Her mate above her.

Against her.

Inside her.

Claiming her.

He moved on her with a hard, relentless rhythm, his
thighs forcing hers wider as he sought to get closer and
surge deeper. She tilted her hips, receptive and eager,
until every thrust rubbed the base of his shaft against
her most sensitive bundle of nerves. Each movement
sent a shock of pleasure through her, making her body
tighten around him, which made him thrust harder
and rub with greater pressure.

She was caught in a feedback loop of arousal, him
stroking her, which made her squeeze, which made him
stroke, until another orgasm began to build inside her.
It writhed low in her belly and sent shivers like ripples
in a pond up and out, until she swore that when she
came, she could feel it in her fingers and her toes and
every strand of her hair.

He wrecked her, but she wasn't going down alone.

While he moved more forcefully above her and inside her, chasing his own climax, Renny let her wolf
have its way. The animal leapt forward, swift and eager,
sharpening her pathetic human canine teeth into proper
two-inch fangs, which it sank deep into her mate's
muscled shoulder.

He howled and poured himself into her, shuddering
through his release. The sound he made was almost
more animal than human, and her wolf recognized and
gloried in the ululating cry. She would have answered,
but that would mean releasing her grip, and she wasn't

ready to do that. She wanted her mark deep and clear on his flesh so that even a casual glance would tell all other females that this male belonged to her.

Mick collapsed on top of his mate and waited for the earth to settle back onto its axis. Somewhere in the middle of that epic mating, he felt pretty sure they had knocked the entire planet out of alignment. He couldn't think of any other reasonable explanation for the experience. Together they had literally rocked the world, laws of physics be damned.

It took hours to catch his breath, but the time passed pleasantly with his lush, fragrant mate serving as his pillow. The heat they had generated had intensified her scent, the sweet, spicy notes strong enough to cut through the musk of sex and embed themselves in his memory. From now on, anytime he smelled the sweet bite of nutmeg and the soft comfort of warm sugar cookies, he would think of his mate and become aroused.

Damn. Christmastime was going to be awkward.

He nuzzled her ear, dragging in one last lungful of delicious female, before rolling off of her and dragging her against his side. Now that he'd claimed his mate, he didn't want to smother her on their first night together. That just seemed rude.

Plus, it would pretty much rule out his hopes for round two a little bit later.

Renny shifted until her head rested in the hollow of his shoulder, one knee drawn up and draped over his. She fitted against him like the missing piece of a puzzle, and she rested there, one hand over his heart, while their skin gradually cooled.

The room had grown dim as afternoon turned to evening, but neither of them made any move to turn on a light. Their lupine eyes could see perfectly well in much darker environments, and moving would remind both of them of the reality lurking like a watchful predator outside their bubble of intimacy.

If he could press a pause button and freeze that moment indefinitely, he would have. He would have kept them pressed together in silence, connected by the act they had just shared and free from the shadows of the past and the complications of the future. Then his shifter metabolism kicked back into gear and his stomach growled at him to replace all those calories he'd just burned off. Kind of a mood killer.

He felt her breath huff against his skin. "Yeah, I could eat a cow," she murmured, her voice husky and blurred around the edges. "We should probably get up and do that."

"I can't pasture cows out here in the woods, but I can keep steaks in the freezer."

"Good enough."

She pulled away from him and sat up, pushing her tangle of dark red hair back over her shoulders. The move exposed the mark he'd left on her shoulder, the reddened imprint of his fangs forming a shape like a crescent moon in the curve where neck and shoulder joined. Hours later it still looked raw and fresh, but then, it always would. She would bear his mark forever, a visible warning to other males that she belonged to him.

Absently, he reached up and felt the evidence of her mark on his skin. His fingers traced the dainty curve, then without thinking moved to the opposite side of his neck where another mark had once decorated his flesh.

She watched him, her expression solemn, and he immediately jerked his hand away from the faded silver remains of Beth's mark.

"Don't," Renny said softly. "It's okay. I know she had you first. I'd never want you to think that I expect you to forget about her. I don't. She's part of you. Always will be. The scar is just proof of what you've survived."

Her smile was crooked, but it looked sincere. Mick tried to believe her, but he was enough of an asshole to have his doubts. After all, if she'd had another mate, seeing the dead male's mark on her wouldn't make him think of everything she'd survived; it would make him think of another male putting his hands on her sweet body.

Yup, he was definitely an asshole. She should probably know that from the start.

She had already risen from the bed and spotted his rarely used bathrobe draped over its hook on the back of the door where it lived and collected dust. She dragged it on while he grabbed the first pair of jeans he saw. They hadn't made it into the hamper, so he assumed they were reasonably clean.

"I doubt I'd be so generous if I were you," he grumbled, following her down the hall to the kitchen. She obviously remembered her way around from the night before.

She opened the refrigerator door and shot him a sideways glance filled with amusement. "So do I. It's the testosterone. Makes you boys less forgiving than we are."

Hell, she was probably right. He reached past her and snagged a package of steaks he'd been thawing. "Guess I should just shut up and count my blessings, then."

Renny sighed and slipped away to take a seat at his kitchen table. "I didn't say that. I just didn't think you'd be ready to talk about this."

Uh-oh. Her tone warned him to tread carefully. He pulled out a giant skillet and set it to heat on the stove top. "About the differences between men and women? I figured we covered those pretty thoroughly a little while ago."

"About you and me. About us."

Yeah, very, very carefully. He aimed for casual as he tore open the package and seasoned the meat. His wolf might be happy to tear into its dinner plain and bloody, but he'd always figured that was just because without opposable thumbs, it had never figured out how to work a pepper mill.

"I guess I didn't realize we needed to talk." He shrugged. "We're mates. We both knew it, we both did something about it. Seems clear to me."

She snorted. "Only because you're a man. It's one of those differences you mentioned."

He drizzled oil into the skillet, then turned toward her while it heated. He kept his expression blank. "Okay, so what did you want to talk about?"

Renny made a face. "I don't *want* anything to do with this topic, no more than you do. I just think we need to know where we stand with each other."

"As far as I'm concerned, we stand next to each other. That's what mates do."

"Even when they never wanted to be mated at all?"

He opened his mouth to demand if she was telling him she didn't want to be his mate, but he couldn't do it. He knew that was a cheap tactic, deflecting his own issues onto her and using them to drive a wedge between them. It would be the easy thing to do, but it wouldn't accomplish anything. It would just cause them both pain, and personally, he'd done enough hurting for this lifetime.

Putting the steaks on to sear gave him a minute to collect himself and to decide how he was going to get this out without it sticking in his throat. It also gave him an excuse not to have to look at her when he finally managed it.

"I don't think it matters all that much what I wanted before today," he said, turning when he heard her sharp intake of breath. He saw the flash of hurt in her expression and struggled to reassure her. "That didn't sound the way I meant it. Shit. I suck with words."

She made a rude noise. "Tell that to the bestseller lists, Mr. Novelist."

"*Graphic* novelist," he corrected. "The pictures tell the story for me. Most of what I write consists of curse words and sound effects."

"I've read the *Hounds of Hell,* series, Fischer. Don't be coy. It doesn't suit you."

He ignored the thrill he felt at knowing she'd seen his work and at the implication that she thought it deserved the accolades it had earned. He'd bled out his nightmares onto the pages of those books, reliving some of the worst moments of his life behind the mask of his fictional characters. In the world he'd created, the villains always faced justice, and the heroes occasionally managed to find some peace. Until Renny, he hadn't thought such a thing existed outside of his make-believe universe.

"I'm not being coy," he insisted. "I'm telling you, *trying* to tell you, why I sound like an idiot when I say this shit. 'Shit' is probably my favorite word. Well, second favorite, after 'fuck.' I use them a lot, in my books and in my life, because they come a lot easier than ones like this."

He paused and took a deep breath. "Renny, it really doesn't matter what I wanted before I met you, because you're my mate. End of story. I can't pretend that I don't need you like I need both arms, even if it would scare me a fuck of a lot less if I could."

"Wow. You really do suck at his."

He growled. "I warned you."

"You're also about to burn our dinner."

Mick swore and quickly flipped the steaks, then removed the pan from the heat and turned off the burner. The cast iron would stay hot long enough to finish cooking the beef and he needed to focus here.

"Mick, I—"

"No." He cut her off. "Let me finish mangling this. It's true that I didn't want another mate. I barely survived losing the first one, and the thought of putting myself at risk for that kind of pain again? I'd rather let Dr. Wilczek neuter me like a cocker spaniel."

She snickered, but he could see the understanding in her expression.

"It scares the shit out of me to have found another mate," Mick continued, "because I *know* what it would feel like if anything happened to you, and I know that right now, you're in very real danger. This isn't a matter of, Oh, anyone could step outside their front door and get hit by a truck. This is, Your front door currently opens onto the fast lane of I-5. Geoffrey Hilliard already wants to hurt you, but now that he knows I'm trying to protect you, he'll want it even more, because hurting you would be a blow to me. If he knew what kind of a blow, he'd kill himself trying to get to you."

"He's been trying for months," she said. "He hasn't managed it yet."

"He's come way too close for my comfort." He crossed the space between them and crouched beside her chair. "Whatever I wanted before is gone. I know I did everything I could to pretend you meant nothing to me, but I think I can stop now, because that ship hasn't just sailed, it's hit an iceberg and been lost at sea. You *are* my mate. So, from here on out, we're going to forget about my idiocy and move forward together. Deal?"

Her lips twitched. "Sounds pretty convenient for you, if you ask me. I just pretend you didn't treat me like a leper for the first eighteen hours of our acquaintance, and you get all the benefits of having a mate without even having to work for it?"

He let himself grin. "Sounds good to me."

"Asshole," she muttered, but since she was pressing her mouth against his when she said it, he decided to let it slide. He had more important things to do.

Like untie the knot she'd put in the belt to keep his robe closed around her petite frame. And then, he figured he'd see exactly how sturdy his kitchen table really was. He'd always wondered.

Finally, afterward, he and his mate could always eat their steaks cold. They *were* wolves, after all.

Chapter Eight

"The coyote's dead."

Mick stared at his friend for a minute, then shook his head. "I'm sorry, what?"

"He's dead," Zeke repeated grimly. "O. D. Nelson found him when he did rounds about an hour ago. He was already cold. There was nothing we could do."

"How the fuck did that happen?" Mick snarled. Renny almost flinched at the viciousness in the sound. Her mate was seriously pissed. "He was in *jail,* for fuck's sake. Where did he get enough drugs to overload a fucking *shifter's* metabolism?"

The lion's jaw tightened. He looked about as happy as Mick sounded. "We don't know for sure, but he must have had them on him when he was booked. Somehow, the officer who did the search missed them during his processing."

From Zeke's expression, Renny was guessing the officer in question would be spending most of the rest of his day removing the boot from his ass. "Okay, so Jordan Heins is gone. What does that really mean, though? I mean, Bryce and the others are still out there. Has all that much changed?"

"No, and that's the problem," Zeke said. "If we'd gotten a chance to question Heins, we'd have an advantage. We'd know where the coyotes are hiding out in the area, possibly what plans they've dreamed up to get to you next time, and we might even have a way to track down Hilliard."

Renny blinked. "Track him down? I can give you his address and phone number right now. Hell, I can draw you a map of Sawmill and mark in all his favorite hangouts, if you want. I had to know all about them if I was going to avoid them. Just give me a pen."

"It's not that simple."

Beside her, she felt Mick stiffen. "Explain."

"That's the other reason I asked you guys to come into town." Zeke ran a hand over his head, and judging from the state of his hair, he'd been doing that a lot in the last few hours. "On his intake form, Jordan Heins listed Geoffrey Hilliard as an emergency contact, so when they found him unconscious, they tried to reach Hilliard."

Something told Renny she wouldn't like what came out of the deputy's mouth next. "And?"

Zeke's lips compressed into a tight line. "And as far as we can tell, he isn't in Sawmill, California, anymore."

Mick let out a string of curses that should have made Renny blush, but she was too busy going numb. It didn't take a genius to figure out why the news would make the sheriff's department so uneasy. If Geoffrey wasn't holding court in the town he controlled, treating the locals like his property, and generally causing misery wherever he went, it could mean only one thing—he'd decided to focus all his attention on Renny so he could find her and redefine the whole concept of "misery" for her from the ground up.

She swallowed hard and tried to fight back her instinctive panic response. She told herself that she wasn't alone anymore, that she didn't have to drop everything and run yet again in a futile attempt to stay ahead of her personal boogeyman. She was in Alpha now, and she had not just allies, but the authorities on her side. She didn't have to be afraid that Geoff would find her isolated and vulnerable and snatch her away while the people around her remained unable and un-protected, or uncaring and unmoved.

Did she?

"What do you know?" Mick demanded, his voice harsh. His big hand closed around hers and squeezed. Until then, she hadn't realized she was shaking.

"Not much yet, but we're digging hard. The sheriff has reached out to the police and sheriff's departments in that area, and we've got people making calls, comb-ing through social media, anything we think could possibly tell us what he's up to."

Mick snorted. "You know damned well what he's up to, and you don't need to surf the Web to figure it out. He's headed this way. I probably pulled the trig-ger when I answered Renny's phone yesterday." He looked down at her, and she could read the regret lurk-ing beneath the anger in his eyes. "I shouldn't have taunted him like that. I knew what kind of hotheaded bully I was dealing with, but I lost my temper."

Renny leaned her shoulder against him and shook her head. "You can't take that on. He's been stalking me for months. If you hadn't driven him to this point, something else would have. Eventually, he was always going to get tired of letting Bryce and the others hunt me down and come after me himself. That was a foregone conclusion."

He didn't look comforted. "Yeah, but I didn't have to push it."

"Let's not waste time with the blame game," Zeke said, leaning his hip against his cluttered desk.

Around them, the sheriff's office buzzed with activity, some of which Renny now knew centered on keeping her safe. The knowledge made her feel guilty even as it offered her a level of reassurance she hadn't felt in what seemed like forever. She had people on her side now, and while she wished their help and protection weren't necessary, she sure as hell wasn't dumb enough to turn it down.

"Anyway, Renny's right. Hilliard's pattern of behavior already established that this was coming. A direct move on his part was inevitable. If anything, you just pushed the time line forward a little."

Renny tried to look on the bright side. "And that's not necessarily a bad thing. I mean, at least if he shows up now, it will bring things to a head, right? I'm all for anything that will put an end to this whole situation."

"Yeah, but not if the end turns out to be him getting his fucking hands on you." Mick's snarl carried more wolf than she'd ever heard from someone still standing on two legs.

Renny snuck a glance at him just to make sure he hadn't shifted into a wereform while she wasn't looking. Most lupines avoided taking the half-human, half-animal shape because it played too much into the horror movie vision of werewolves that humans held in their heads. The Others still had to go out of their way to keep the larger "normal" population comfortable with their presence among them. No one wanted to encourage fear or panic, because those would just lead to persecution. Their kind still remembered the days of vampire slayings and werewolf hunts perpetrated by humans who had learned of them before the Unveiling. Those days needed to stay in the past.

Besides, holding a wereform took an insane amount of energy. Most lupines reserved it for ceremonial occasions, like Mate Hunt challenges, and even those almost never happened anymore. Thank the Moon. As far as Renny was concerned, some of the old ways in lupine culture had made human misogyny look like a tea party.

She tried to reassure her mate. "He won't get to me, not now. Before, it was always a danger, because I was on my own and being constantly on the run meant I couldn't form any ties to anyone long enough for them to notice or care if I just disappeared. But he'd be crazy to try and grab me now. Too many people know who I am, where I am, and what I've been up against. For Pete's sake, I even have the police looking out for me now."

Mick let go of her hand, but only so that he could wrap a tattooed arm around her and drag her even closer against his side. "I'm not convinced crazy isn't a factor."

Zeke nodded. "Me either. Stalkers are all unbalanced to one degree or another. Normal people don't do this kind of crap. But Renny's right about one thing. The fact that she's here and we know about her situation means that we can protect her. We just need to put some safeguards in place."

"She gets twenty-four-hour protection," Mick immediately agreed. "A guard goes with her everywhere that I can't. If the department can't handle that, Jaeger will have to make arrangements himself. He's the closest thing we have to a town alpha. People will take orders from him if he gives them."

Renny thought about having a bodyguard dogging her heels every moment of the day and experienced an unexpected resurgence of her independence. That did not sound like fun.

"Let's not get carried away, guys," she said. "I'm not eager to get myself kidnapped, but don't go overboard. How often would I be in real danger? Living with Molly means I'll almost never be home alone—"

Mick growled. "Living with Molly is not happening. You're moving in with me."

She cocked her head to the side. "I'm what, now? I think I must have missed something, because I don't remember us having this discussion at any point in the last two days."

He scowled down at her. "What's to discuss? We're mated, with the marks to prove it. Did you think we wouldn't be sharing a den?"

"I *thought* it was something we'd have to talk about, but I know for sure it hasn't come up yet. I think it's the kind of thing I'd remember."

"Is it the kind of thing you want to fight about?" His tone offered a clear challenge, and his face told her he fully expected to come out on top.

Was it wrong that she experienced a little thrill of

arousal at the show of dominance? She knew Alpha had a medical center, but she wondered if they had a psychiatrist on staff. Maybe it was something she should look into. . . .

She could admit that Mick was right, though. Once they had mated, living together became the inevitable consequence. Neither of them could stand to be parted now, so trying to assert her independence at this point would be like going blond—she could bleach her hair, but she'd still be a redhead underneath, and her roots would prove that to the world sooner or later.

"No, I don't want to fight"—she sighed—"not about this. I'm pretty sure we'll find another reason sooner rather than later. But I also don't want to be left out of the discussion about my own safety. I'm not an idiot, and I don't want to take any unnecessary risks, but I also won't sit my meek little ass in the corner while you big, strong men rearrange my life for me."

She thought she saw Mick roll his eyes, but he was smart enough to look away while he did. "Trust me, sweetheart, no one is going to start calling you meek."

Zeke grinned. "Definitely not the word I'd attach to your ass, Renny."

"My mate's ass is not open for discussion, and you should keep your eyes off it." Mick gave his friend a low rumble of warning, offering Renny her own excuse for an eye roll. Alpha wolves could be stupid possessive, especially considering how hard this one had fought to pretend they weren't mates.

Zeke completed the eye-rolling trifecta. "Settle down, Fido. I'm not making eyes at your woman. I just don't happen to be blind. I swear that any notes I may have made about your mate's ass all happened before you claimed her and will not, under any circumstances, be repeated. Satisfied?"

Renny stepped forward. "Can we get back to the matter at hand, please?"

"The matter of placing you under guard, or the matter of you arguing about it?"

"I told you, I won't argue, not as long as you at least include me in the discussions. I don't think it's too much for me to ask for a say."

"Of course not." Zeke nodded. "You can say exactly when you'll be moving your things to Mick's place."

She blew out a breath. "Considering that my 'things' currently consist of the contents of your sister's truck, I'd say as soon as she drops them off. I don't think she'll be lending me the truck itself after Mick stole it yesterday."

"I didn't steal it. I borrowed it. She has it back now, doesn't she?"

"You took it without permission, used it during the commission of a felony, and kept it overnight. And I think it's an overstatement to say you returned it when you just drove it back to town this morning and sent her a text that it was parked outside if she wanted to come get it."

"Felony?"

"You kidnapped me!"

"I rescued you."

"Children." Zeke couldn't hide his amusement. "Don't make me turn this car around. Let's just assume that we can get Renny's new things to your place sometime in the next day or so. Does that work?"

Renny nodded. "Please. I can only borrow so many

things to wear. I want my clothes, even if most of them are secondhand."

"Okay, I'll make sure it happens. I think we can assume that Mick will take charge of your safety while you're at his place, so that's the night shift covered." Zeke stepped around to sit behind his desk and started making notes. "We'll just need to work out a rotation for the days, then. The department can make sure it sends patrols past your place a couple of times a day, but we don't have the manpower to assign officers around the clock. I'll touch base with Jaeger about rounding up some volunteers from the community."

Mick grunted. "I'll be with her day and night. It's not like I have to leave home for work."

Renny supposed that meant he kept a studio in the house where he produced the art and stories that made up *Hounds of Hell*. She practically salivated at the idea of getting to see it. She would love to take a peek into how he put together his graphic novels. As both a reader and a librarian, she found the notion fascinating and unutterably tempting. She could see his process, maybe even get a look at the production of a manuscript from beginning to end. That would be awesome.

Then she stopped to think beyond her fantasies of watching her mate work to what it would mean for her to never leave his side. She'd go stir-crazy.

"Hold on," she said, shaking her head. "If you're working, you can't be in charge of my safety twenty-four seven. I'd never be able to go anywhere outside the house."

"So?" He looked confused by her protest.

Renny gave him a dubious look. "So? The whole

point of me running to Alpha was so that once I got here, I could have a life again. Not running any-more was supposed to mean settling down in the real sense—getting a job, shopping for groceries, going to the coffee shop. I can agree to having someone keep an eye on me, because I know Geoffrey hasn't given up, but I don't want to be under house arrest."

"It wouldn't be forever," Mick said. "Just until we locate him and let him know where things stand now."

She lifted an eyebrow. "You mean the way you did over the phone yesterday? As I recall, you already ex-plained to him that I was being protected from him, and how did that go? Oh, yeah. He sent his minions out to snatch me from a public parking lot. Doesn't sound like he's discouraged yet."

His eyes flashed with a feral light. "Oh, I'll discour-age him. Trust me."

She patted his shoulder. "Down, boy. I just mean that if we can spread out the responsibility for my pro-tection, I think we should. I don't want to be confined to your house like a parolee, but I don't want you to have to change your life for me either. You need to be able to go about your business and do your work like you normally would."

"Little red, you are my new normal." He looked down at her, and his gaze heated. "You've already changed things for me, just by being you."

Okay, that may have melted her insides a little. She licked her lips. "But I don't want you to regret that."

"Not going to happen."

He kissed her, his mouth hard on hers, and Renny wrapped her arms around him without thinking. Al-ready it had become instinct to hold on to her mate.

A sharp cough shattered the moment. "Hey, cut that out. Do you want me to have to cite you for public lewdness *inside* the sheriff's office?" Zeke griped. "Keep it clean, please."

Renny felt herself go red, but Mick just brushed his thumb across her lips and smiled. More melting ensued. This having a mate thing was hell on her knees.

"I'm still going to want to do the heavy lifting," Mick said, his eyes never leaving her face. "I'll be with her whenever it's conceivably possible, but go ahead and talk to Jaeger. It can't hurt to have backup, just in case something comes up."

"I agree. We know Hilliard is obsessed, determined, and frickin' persistent," Zeke said. "The more eyes we can keep on your girl, the better."

"I can also tell you from what I remember that he's a devious, cowardly, backstabbing excuse for a male." Mick grimaced, his distaste for the coyote clear. "He won't give up because Renny is protected; he made that clear to me on the phone. But he won't want to risk his own skin to get to her, either. He'll do whatever he can to trick or threaten her into a vulnerable situation, and that includes trying to lure me away from her with some kind of ploy. Everyone needs to understand that she's never to be alone. I don't care if someone's standing outside with their mama holding a gun to the old woman's head. They don't leave Renny until someone else comes to relieve them."

She made a face. "Gee, won't I be the popular new girl in town."

Zeke nodded slowly, clearly running through scenarios in his head. "If that's true, it's even more important for us to find Hilliard's little band of bullies. It's a lot easier to guard against a single enemy than a handful of them. That's one of the reasons I wanted to question Heins while he was in custody."

"Got a Ouija board?" Renny joked, forcing a grin.

"Fucking addict," Mick sneered. "What kind of shifter needs a high so bad, he's got to kill himself to get it?"

"Apparently, one like Jordan Heins. He had a rap sheet going back almost a decade. And considering what kind of quantities of drugs it takes to get one of us high, he's probably single-handedly responsible for financing one cartel or another."

Renny wouldn't doubt it. Shifter metabolisms ran so fast that it was nearly impossible for them to get drunk on anything less than several bottles of liquor, and most chemicals didn't have time to take effect before they burned them off, including medications. It made them resistant to being unwittingly drugged, but it also made certain conditions difficult to treat. Good thing they healed so fast and were resistant to so many of the diseases that plagued humans.

"Too bad none of the others smelled like users," Mick said. "We could just treat them to a night out and let them all off themselves for us. Save us the trouble."

"Nothing's that easy." Zeke leaned back in his desk chair. "But we do need to find the rest of them. I got the scents of the four from the parking lot, but didn't you say there were five of them in the hunting party?"

"Yes. Bryce wasn't there yesterday when Molly and I got jumped, and since he's the leader, I'm assuming Mick's shot must have caused him more trouble than we thought. If he wasn't hurt, he'd have definitely made a grab for me himself."

Zeke nodded and reached for a pen. "Bryce. What's his last name, honey?" He smirked when Mick audibly objected to the endearment.

"Landeskog."

"Give me the names of the others, too. I can run them. Might as well get an idea of what we're up against. Maybe I can also put out some feelers to see if anyone's spotted them or their names in the area, like at the front desk of a motel or something. That's probably too easy, but it doesn't mean I won't check it out."

Renny reeled off the names of her four remaining pursuers. They already knew Geoffrey's name. "Aside from Jordan, the ones there yesterday were Will and Tommy Molina and Eric Ayala. Will and Tommy are cousins. Tommy's an asshole, but Will's a little . . ." She paused, memories making her skin crawl. "He's just not right. I mean, all of Geoff's friends are nasty bastards, but Will takes it a step further. He doesn't just get off on being one of the pack's enforcers; he gets off on hurting people."

Mick flashed a mouthful of fangs. "Oh, good. We've got a little sociopath to play with. Won't that be fun?"

"Okay. I'll start getting some information together. I'll also talk to Jaeger," Zeke said. "He can come up with a list of potential guards to have on standby. Renny, I know it won't be fun for you to have a shifter shadow following you around everywhere you go, but hopefully it won't be for long. I'd like to find these bastards as soon as possible. At the very least, the Northwest Council will need to hear about them."

"I'll deal," she said with a reassuring gesture. "Trust me, a bodyguard will be a lot more fun than what

Geoffrey has planned for me, and I know it. I can't promise to be happy about living under constant surveillance, but considering the alternative? I'll deal."

Mick's toothy grin took on an entirely new edge, one that had Renny's thighs clenching together.

"I'll do what I can to keep you occupied," he promised in a voice that made her wonder which male in the room was really the feline shifter. "I'm sure I can come up with something."

Renny felt her heart speed up. She was sure he could, too. And if not, maybe she could put her own twist on things. If he had trouble with ideas popping up, she knew the first thing she'd be happy to go down on.

With.

With. She cleared her throat and hoped Zeke would ignore the way her cheeks had just gone flaming red. She'd meant "down *with.*"

Really.

Chapter Nine

Apparently, there genuinely was such a thing as too much sex. Go figure.

Renny stretched to ease sore, tight muscles and sent up a little prayer of thanks for her lupine healing ability. Without it, she felt pretty sure she'd have lost the ability to walk at least three or four days ago.

From what she had seen (and felt, and orgasmed), her reluctant mate seemed to have left his doubts behind him once they had claimed each other. No more did she feel as if he were doing everything in his power to pretend she didn't exist. Instead, he was doing everything he could to ensure that she never wanted to get more than a couple dozen feet away from him. He'd kept her half-drunk on sex for an entire week.

She'd heard about the new-mating honeymoon phase that bonded wolf pairs went through, but she'd always thought of it as a romantic sort of fairy tale. It was said that once a couple found and marked each other for the first time, they would go for several days without being able to stop touching each other. Direct physical contact would become a necessary thing, and too long without it would lead not just to irritability, but to real physical and emotional discomfort. Sex would be frequent, intimacy would develop rapidly, and the new mates would gorge themselves on each other's bodies and company until the bond had time to cement itself.

Boy, had they really meant that stuff. If anything, the stories had underplayed the situation. Her desire for Mick had become like an itch under her skin, and if she didn't scratch at regular intervals, the itch became a burning kind of ache. She thought he must be experiencing something similar, judging by how often he touched her, or kissed her, or bent her over the nearest horizontal surface and ravished her until her brains leaked out her ears.

It was fricking amazing, if a little hard on certain portions of her anatomy.

She grinned to herself and stood, leaving the softness of the overstuffed armchair behind her. A week may have passed, but Renny still preferred not to sit on Mick's sofa if she could avoid it, and definitely not when she was alone. Some moments in her life did not need revisiting. Especially when there were so many more pleasant memories beginning to take their place.

Her stomach rumbled, and she padded through the deserted living room toward the kitchen. Time for lunch.

She'd sent Mick into his studio to work just after breakfast. It had taken some persuading (and a bribe that left her with an interesting bruise on her jawline and a patch of rug burn on one knee), but he'd admitted that the past week had put him behind on the deadline for his current manuscript. Renny had shooed him toward his drafting table with joking demands that he give her a chance to rest. But that had been hours ago, and some time alone with a good book had allowed her to work up another appetite. Or two.

Beginning to feel at home in her mate's den, Renny raided the fridge for the makings of sandwiches and set up a mini assembly line on the table. The first day or two had felt really awkward for her. Mick did his best to make her welcome, but it was hard for her to shake the hostile impression he'd left before he accepted their mating. A part of her had still feared making him angry somehow, had thought that he'd change his mind again and go back to denying that he'd found a second mate. She thought it might have killed her if he had.

Renny snorted as she smeared mustard on rye. Thought, hell; at this point she *knew* her mate's rejection would kill her. Their honeymoon phase had done its job, and she was now bonded to Mick Fischer with a vengeance.

It had helped when Zeke and Molly had dropped off all the items Renny had bought during the girls' shopping trip. Not that she needed her own bed anymore, but that was stored in the loft above the garage, and at least she had clothing of her own now. It might be mostly secondhand, but it was hers and all of it fit the way it was supposed to. At this point, she could be grateful for the little things.

Of course, now that she'd moved in with a man and not another woman, she had started a mental list of things to buy on her *next* shopping trip. Mick had set up a perfectly functional bachelor household, but it could definitely use a woman's touch.

Take, for instance, this lunch, she thought with a smile. Here she was loading plates and bowls and glasses onto a baking sheet, because what single man stopped to think he might need a serving tray at some point?

Next time, she promised herself. Once she got a little more settled and found herself a job, she'd let Molly take her on another spree. Earning money again might even make her feel something close to normal after all these months on the run.

Mick had left the door to his studio partway open so that he could hear her in case there was trouble. She had resisted rolling her eyes at the time, because she doubted even Geoffrey was stupid or suicidal enough to break in and try to snatch her from an alpha wolf's den in the middle of the day while the wolf himself was there. But her mate insisted, and Renny had humored him. Now she was glad, because it meant she could just nudge the door open with her foot and carry their improvised lunch tray into his domain without having to juggle a hand free.

He must have heard or smelled her coming (and maybe the roast beef in the sandwiches, too), because he was already standing and reaching for the baking sheet when she stepped over the threshold. He grinned at her and set the burden on the top of a table near the wall.

"You've got pretty good timing there, red." He slipped his hands over her hips and tugged her against him, letting her bounce playfully off his rock-hard abdomen. "I was just thinking about getting myself something to nibble on."

His wolfish grin drew an answering smile from her. She reached up and tangled her fingers in the back of his hair, leaning more heavily against him. She could feel his interest rising in his jeans.

"Is that right?" she purred, trying her most seductive voice. She hadn't had all that many moves in her arsenal before Mick, but her mate seemed happy to let her test them out on him, no matter how pathetic she figured some of them must be. He was turning out to be an easy lay, and Renny was okay with that.

"Mm." He suited action to words, nuzzling his way across her cheek to catch her earlobe between his teeth. She shivered at the sensation.

"Uh, maybe lunch can wait for a little while?" Renny wanted the question to come out all husky and inviting, but she feared it sounded more like a breathless squeak. Still, Mick didn't seem to care.

He rocked his hips against her and tightened his grip, lifting her up and into his body. Automatically, her legs wrapped around him to maintain her balance.

"I'd say it can," he growled just before his mouth claimed hers.

Good Goddess, but the man could kiss, she thought, the last coherent one she expected to have for a while. The rumble in her stomach had subsided to a much more demanding ache centered a few significant inches to the south. Right now, the only beef she wanted to taste was more appropriately termed beef*cake*.

The doorbell shattered the moment with a rude peal of chimes.

Mick tore his mouth from hers to glare in the

direction of the front door. "Who the hell could that be? I hope whoever it is has a damned good reason for showing up uninvited, because I'm in the mood to pound something."

Renny had hoped he'd be pounding her in just a minute, but instead, it looked like they were going to have company.

She hurried to follow him into the main part of the house, reluctantly obeying his gestured order to keep out of the direct line to the door until he had a chance to determine who was on the other side. Before he could ask, the bell rang again, followed by an impatient rapping of knuckles.

"I know you're in there, young man," a woman called out. She had the voice of someone older, strident, but a little thin, and the precision in her consonants made Renny think of a schoolteacher she'd known in her youth. Mrs. Bertram had come up with some fiendish punishments for anyone caught saying "yeah" instead of "yes" in her presence.

Without thinking, she straightened her spine and tugged her shirt into place. Some lessons just stuck with a girl.

Mick groaned and let his head drop back to his shoulders. He must have studied just as hard at some point.

"And I heard that," the voice threw out peevishly. "If you can't be bothered with pretending to be happy to see me, then I won't fret about my manners and worry about ordering you around in your own home. Send that new mate of yours to the door instead. There's a reason why we refer to a woman as a man's better half, you know."

Renny watched her mate disarm the security system with an expression normally reserved for the faces of five-year-olds about to be served brussels sprouts. He opened the door to a comfortable, gray-haired matron carrying a large alligator handbag and pursing her lips in disapproval.

"Hello, Marjory," he intoned with all the enthusiastic energy of a pallbearer.

The woman didn't wait to be invited inside. She swept over the threshold like a luxury ocean liner, all polished and shined and as unstoppable as an iceberg. Then her eyes settled on Renny, and her face dissolved into a delighted smile.

"There you are." She extended her arms in a universal gesture of welcome and positively beamed at the younger woman. "You must be Ms. Landry. Young lady, I cannot tell you how delighted I am to hear you've decided to settle in Alpha. You, my dear, are the Goddess's answer to my prayers."

Wow, talk about the Welcome Wagon. Renny tried to digest the effusive greeting. "Thank you, um, Mrs. . . ."

"Oh, none of that, dear. My name is Mrs. Marjory Caples, but I expect you to call me Marjory. Mr. Caples died more than seven years ago, and you and I are going to be working together very closely for a while, so don't stand on ceremony."

The visitor certainly didn't. Ignoring Mick as if he'd ceased to exist, the small senior citizen with the mighty presence drew Renny into the living room and settled them both on the sofa, half turned to face each other. Any minute, Renny expected to watch her snap her fingers at Mick and order him to ring for tea. The woman had that kind of presence.

"Thank you, Marjory," she said, smiling and hoping her confusion didn't overwhelm the effort. "Um, forgive me for sounding rude, but do we know each other?"

Renny knew very well they didn't, even if the name sounded vaguely familiar, but demanding what the hell the old woman was doing here seemed rude. Not to mention that she got the distinct feeling Mrs. Marjory Caples wouldn't take kindly to being ordered point-blank to state her business.

"Not yet." The woman patted Renny's hand where it still lay captive between her own. Her skin had that curiously soft and yet unsupple texture age seemed to bestow. "And that is why I have come to see you, Ms. Landry, so that we can get to know each other. I do believe very strongly that co-workers should establish rapport early, in order to minimize distractions and misunderstanding in the workplace."

"Call me Renny, please," she insisted, partly because it seemed inappropriate to call the woman Marjory while insisting on Ms. Landry for herself. The rest of the reason had to do more with buying herself a minute to think. *Co-workers?* What was the old woman talking about? Was she some kind of senile local eccentric that nobody in town had bothered to warn her about? "I'm just afraid that you might be a little confused. We don't work together, Mrs.—uh . . . Marjory. In fact, at the moment, I don't work anywhere. I'm kind of between jobs, since I just moved to town."

Marjory chuckled and shook her head. "My dear, you're really going to have to get a better grasp on the local gossip network if you're going to survive in Alpha. No matter how big our population grows, we're still a small town at heart. Nine out of ten of us had heard of your arrival before you even set foot downtown, and the other one was just sleeping late."

Mick relocked and reset the alarm while Renny tried to keep up with their visitor's chatter. She knew because she kept shooting him glances, wondering when the heck he was going to get around to rushing to her rescue. But judging by how long he took at the simple tasks, she got the sinking feeling he was debating just leaving her on her own and making a break for it.

Coward.

Finally, he joined them in the living room, but he managed to hover just inside the doorway, as if he still hadn't decided not to bolt. "Marjory, what a surprise. I can't say we were expecting you to drop by today."

Renny tried to decipher her mate's mood, but he had her baffled. On the one hand, he seemed to be treating the unexpected visitor with the formal respect of someone deferring to a valued elder in the community, but on the other, he looked like he had to grit his teeth to force the pleasantries from his lips.

Marjory returned his nod with a minute, but regal, tip of her chin. "Why, yes, thank you, Michael. A cup of tea sounds lovely. Something plain, please. A little milk, three sugars."

Renny choked back a guffaw. She couldn't decide which was funnier: the way Marjory just straight out ordered an alpha wolf around in his own den or the way Mick reacted to it. She wouldn't have put it past him to kick their visitor out right then, prickly, private, my-home-is-my-castle male that he was, but he looked more amused than angry at being treated like a butler in his own house.

"I'll be right back." He made it sound like a vow, or possibly a threat, before retreating into the kitchen.

"Good. Now that's out of the way, we can talk."

Marjory released Renny's hand and neatly deposited the alligator bag on the low coffee table. She shrugged out of her coat, folded it, and draped it precisely over the top. When she turned back to Renny, her expression was serious and the look in her eyes sharp as nails. This was not a senile old woman. In fact, if Renny had to guess, she'd put the smart money on Marjory Caples having a mind like a steel trap and a will of pure titanium.

She could tell the woman was a shifter, which was to be expected in Alpha, but for a second after she caught the scent, the identity of Marjory's animal eluded her.

Was that . . . She sniffed again. Oh, my goodness, was that wolverine she smelled coming from the prim and immaculately dressed matron? She let the thought percolate in the back of her mind while she waited for the other woman to explain herself.

Marjory smoothed the knees of the tweed trousers and fixed Renny with a level stare. "I hope you'll forgive me for not giving you more time to settle in, Renny, but I'm too excited and too determined to wait. I had to come today, as soon as I spoke to Molly."

"Molly?"

"Your friend. Molly Buchanan." Marjory nodded. "She stopped by the library on her way to work today to return a few books, and she filled me in on a few details about your background."

She must have seen the look of discomfort on Renny's face, because she hurried to reassure her. "Oh, I don't mean your personal history, dear. Although Alpha is a small town, so you'd be wise to give up any expectations of privacy right now and save yourself some headaches. No, I mean that Molly told me of your professional background. Are you really a qualified librarian?"

No one had ever asked Renny that question in quite the same tone of voice. Oh, she'd gotten used to disbelief, but the suppressed excitement was entirely new. She frowned and offered a puzzled smile.

"I have my master's degree in information sciences, if that's what you mean," she said, still confused. "But mostly, I've just worked as an associate reference librarian."

She no longer counted her brief stint as head of information services at the Sawmill Free Library. First, because she no longer felt certain her qualifications had landed her the job to begin with; and second, because she'd learned quickly that nothing in Sawmill operated the same as its counterpart in the world outside of Geoffrey's domain.

Marjory beamed and looked toward the ceiling as if offering up beatitudes. "My dear, I thought so. I don't care what your titles have been at your previous positions. As far as I'm concerned, I'll have your business cards printed up to read 'Savior and Messiah,' if that's what you want. Just say you'll take the job."

"What job?"

"My job. Please. I've been trying to retire for a decade." The woman chuckled. "I apologize, dear. You look confused. I thought Molly said she'd mentioned my name to you and that I'd probably react to your arrival in town just as I have."

A vague recollection teased at the back of Renny's mind, but she couldn't nail it down. Before she struggled too hard, the older woman continued.

"Renny, I am currently the director of the Alpha Public Library, a position I've held for more than forty years, the last ten very reluctantly. Frankly, I'm done. I want to hire you to train as my replacement."

Renny accepted the mug Mick pressed into her hand without bothering to be surprised by his return from the kitchen. She had no room left for surprise; it had all been taken up by Marjory's announcement.

"I'm—I'm . . . well, I'm flattered, Marjory," she finally stammered, looking helplessly at Mick as he passed a second mug to their visitor. "But I don't see how that's possible."

Marjory didn't even glance at Mick. She set her tea untouched beside her purse. "And why not? What strikes you as impossible about working in the profession for which you have studied and trained? I would have used a term more like 'logical.' Or perhaps 'suitable.' "

"How about 'miraculous'?" Renny blurted out, shaking her head. "Mrs. Caples—"

"Marjory."

"Marjory. Don't misunderstand me. It's not that you haven't just sat down and offered me my dream job, because you definitely have. But I'm having a hard time processing it, for a whole host of reasons."

The old woman gave another regal nod and reached for her tea with calm deliberation. "Please elaborate, my dear."

Renny glanced at Mick. He said nothing, just took a seat in the chair closest to her and let her figure things out for herself. At least he remained close in case she needed him. She had even almost started to expect it. Alpha though he was, Mick never tried to control her words or behavior.

Well, okay. Almost never. He'd put his foot down a few times where the question of her safety was concerned. He refused to allow her to place herself in harm's way, but he respected her intelligence and her independence. The way he put it was that he had a hard enough time making his own decisions; he had no desire to try to make hers as well. He just wanted to be part of the process.

Her mate had become her rock in the last week, something to cling to while everything around her seemed to be changing. Admittedly, they were positive changes, but still. It was a lot to deal with.

She told Marjory that very thing. "I haven't exactly been living a normal life for the last few months. Being on the run, trying to stay a step ahead of the pack that's been chasing me, it's been like being adrift. But now, all of a sudden, I've got a new home and a new mate and the beginnings of a new life, and I feel like I still don't quite have my land legs back."

"That's perfectly understandable, but of course I'm not demanding that you report to work this afternoon, my dear. I only came by to let you know there's a position for you if you want it. I want to retire, badly, but I'm not ready to collapse just yet. Still, you're the first qualified candidate I've seen in years. I couldn't just let you slip through my fingers."

"She's not going anywhere. Trust me," Mick offered,

sounding assured and possessive, possibly bordering on smug. She shot him a look. It was a good thing he was cute.

"Of course she isn't. She's one of us now." Marjory sniffed, as if to even suggest otherwise was worthy of disdain. "However, I've lived in this town too long to become complacent. I know I won't be the only one offering Renny a job, but I *am* offering the one best suited to her talents and her education. As far as I'm concerned, your new mate is the answer to my prayers, Michael."

He smiled, the expression way too sexy for innocence. "I've never been a religious man myself, but I'm not about to argue with that assessment. I've gotten used to having her around." He focused on Marjory again, and his expression sharpened. "Which is why there are certain requirements for any job she might consider taking."

"There are?"

"There are?" Renny echoed, frowning. "Um, I don't remember laying any out, so would you mind sharing with the rest of the class, Mr. Alpha, sir?

His face told her he knew he'd sounded high-handed without her pointing it out, but that this was something he'd decided was worth the pushback. "Relax, red. Don't get your hackles up. I don't plan to negotiate your salary or 401(k) benefits. I just mean that your safety is my priority, and right now it's still in question. I know Alpha's grapevine is a well-oiled machine, but before you go back to work, you need to consider the potential ramifications. And so does whoever hires you."

Marjory straightened. "You are referring to the fact

that your mate is currently being stalked by a poor excuse for a coyote who has resorted to sending his bully boys to do his dirty work for him?" She sipped her tea calmly. "Yes. I am aware."

Renny looked back and forth between her mate and their visitor. Apparently, all those jokes about gossip and small-town life hadn't really been meant to be funny. "Was there some kind of newsletter that went out about my life? Because I never got my copy."

"Of course not. Haven't you heard, Renny? Print is dead." Marjory's eyes sparkled. "Michael, I am well aware that Renny is still in danger from her unwelcome pursuer. I have no intention of putting her at risk. If the two of you believe it would be better to fully resolve the situation before she begins work, that's perfectly fine. The position's been open for years. It's not going to be filled in the next few weeks. Or months."

Oh, no. Renny was not prepared to wait months before she started building her new life. A week's honeymoon with her new mate was one thing, but she was done running. Now she wanted to be normal again. She wanted to go back to work, live on a schedule, have a boring, everyday life again.

She forced a smile. "That's completely unnecessary, Marjory. If you're anxious enough about retirement to come all the way out here to offer me a job without even checking my references, you won't want to wait for me to get started. Besides, it's not like I have to give my current employer two weeks' notice."

"No," Mick drawled. "But you do have to give your mate time to coordinate with Zeke and Jaeger so that we know we can keep you safe if you start going to a predictable place on a predictable schedule. You know the rules, Renny."

"You know I hate that word," she grumbled. "You also know I don't want Geoffrey to get near me any more than you do. But it's not like I'd be going somewhere all alone and remote and cut off from help. A library is a public place. There would be people around all the time."

"And those people would have big tall stacks of books to hide behind, as well as multiple points of entry and exit from the building. You haven't even seen the library yet, red. It's in a converted, old Victorian house. There are windows and doors in every single room."

Her eyes narrowed. "Are you trying to tell me you won't let me take the job?"

He snorted. "Do I look like I've lost my damned mind? I'm just saying that this is a big change and we'll need to do some planning before you can start. If you decide you want the job, I mean."

Did she want the job? Renny could feel the grin nearly stretching her cheeks to their limit. "Oh, I do. I absolutely want it."

"Wonderful. Then that's settled." Marjory set her mug aside and gathered up her coat and purse. "The mayor has assured me that I have full discretion in hiring my replacement, so we won't bother making you fill out a silly application form. I'd like copies of your CV and credentials for the records, of course, but you've already aced the interview, so I'll start getting the paperwork together to make it official."

Renny laughed. "This was an interview? I don't

remember you asking me anything beyond whether I have my degree."

"That was all I needed to know." The woman handed her coat to Mick and waited until he caught on to her unspoken demand. He held the garment for her while she shrugged into it. "I might be old and ready to retire, but I'm still a shifter, my dear. I always trust my instincts."

Mick escorted her to the door to turn off the alarm while Renny trailed a little behind, still trying to process what had just happened. In the space of a week she'd gone from fearing for her life and struggling to survive on the run, to having a home and a mate and now the job she'd been dreaming of since she was a child. Maybe she should try jumping off the roof next to see if she could fly, because with Landry's Law lying broken at her feet, could the laws of physics be far behind?

Marjory said her goodbyes and left, her exit as majestic as her entrance. Renny stood staring at the closed door for a good two minutes before Mick chuckled and spun her into his arms.

"Want me to pinch you?" he asked.

"I already tried pinching myself, and somehow, I haven't woken up yet."

"That's because you're not dreaming, little red." He grinned down at her, holding her against him with one hand while he lifted the other to trace his fingertips over the edges of her mating mark. "Of course, if you felt like you should lie down for a while . . ."

Renny felt the caress all the way from her neck to her toes, but it was the places in the middle that sent up the most enthusiastic response. Suddenly, she felt like celebrating.

She hooked her arms over his shoulders and boosted herself onto her toes. "Lie down? But we never got to have our lunch, remember? Marjory interrupted before we could eat."

With their bodies aligned, she could feel his erection nestling against her belly. She undulated slightly, teasing him with rolling hips and a sly smile designed to remind him of exactly what they'd been doing when the doorbell rang.

"Oh, I am positively *starving*, little red," Mick growled, scooping her up into his arms and striding straight for the bedroom. "In fact, I'm planning to just eat you all up."

Renny smiled up at her big, bad wolf and licked her lips. "I can hardly wait."

As it turned out, she didn't have to.

Chapter Ten

The sound of the alarm startled Renny out of sleep. For a second, she couldn't quite figure out where the annoying noise was coming from. Then, her fumbling hand knocked her cell phone to the floor and memory returned. It had been a while since she'd had to get up early for work.

She smiled without opening her eyes. Today was Monday, and damned if she wasn't so excited she could spit. It was her first day as Alpha Public Library's assistant director. She could hardly wait to get started.

Before she could reach for the blankets to throw them off, a muscled arm snaked around her torso and pulled her back against a wall of warm steel. Mick nuzzled the nape of her neck and rumbled out a happy sound of greeting.

"Morning, little red." His breath stirred her hair and made her shiver. Or maybe that was caused by the hand that went from pulling her back against him to cupping her between her thighs. "You've got a big day ahead of you."

"I know." She tugged at his wrist, shuddering when his fingers simply burrowed deeper. He parted her folds and found her clit with wicked skill. It still stunned her how he could have her wet and ready for him with a single touch. "That's why I have to get up now."

"I'm already up." He pressed his erection against her bottom for emphasis.

Renny snorted. "Yes, I can feel that, but you'll have to put it away. I can't be late for my first day."

"Right."

He sighed, and she expected to feel his hold loosen and his hands fall away. For a moment they did, but then they grabbed a new hold and flipped her unceremoniously to her back.

He grinned down at her. "Don't worry, sweetheart. I can make this quick."

"Is that supposed to be persuasive? Because if so, you might need to rethink your argument. Speed is not sexy."

Mick hooked one arm under her knee and slid home with an easy thrust. "Really? Tell me more."

She would have, but it was hard to form a logical summary of facts when her eyes were rolling back in her head. He did this to her every time. Just the feel of him lodged inside her was more arousing than any sex she'd ever had in her life. He didn't even have to move. His thick cock stretched her just right, filling and pressing against all her most sensitive spots.

"Jerk," she moaned, lifting her hips to urge him deeper. "Fine. Fuck me already."

"Working on it." He chuckled, hitching her knee

higher. Then he began to power into her with quick, deep thrusts.

She lit up like a Christmas tree, eagerly matching him move for move. This marked the beginning of the third week that she'd spent every night in his arms. She kept expecting the mating frenzy to subside, for them to sate themselves with sex and each other, but it never happened. Every time she had him, she wanted him more.

She had to show him.

Twining her fingers in his hair, she pulled him down to a kiss. Their mouths met and mated like their bodies, lips caressing, tongues tangling, breath and pleasure shared.

When she squirmed beneath him, the hair on his chest abraded her nipples, making them ache and tingle. She repeated the movement and felt him groan above her. That's when she stopped trying to make him hurry.

Forget about her schedule. She wanted to savor the feel of her mate inside her, pinning her body beneath his as he rocked them both toward completion.

She wrapped her legs around him, digging her heels into his back in a quest for more leverage. She needed him harder, deeper, higher inside her. Hell, she needed him to climb beneath her skin until she couldn't separate where she ended and he began.

Breathless and gasping, she tore her mouth from his and threw her head back, desperate for air. The need within her was growing and expanding until she thought it must be taking up all the room inside, making it impossible for her lungs to draw in the oxygen they craved. Only release could disperse the need and restore her breath. It honestly made her feel like she had to come or she'd never survive.

She heard a high, thin sound and realized it was coming from her. She was whining deep in her throat, the sounds driven out of her in time with her mate's increasingly frantic thrusts. He, too, struggled with short, panting breaths, sweat beading on his skin, his jaw clenched as he worked her harder. What had started with a lighthearted spirit had become deadly serious, driven by hunger and need.

Renny tried to speak, to beg, to make some plea for the release she could feel hovering just out of reach. Her clit throbbed and burned, her thighs trembled, her nails dug furrows into her mate's back. She felt entirely out of control, unable to move, to breathe, to do anything but feel and yearn.

Their bodies slammed together, each straining toward climax. Renny thought she might lose her mind when Mick suddenly jerked back, freeing himself from her body and leaving her empty and confused.

She opened her eyes and stared dazedly into his face. Or she would have, but she barely managed to focus on his tight, feral expression before he dragged her down the mattress and flipped her to her stomach. Rough nudges maneuvered her onto her knees, and a hard palm pressed between her shoulder blades to keep her head down. She wound up curled over herself, chest flattened against tangled sheets, hips raised to expose her pussy like an offering to appease a hungry god.

Her head spun and she turned so that her cheek pressed against the soft surface and she could see her mate at the edges of her vision. He rose up behind her, positioned himself at her entrance, and then drove into her with a snarl of satisfaction.

Renny gasped and jerked, but his hand kept her upper body pinned in place. He felt twice as big in this position, his cock reaching so deep inside, she felt like she could taste him in the back of her throat. Mick set up a fast, punishing rhythm, driving into her hard and deep until the movement of his hips became confused with the beat of her heart. He was the thing pushing the blood through her veins, the power that animated her, and if he stopped fucking her, she would die.

The irrational thought swirled around in her head for an instant, then dissolved in a shower of explosive sparks. The climax crashed over her like a tsunami, dragging her under with the force of her pleasure. Dimly, she felt Mick jerk against her and she thought she heard him howl his pleasure. But then again, she couldn't be certain she was still alive, so she might have just imagined it. Wasn't the brain supposed to randomly fire off synapses at the moment of death, inducing hallucinations and explaining all those stories about white lights and tunnels?

Renny had just become a believer.

Her mate collapsed on top of her, making her grunt. Immediately he rolled to the side, pulling her along with him. Her back nestled against his chest, and she couldn't even summon the energy to push aside the curtain of her own hair that had fallen over her face. Who needed to see? She wasn't even sure she still *could* see. He might have fucked her blind.

From somewhere beneath the bed, her cell phone

alarm began to chime. Her second, just-in-case-I-sleep-through-the-first-one, emergency backup alarm had gone off.

Behind her, Mick chuckled and nudged her off the bed. "Hurry up, baby. Go grab a shower. After all, you don't want to be late for work."

Renny was still cursing him when the bathroom door closed behind her.

Mick whistled a happy tune on his way to Jaeger's office. He'd dropped his mate off at her brand-new job, a bear shifter was on duty outside to ward off any trouble, and he'd gotten to start his day with some pretty phenomenal sex. All in all, it was a very good day to be him.

The good mood helped him balance the lingering sense of discomfort he felt at leaving Renny's side for an entire day. For two weeks, they had basically lived in each other's pockets. She'd gone out a couple of times with Molly, once for coffee and "chocolate goodness," as they called it, and once to browse the bookstore. Both had been brief trips to well-populated public places, and he'd extracted solemn vows from both women that they would remain on guard and wouldn't even get out of their vehicle if they sensed a possibility of danger. Still, he could admit he might have done a little bit of pacing until his mate returned safely to his side.

His intense feelings for his little she-wolf terrified him if he spent too much time thinking about them, so he did his best not to. He'd known Renny for such a short time, but already the strength of his attachment to her rivaled what he'd felt for Beth after a couple of years together. He hadn't thought it possible for their bond to grow so strong so fast. If he had, he'd probably still be pushing her away.

Turned out he was a fucking coward, he acknowledged, steering his truck toward the town hall. At his very core lived a primordial fear that he could lose another mate. If he did, he knew without a shred of doubt that this time, the pain would kill him.

Death wasn't what scared him, though. If it came to that, he knew that he'd welcome the oblivion, because he'd rather follow Renny into the darkness than live with the constant knife blade of grief stuck in his gut. He'd done that before, and he'd burned the fucking T-shirt.

Mick parked and climbed out of the pickup, slamming the door behind him. This was why men didn't dwell on their feelings, he noted. Not because they didn't have them, but because they knew they had no control over them, and no man wanted to admit that kind of helplessness. Their Y chromosomes forbade it.

He nodded to Vonnie at her desk in the foyer on his way up to Jaeger's office. The badger shifter waved him by, not even pausing in her conversation with whoever was on the other side of her phone line. Mick took the stairs two at a time and knocked briefly before letting himself in to the mayor's inner sanctum.

Jaeger stood at the window behind his desk, but his eyes weren't on the view. They were fixed on a large, movable bulletin board that had been positioned to be visible from almost any spot in the room. A map of Alpha and the surrounding area had been tacked in the center, with a series of photographs pinned around the outside. It looked like something from a television police drama. Mick was tempted to look around for Richard Belzer.

Plus, he felt a sudden craving for doughnuts.

"Come on in." Jaeger waved him forward. Several other figures already occupied a variety of seats, most of them moved in from other rooms to accommodate the small crowd. "I thought about moving this to a conference room, but I want this operation based where I can keep an eye on it personally."

Zeke looked over his shoulder from where he stood adding index cards of information to the bulletin board. "And the sheriff wants it run from his office, so here I am, duplicating all my damned work word for word just to keep the muckety-mucks happy. A deputy's work is never done, I tells ya."

Mick snorted and looked around at the others gathered. Three other officers from the sheriff's department clustered in one corner and talked among themselves. He also recognized a couple of members of the local fire and rescue squad (sometimes co-workers of Molly) and a few of the town's more colorful business owners, like Linus Russu, the tiger-shifter owner of the Twisted Shifter, Alpha's favorite brew pub.

Opposite the others, in one of the large chairs closest to the mayor's desk, the real elite of Alpha society sprawled at his leisure, expensive suit and silk tie somehow *not* making him look like an overly gentrified fop.

Recognizing the man who owned half of Alpha (and whose family used to own the rest), Mick crossed to him and extended a hand. "Jonas."

The bear shifter stood to greet him, all six feet and some odd inches of him unfolding itself with lazy grace. He smiled and nodded as he shook hands. "Mick. Good to see you again."

"You, too. Been a while."

"Been busy."

"Busy honeymooning." Jaeger's grin carried a mocking half leer. "How is the good doctor, by the way?"

"Fantastic," Browning rumbled, his expression taking on a rather satisfied smirk.

Jonas Browning had given up his playboy ways just the year before, Mick recalled. The entrepreneurial grizzly had mated another newcomer to Alpha, a previously outcast wolf shifter with a series of letters after her name and an IQ that made half the town's population look like drooling idiots. Annie Cryer now worked overseeing the lab at the Alpha Medical Center, in addition to pursuing her own research interests.

"I'm sure she'll want to meet your new mate, Mick. Annie misses having a pack around, in spite of the way her old one treated her." Something violent flickered in the bear's dark eyes but was quickly suppressed. "You should bring her over for dinner. What's her name, again? Wendy?"

"Renny," Mick corrected.

"Unusual."

"She's named after her grandmother, who was French Canadian, I think."

A last group filed into the room and settled into the remaining chairs. Mick saw the mayor run his gaze over the assembly and give a small nod.

Jaeger stepped up to his desk and rested his finger-tips on the blotter. "If I could have everyone's atten-tion, please."

The background chatter subsided as Mick took a seat in the other chair next to the desk. All eyes now focused on the cougar in chief.

"Thanks, everyone, for carving out the time to deal with this," Jaeger said. "I'm sure most of you know the basics of our current situation, but just to make sure we're all on the same page, let me sum it up for you."

Mick watched the faces of the group while Jaeger gave a succinct account of Renny's arrival in Alpha and the events that had brought her to their commu-nity. He'd heard the story a handful of times already, and it still made his jaw clench and his lips curl when he listened to the history of Geoffrey Hilliard stalk-ing, harassing, and attempting to kidnap his mate. Judging by the expressions of the other people in the room, they shared a similar distaste for the coyote's actions.

Good, Mick thought. They needed everyone in town to know what his mate had been through and what kind of risk Hilliard and his bully boys still posed to Renny's safety. It would keep everyone alert and give them a stake in finding the coyotes before they could make another attempt to grab his mate.

When Jaeger had finished his summary, he gestured to Zeke, still standing beside the bulletin board. "Zeke and Sheriff Lahern have worked the last few days to get us some real concrete information on this bunch, so I'm going to let him take it from here. Zeke?"

The deputy shifted forward, tangibly focused and

ready for action. "Right now, we're aware of two main threats. Geoffrey Hilliard is, of course, number one, because he's the one driving all this. Number two is the hunting party that works for him." Zeke pointed to a photo at the top center of the board, above the map. "Get a good look. So far, we believe he's been staying in California and running things remotely, but he's been trying to get his paws on Renny Landry for months, and we can expect that sooner or later, he'll decide to take matters into his own hands."

Mick almost wished Hilliard would. He'd pounded the little shit once over the way the coyote had treated his half sister; he wouldn't mind doing it again. In fact, he'd damned well walk away from that righteous ass kicking with a smile on his face and a song in his fucking heart.

"These five individuals made up the hunting party we believe is currently in the area." Zeke had tacked photos of five men in a ring around the map. Mick recognized all of them, and he wanted all of them to pay for terrorizing his mate. "These four attempted to grab Renny from the parking lot outside the East Plaza Shopping Center on Saturday the seventeenth. She and my sister were both attacked, but Mick and I managed to intervene and drive three of them off. The fourth, this man—Jordan Heins—was taken into custody, but died later that night of a drug overdose."

"You're shitting me." Linus looked like he couldn't decide whether to laugh or spit. "An overdose? Of what? Stupidity?"

"According to Dr. Kirby? Meth. He managed to smuggle it into the jail at the time he was booked, and ingested a fatal dose. It appears that he was a regular user, so we can't determine if the OD was accidental or a deliberate move on his part."

"And this putz was a member of the coyote alpha's elite hunting party?" The tiger snorted. "What the hell kind of a pack is this Hilliard running?"

"A highly dysfunctional one." Zeke moved to point out each of the other coyotes in turn. The photos he referenced looked like they'd been taken from official ID pictures or, in a couple of cases, from police mug shots. Somehow that didn't surprise Mick.

"These three are still at large and, we believe, still in the area. William and Thomas Molina. Cousins. Both have records in California, but our friend Will's here is considerably more extensive, with charges ranging from petty vandalism, to assault with a weapon, to animal cruelty. Apparently, he didn't restrict himself to hunting in his fur, and he didn't always bother to make his kills clean before he tore them apart. That gets especially disturbing when you understand that Will is an expert marksman. As in, he's won competitions and even got a serious look from the U.S. Olympic Committee. Presumably until they saw these."

Goddess. Mick felt a little sick when Zeke illustrated his point by adding a series of gory snapshots to the space beside Will Molina's picture. They looked like a cross between crime scene photos and test shots for a slice-and-dice horror film. At one time, the subjects might have been rabbits or deer or even—fuck him sideways—someone's poor Labrador retriever, but it was hard to tell with all the pieces scattered around like that.

It wasn't the blood that bothered Mick. Hell, he'd

spilled more than his share of the stuff during his life, some in skin and some in fur. No, it was the wanton glee displayed in those photos that turned his stomach. They looked like some psychotic kid's idea of finger painting gone horribly, horribly wrong.

"The notes in William's file make for some pretty interesting reading," Zeke continued. His mouth firmed into a grim line. "At least two different police departments ordered that he undergo preliminary psychological testing after subsequent arrests. Both times, the doctors who spoke with him noted marked evidence of a sociopathic lack of empathy, violent aggressive tendencies, and possible delusional thought patterns. Both times they recommended further testing and possible involuntary commitment, but both times, Molina was released when his accuser either disappeared, or mysteriously dropped the charges, *then* disappeared."

One of the junior deputies piped up. "So, he's a real people person, huh?"

Several in the room chuckled.

"If by 'people person' you mean person who targets other people for his own sadistic purposes, then yeah." Zeke moved on to the next picture. "This is Will's first cousin and closest companion, Thomas 'Tommy' Molina. His father and Will's father are brothers. Tommy's record is mostly straight-up violence, usually committed on behalf of his cousin. Sometimes it looks like he was backing his cousin up, sometimes he may have been trying to clean up Will's messes. But in either case, Tommy can and will use his fists, his claws, or his fangs to take care of business. Both these guys should be considered dangerous.

"Bachelor number three is Eric Ayala. From what I've been able to put together on him, I think he's only recently earned a promotion from errand boy to evil henchman," Zeke said, earning a few more chuckles. "His criminal record is pretty clean, other than a few minor dings here and there for typical stupid kid shit. Our sources think he's a scab brought in to replace another member of Hilliard's pack who got ideas above his station. There's a missing persons report with Trinity County for a male, twenty-seven years old, six feet tall, two hundred pounds, resident of Sawmill, California, whose employer is listed as GH Holdings, also of Sawmill."

"You think he took out one of his own men?"

Zeke shrugged. "No idea. But I think he's unstable, and from what Renny told us, he runs his pack like a little rebel army, offing anyone who challenges him, no matter who they are."

"It fits what I know," Mick said, scowling. "The Geoffrey Hilliard I know is a cowardly, treacherous, backstabbing little pissant who wouldn't hesitate to knife the Goddess Herself if She tried to stop him from doing what he wanted."

Linus turned his head to look at Mick and raised an eyebrow. "You've met the charming gentleman?"

Mick nodded brusquely.

"Anything you'd like to share with the class?"

Oh, about as much as he'd like to invite them all along on his next visit to the proctologist. He'd spent the last eight years not talking to anyone about his past, and that was the way he fucking liked it. What he'd gone through was no one's business but his own.

And maybe his mate's.

Maybe.

Still, he was going to have to rely on these folks to help him keep Renny safe. Did that mean he owed them something? Shit, he was out of practice with all of this. Life had been so much easier when it was just him in his cabin, in his woods, drawing his pictures, and ignoring the rest of the town/world/universe.

He weighed his sense of obligation against his loathing for giving out personal information and settled on a bare truth. "I grew up in Sawmill. It was before Hilliard took over. But I knew him, a bit."

The tiger's gaze bored into him, eerie amber-gold eyes intent and unblinking. He'd never gotten a good read on Linus. The feline was on friendly terms with almost everyone in town, but close to no one. Like many of his kind, he tended toward solitary habits, something Mick was in no position to criticize.

After a long moment, Linus nodded. "All right, then. Sounds like the kind of fellow who deserves a real Alphaville welcome." When he smiled, it revealed a lot of teeth and little mercy.

"As does his right-hand man." Zeke tapped the last unidentified photo. "This is Bryce Landeskog, leader of the hunting party. Judging by the information I got from the Cali State Police, he might turn out to be half coyote, half Teflon—nothing sticks to him. Any arrests have been wiped, any charges dropped, any accusers gone silent. Might have something to do with Hilliard, might have to do with the fact that his father's connected. Not to the Mafia, to the statehouse."

Jaeger explained, "Landeskog senior is a lawyer who left his practice to start a lobbying firm in Sacramento. Their Web site says they 'seek to define and defend the rights of Others on a state and national level.' Sources say their business has more to do with accumulating financial and political power and using it like a club to beat down anyone who opposes them."

One of the deputies snorted. "Talk about a blood-line breeding true."

"Yeah. Junior here does seem to take after daddy. We're pretty certain he was injured in the initial attack on Renny Landry the night she arrived in Alpha. We assume that's why he didn't participate in the attempted kidnapping the next day, but he's a shifter, so chances are that by now, whatever wound he sustained has healed. We need to expect that he's back up to full strength and back in charge of the others."

Jaeger folded his arms over his chest, his usually good-humored expression gone serious. "But that still leaves us with four coyotes known to be in the area, with the potential that Hilliard himself will be joining them anytime."

"More than potential," Zeke said. "Based on the established pattern of his behavior and the rate of escalation, it's a pretty sure bet that he's not going to stay in California much longer. Stalking behavior like this *always* escalates, and even if he's left it to his minions for this long without results, he's going to take matters into his own hands one of these days. And in the meantime, it's safe to assume he'll be applying more and more pressure on the hunting party to get some results."

Jaeger nodded. "Then I'd say it's time to have a face-to-face with our visitors and explain to them exactly why they might want to be moving along back south."

"First, we have to find them, and that's why you're all here." Zeke picked up a highlighter marker and turned to the map that occupied the majority of the bulletin board's surface. "We all know this area. There aren't many population centers, so we're assuming that if they're not roughing it, they'd have to set up a base in Cle Elum. If they want any chance of sailing below the radar, it'd have to be in Ellensburg. To really blend into the woodwork, we're talking Renton, and that seems unlikely. That kind of distance would put them at a real disadvantage when it came to seizing an opportunity to get at Renny."

It made sense. This was a pretty sparsely populated area of the state. A lot of it consisted of state and national forest with the few towns that dotted the map being mostly small and remote. Alpha itself represented the biggest population center outside of the human towns Zeke had mentioned.

"We've been checking around hotels in Cle Elum and Ellensburg with no results, so chances are the coyotes are staying away from towns. Camping out makes them harder to find and gives them a lot more options. If they stay in fur a lot, it means we won't even have the general signs of temporary shelters and cooking sites to look for, so this search is going to take some doing."

Mick listened while his friend went on to outline the plan of action he and the sheriff had come up with. The bear hadn't been happy to cut short his vacation, but Sheriff Lahern was good at his job. He and the deputy had identified how close to town the coyotes were likely to remain for their best chance at Renny and developed a search radius based on that. It was a big area of rough country, but they would assign small teams of volunteers to individual sections and suggest tracking techniques and search parameters.

Teaching shifters to hunt in the woods was a lot like teaching chickens to lay eggs, but Mick acknowledged the wisdom of having a system in place to ensure nothing got overlooked. He just wished everyone who'd volunteered to help with the search could focus all their attention on it, instead of working their shifts in around work and family schedules. This was his mate's safety they were talking about.

By the time everyone's questions had been answered and check-ins had been arranged, the anxiety Mick had mostly shoved aside for two weeks with sex and staying safely denned up with his mate had come flooding back. His skin itched with the desire to get into his fur and find the coyotes threatening Renny. Tearing them into bloody little chunks would go a long way to making him feel better.

Maybe he should drive by the library on his way back home, he decided. He could just check up on his mate and make sure her first day at work was going smoothly. After all, the bear guarding the building had been instructed not to intrude, so he might not know if anything unusual had occurred inside.

Yeah, he'd just stop in for a minute, maybe steal a kiss as an excuse for butting in, he decided as the meeting broke up and shifters filed out of the mayor's office. He knew Renny had told him not to worry, that she'd be inside a building under guard and by Marjory's side all day, but it never hurt to double-check.

At least, he hoped it wouldn't hurt. He suspected his

mate's bite felt a little different when she wasn't clamping down on his skin in the heat of passion.

"This is really sweet of you, Marjory, but it's not necessary." Renny settled into the booth at the Timber Top Café across from her new boss. "I swear I brought lunch with me. We didn't need to go out."

The older woman ignored her protests and opened the menu their waiter had left. "And I told you I was taking you out to celebrate your first day at the library. If it makes you feel better, I suppose you can think of it as celebrating my first *last* day. Personally, I am so excited at the prospect of my upcoming retirement, I wish we had time to do lunch in Seattle at someplace ridiculously expensive and terribly stylish, but our lunch hour doesn't extend to a ninety-minute drive each way."

"You can't be any more excited than I am." In fact, Renny was still having a hard time not bouncing in her seat. Even after a morning of filling out boring paperwork and doing nothing more strenuous than touring the facility and familiarizing herself with the staff and schedule, her excitement at being back to work was hard to contain. "I feel like I'm finally getting my life back."

"After hearing what you've been through, I can imagine." Marjory had been briefed on Renny's background, officially this time, as opposed to just through the grapevine. It wouldn't have been fair for her to be working at Renny's side without knowing the danger Geoff and the hunting party still posed. "I hope your mate is contributing to those feelings."

Renny noticed the twinkle in her companion's eye

and blushed. Mick had left her on the library steps this
morning with a goodbye kiss that threatened to set her
panties on fire. Jerk. He'd done it in front of Marjory,
the bear on guard outside, and all the passersby at the
library's front door, too. She'd been tempted to kick
him in the shins, but her knees had been too weak to
manage it.

"Yes, well . . ." She coughed. "I suppose you could
say we're still in our honeymoon phase."

"Ah, yes. I remember my own, lo those many years
ago. My advice is to enjoy it, thoroughly."

"Did you?" She scanned her own menu, mentally
debating between eating like a healthy, responsible
adult human and devouring her food like a ravenous
carnivore. Breakfast had been a long time ago.

"Oh, lady, yes." Marjory chuckled, and Renny noticed the older woman didn't waste any blushes. Maybe
someday she'd get past that reflexive coloration. "Of
course, it was different for me. Harold and I loved each
other, but mating isn't the same for us as it is for you."

They placed their orders—stuffed chicken breast
for Marjory and a compromising steak salad for
Renny—and turned over their menus. "What do you
mean?"

"Our animals approach the whole thing very differ-
ently, of course." Marjory shook out her napkin and
spread it over her lap. "Wolverines of the mundane variety don't form monogamous pairs. Usually, males
attach themselves to two or three different females and
move between them. It's not the sort of arrangement
favored in human society."

Renny had a fleeting image of sharing Mick with

other females and almost let her claws pop out. It wasn't something she would favor, either, and she had a feeling her inner bitch would try to rip its throat out.

"When wolverines mate, it's our human halves that choose to be faithful. Our animals aren't so finicky. Things are different among you wolves. Your animals are even more pair-bound than your human selves. From what I've seen it makes for an entirely different level of intimacy."

"That's the idea." Renny tried to hide her grimace behind her water glass, but judging by the older woman's curious expression, she didn't think she had succeeded. She shrugged and aimed for casual. "I think it must be different for Mick. I'm his second mate, after all. Most wolves don't survive losing the first one. I think he's kind of leery about the intimacy thing."

"That's not what I observed this morning."

Renny flushed at the teasing. "No, physical intimacy isn't the problem. We've, uh, got that covered. I mean emotional intimacy. He doesn't like to talk, and when I try, he's always distracting me with something."

Marjory leaned back to allow the waiter to serve their entrées, and her entire face glowed with humor. Sheesh, at this rate, Renny would end up with her mouth too full of her own foot to eat her salad.

"Get your mind out of the gutter. Do you want me to think of you as a dirty old woman?" Renny picked up her fork and toyed with it. "He just doesn't want to talk about the past or about anything . . . deep. He doesn't tell me how he feels, not about me, not about his last mate, not about anything important. Well, he spilled a little bit, that first night, when he broke down and claimed me, but since then, it's been a no trespassing zone."

Marjory looked thoughtful as she chewed and swallowed a bit of chicken. "Does he show you?"

"Show me?"

"Do his actions demonstrate his feelings in a way that makes his emotions obvious? A lot of men have trouble talking about their feelings, humans and shifters alike. We have an entire shelf at the library dedicated to the phenomenon. For our kind, especially for alphas like your Mick, it can be a particular challenge to use words to express emotions when their minds are oriented much more toward physical action."

Renny's fork stabbed a slice of rare beef with what could be construed as excessive force. "He expresses possessiveness, but what wolf doesn't? I know he's my mate, and I know we're bonded together. I can feel it. We're . . . aware of each other. I can tell if he's close by, if he's tense, if he's healthy. I can even tell if he's angry, but that's just part of the bond. It doesn't tell me how he *feels*."

"Have you tried asking him? . . . No, don't glare at me like that, young lady. It was a serious question. Of course, you can't read his mind, any more than he can read yours. If you want to have a discussion about emotions, chances are that he won't be the one to initiate it. He is a man, after all. They don't look at things from our perspective."

"It's a little awkward, don't you think? 'Excuse me, Mick? Are you still in love with your dead mate? Do you think you could forget about her and concentrate on me instead? Because while the sex is amazing, I can't help but get the feeling at times that you still wish I had never come barging into your life.' That would be a fun evening at home."

Marjory patted her napkin against her lips. "Then you have to decide which is more important."

"What do you mean?"

"Which is more important to you?" she asked baldly. "Is it avoiding the potential for an unpleasant scene, or knowing the truth and having the facts of your mating out in the open? That's your decision, and no amount of advice is going to make it seem any easier to choose."

Chapter Eleven

Her steak salad turned out to be delicious, covered with enough rare beef to make the vitamin-packed greenery go down like so much gravy. It was the conversation over lunch that threatened to give Renny indigestion.

She hadn't been able to get it out of her head all afternoon. While she reviewed library budgets, perused catalogs, explored computer systems, and met part-time employees, her mind remained fixed on the problem of one Michael Kennedy Fischer and the electrified, barbed-wire-topped, fifteen-foot stone wall he had erected around his feelings. So far, she hadn't been able to find any way over it, so now she supposed it was time to consider the other choices: Go under, go through, or go home.

The going home part being figurative, since her home was now beside him. And that, Renny had concluded, was what made the whole damned question so terrifying. However Mick felt about her and their mating, it didn't change the fact that they *were* mates.

Nothing could change that. They now relied on each other to the point where a lengthy separation would kill them, so her choice wasn't to stay or to leave; it was to push for more or to accept what he had already given her.

Gah. It made her feel like the heroine of some Hallmark Channel afternoon movie. *Desperate for the love of her man, one woman will risk it all for the chance to find the ultimate happiness.* Her more cynical instincts wanted to hurl at the sap factor, but she had to admit the question wasn't going away, and the only way to get an answer would be to take her thumb out of her mouth and ask.

Mick picked her up a little before six. With the time change not coming for another couple of weeks, the sun had already set, leaving Alpha wrapped in a cocoon of evergreen forest beneath the starry northwestern sky. For a while, Renny simply watched it roll past the truck windows in silence. A girl had to gather her courage, after all.

"I thought you'd be chattering like a magpie about your first day." Mick's voice rumbled into the quiet, interrupting her brooding. "Didn't it go well, red?"

"No, it went fine. I've just been thinking."

She let the sentence drop and watched his face in the lights of the dashboard. The road between Alpha and his house in the woods didn't boast much in the way of street lamps.

"Uh-oh. That sounds ominous." He didn't tense up. In fact, he looked more amused than anything else. "Did Marjory spend the afternoon telling you stories of my poor manners and misadventures?"

"Of course not. We did have an interesting talk over

lunch, though. She took me out to the Timber Top Café."

"They make a hell of a steak sandwich."

"I had a salad. A steak salad," she clarified when he shot her a look. "It was good. More steak, less salad."

He nodded. "They know their clientele."

Okay, Renny decided. It was now or never. She scraped together her courage and hoped like hell that the tightness in her chest and the trembling in the rest of her wouldn't color her voice. She was striving to sound casual here.

"We talked a little about relationships."

"You mean about sex."

Renny rolled her eyes. "No, Mr. Horn Dog, that's what men mean when they say they talked about relationships. We talked about *relationships*. She told me a little about her husband, Harold."

"I only met him a couple of times. He was already sick when I moved here, but I remember him as a nice guy. He let Marjory steamroll her way through everything while he just watched and smiled and found a way to work around her." He paused. "They were good together. You could see it. She took it pretty hard when he died."

"He had cancer?" It was one of the few human diseases to which shifters didn't have any more immunity than any other species.

Mick nodded. "I don't think he suffered, though. Marjory wouldn't have stood for that. The end came pretty quick, but I don't suppose that made it any easier." He paused and corrected himself. "I *know* that doesn't make it easier."

And there was her opening. She thought for an instant about letting it pass, but her mouth opened before she could stop it. "Yeah, you do know. Beth's death was sudden, but you didn't know it was coming. At least Marjory had that."

She looked out the windshield while she said it, but she could still feel the way he tensed beside her. The raw nerve was no less raw than before. For a while she didn't think he would even respond, and she searched for a way to muddle forward without his cooperation.

"If I'd paid attention, I would have known," he finally said. She almost gasped to hear his voice, gruff though it sounded. She hadn't thought he would continue speaking. "Abraham never made any secret of how he felt about Beth. Tried to forbid me from mating her in the first place, and never let a chance slip by when he could be telling me I should get rid of her. Should have known he'd eventually decide to do it for me."

Renny clenched her fingers to keep from reaching out and curling them around his arm or leg or anywhere she could reach. She wanted to comfort him, but she couldn't take the chance that he'd slam this door shut again. This was the first time since she'd worked out his identity that he'd willingly discussed his past with her. Every other time, he'd cut her off at the knees.

Or, you know, someplace between them.

"No, you shouldn't have," she said, barely above a whisper. "No one should ever have to expect their own grandfather would have their mate murdered. That's not how it's supposed to work."

He snorted. "You never spent time in Abraham's

pack. It worked the way he said it worked, or it bled out."

"That doesn't make it right."

Mick lapsed back into silence, but Renny wasn't ready to give up. She'd gotten this far, gotten him to at least mention the past; that couldn't be easy for him. Maybe it was time for her to meet him in the middle and mention the thing that scared her the most.

"Mick . . ." She struggled for words. Goddess, this was hard. And terrifying. And why the hell did she want to go here again? "I know that what happened to you, what happened to Beth, was devastating."

He said nothing, but she could see his knuckles turning pale on the steering wheel. She felt like she had a knife in her hand and was taking turns stabbing it into each of their chests, just for funzies.

"I can't pretend that I understand exactly how you feel, how you felt, about it, or about the fact that you . . . stayed, when most wolves don't. I can never really get that, not fully."

She took a deep breath, or tried to, but the fist clenched around her trachea made that kind of tough. She had to settle for what air she could get, but maybe she could blame her slightly dizzy, out-of-body feeling on oxygen deprivation. You know, instead of abject emotional terror.

"But I hope you know how grateful I am that you're still here." She forced the words out and let them ring in her ears while she tried to get it all out into the open, instead of letting it fester in her belly. "I know you didn't want a second mate, but you got one. I'm here, and I'm not going anywhere. I might be a second choice for you, but you're it for me. You're what the Goddess gave me, and no matter what happens, I'm going to find a way to do this."

"Then tell me, red, why does it sound like you're giving me a great big farewell speech?" His growl made the hair on her arms stand up, made her skin itch to grow fur. It made his wolf sound awfully close to the surface. "You know damn well I won't let you run now. I already told you all this. You're my mate now. *We* are mated. It's done."

"I know that, Mick. Trust me, I know. Like I said, I'm not going anywhere. Not ever." She swallowed hard. "But I need to get a few things clear, because my staying isn't an issue, but *how* I stay is still up in the air."

He glanced at her, and his eyes glowed in the darkness. They weren't human eyes anymore. His wolf stared out at her from under those dark brows. "What the hell is that supposed to mean?"

Shoving her fear down to churn away in the pit of her stomach, Renny revealed her worst fears. She threw her heart out on the road and waited to see if he'd run right over it.

"I need to know how you feel about me, Mick, because I'm already most of the way in love with you. What I want more than anything is to know that you're able to love me back, but at this point, I'm honestly not sure. Part of me thinks you loved Beth so much that you don't have anything left for me. And if that's true, it doesn't change that we're mates. It doesn't change that I'm here, and I'm staying forever, but it does change how I'm going to deal with that. If you can't love me back, I'll be building a very different life than I will if you can."

Mick felt like he'd just had a piano dropped on his head and a mule kick him in the balls, simultaneously. Where the fuck had this come from?

Renny wanted to know if he loved her?

Seriously, she wanted to know if he possessed the *ability* to love her? What the fuck did she think he was, some kind of robot? Did she think he could just ignore the mating pull and pretend the Goddess hadn't designed them for each other? Hell, he'd tried that for about seven seconds, and it had gotten him fucking nowhere. They were *mates* now. They'd spent the past two weeks wallowing in each other, hands on each other more than they'd been off. Did she really think that meant nothing to him?

Was she stupid?

No, he knew his mate wasn't stupid, but he had to wonder if she might be a little crazy. Or just oblivious. She'd have to be one or the other not to have noticed the way he acted around her. He wanted to be with her all the time, in plain sight if that was all he could get, but preferably touching if he could manage it. He craved her taste and her scent like he craved the feel of pine needles under his paws. He couldn't stop thinking about her, even when he should be concentrating on other things, like his work, or meetings with the mayor, or keeping her safe from a pack of fucking lunatics.

Goddess, the idea of her in danger almost made him lose control. He'd have to take up fucking Zen breathing techniques to keep from sprouting fangs every time he so much as thought about the coyotes trying to hunt her down. He could barely maintain his fucking sanity, and she was wondering if he was *capable* of falling in love with her?

Fuck, he'd already landed on his head hard enough to cause a concussion, and he had a feeling he hadn't even hit bottom.

He opened his mouth, feeling the way his teeth had already sharpened into fangs, and hoped he'd still be able to manage enough human language to get his point across. Then again, it might be a good thing if she couldn't understand the first few words that wanted to come out of his mouth. 'Cause them were fightin' words.

Mick never got a chance to insult his mate's intelligence, perception, or instincts. He was too busy reacting to the large, solid mass that suddenly appeared in the middle of the road in front of him.

Deer.

He hit the brakes hard and jerked the wheel to the right, doing his best to avoid the stag that burst out of the tree line and across the expanse of asphalt. The truck swerved, headlights raking over the animal's hide and revealing bloody traces of tooth and claw along its hindquarters.

That brief glance told him three things: one, that the deer bore the marks of being harried by predators, which meant it was not the only thing out in the woods tonight; two, whatever was after the deer would have been able to hear their vehicle approaching well before the deer made for the road; and three, his mate had just been endangered. Again.

Beside him, Renny hadn't made a sound, or at least

not much of one. She'd squeaked briefly at the first
sight of the deer, but then she'd gotten control of herself and braced against impact. Mick managed to
swerve and avoid a wreck, but he had to run them off
the road to do it, narrowly missing the trunk of a mas-
sive spruce and bringing them to a jerking stop in the
middle of a patch of brambles. The thorns made hissing squeals as they scraped against the metal truck.

He looked immediately to his mate to make certain
she wasn't hurt.

"Did we hit it?"

Snapping branches and rustling leaves as the buck
scrambled and crashed through the underbrush answered her question, but it raised new ones for Mick.
Whatever predator had injured the deer should be
moving in for the kill, which meant they should be able
to catch a glimpse.

Unless the deer wasn't the real prey.

He had a bad feeling.

"Shh. Get down." He reached over, releasing her
seat belt with one hand and using the other to press her
toward the floor.

"Mick, what—"

"Quiet."

He flipped off the truck's ignition and counted the
heartbeats it took for his eyes to adjust to the dark of
the deserted roadside. *Three. Four.*

There.

He blinked and focused on an irregular shadow
creeping forward from the trees where the deer had recently emerged. His eyes registered the movement
more than the shape, because nature had provided it
with effective camouflage. Dense fur in the shades of

forest darkness blended into the background, but the glow of pale yellow eyes revealed the stalking form of a coyote.

Yeah, a really bad feeling.

But then again, Renny's conversational gambit had put him in the mood to attack something, and what better target than a sneaky, low-down coyote out to harm his mate? Hell, maybe his evening was looking up.

He began to peel off his shirt, ignoring Renny's protests. "Stay here, keep the doors locked, and stay down," he ordered, eyes fixed on the approaching shifter. "I'll be back in a minute."

"Mick!"

He ignored her shout, stripped down to skin, and climbed out of the car, hitting the door locks on the way out. He didn't think this would take long, not the way he was feeling.

With a feral smile, he stretched his muscles and shifted.

Renny cursed a blue streak and fumbled around on the floor of the truck for her bag. Damn him, but her mate was about to get himself seriously mauled unless she did something to stop it. She'd been through this before, and she knew damned well that where one coyote appeared, others would not be far away, not when they were on the hunt.

She grabbed her purse and fumbled to free her phone. This setup had all the earmarks of a trap, and she'd nearly been caught in enough of them to recognize one when she saw it.

The deer had been a distraction, not prey. While

shifter packs hunted large prey more often than natural coyotes, they still employed similar tactics of swarming the victim. Wolves would bring an animal down from the rear, attacking from behind, crippling, and then moving in for the kill, but coyotes liked to take their victims head-on, going for the head, throat, and neck. The fact that the deer that had run in front of Mick's car had borne injuries only to its hindquarters meant that the coyotes hadn't been hunting it; they'd been driving it ahead of them, forcing it into the road and in front of Mick's truck. Left with no choice but to run off the road or crash into the big buck, either way, Mick would have to stop on this stretch of deserted road and give the coyotes a chance to kill him.

Well, fuck that with malice aforethought.

Renny punched a number into her phone and prayed for a swift response. She wasn't going to let her mate get hurt on her watch.

She knew she was really worried when she didn't even bother to drool over Mick's naked ass during the brief moment before he shifted from man to wolf. Her instincts proved correct when just seconds later, three more coyotes leapt from the shadows at the side of the road and surrounded the lone wolf.

"Alpha 911. Please state your emergency."

"I'm on Hidden Fork Road northeast of Browning Creek. My mate is being attacked by coyotes. Send deputies out now!"

"Ma'am, I need you to stay calm," the voice told her. "I'm contacting the sheriff's department, but it may take a few minutes for them to reach you. Remain on the line. Can you tell me—"

Renny stopped listening. Her eyes were glued to the

motion outside the truck. The four members of the Sawmill hunting party had surrounded her mate and were circling him like furry sharks, waiting for an opening in his defenses. For his part, Mick stood tall in the center of the road, his posture stiff and challenging but not at all intimidated by the coyotes' superior numbers.

"Stupid wolf," she muttered, wincing when the first coyote—Bryce—lowered itself into a crouch and then sprang at the wolf's head.

Mick didn't fall for it. He stood his ground until the last moment, then feinted right and spun to meet Will, who had darted in to bite at his flank. A flash of fangs met the smaller canine, tearing open the skin over the coyote's sharp muzzle. The shifter yelped, and the remaining two pack mates leapt into the fray.

"Ma'am!" came the voice from the phone, distant and muffled, but that was probably because Renny had dropped the device to the floorboards and was busy fumbling her way out of her first-day library clothes. Her mate was outnumbered.

"Shit."

Her trousers tangled around her ankles, reluctant to come off over the low-heeled boots she'd forgotten to remove. She heard seams ripping and couldn't be bothered to care that she was destroying one of the few suitable outfits she had for her new job. She'd work at the library naked if she had to. Mick needed her help.

It took three slaps at the button on the driver's-side door to disengage the locks, and then she went sailing into the darkness, skin shivering into fur before her paws even touched the ground.

Instead of welcoming her, her mate snarled at her approach, opening himself to yet another attack. A tawny coyote—Tommy—darted in under his guard and managed to get a mouthful of fur before Mick shook him off and batted him away with a strike of his huge paw.

Renny ignored the sign of displeasure. One wolf against four coyotes was not good odds, especially not when the coyotes had been working and hunting together for years. Their numbers gave them too great an opportunity to surround the wolf, and even a battle-tested alpha couldn't keep watch in four directions at once. She would have to watch his back, and if he didn't like it, that was his tough nougat.

She dove forward to put herself between her mate and the darkest of the coyotes. Eric had thought to take advantage of Mick's distraction and strike while the wolf was focused on his mate, but Renny put a stop to that. She slammed her shoulder into the attacking male, sending him stumbling back a few steps. A similar blow from Mick would have sent the coyote tail over ears, but her smaller size made her no larger than the males of the other species. It left them on equal footing.

It also seemed to give the pack ideas. They saw how Mick reacted to his mate joining the fight, and they immediately began to exploit that weakness. The four coyotes fell back from their attacks on Mick and began to focus their attention on Renny.

Beside her, she could practically feel the growl vibrating in her mate's chest. He crowded close to her, attempting to herd her back toward the truck, but she uttered a rumbling protest of her own. He might not want her in danger, but she'd be damned if she'd let him face down four coyotes all by himself. She just hoped the cavalry was already on its way.

Will, his wounded muzzle still welling blood, lowered himself toward the ground and began to slink closer, as if Renny were a rabbit he intended to have for dinner. Mick snarled a warning and moved toward the threat, but Will had only been setting the stage for his cousin to strike. Tommy dove in from the right, forcing Mick not away from Renny but into her. She stumbled, thrown off balance by the impact, and Eric immediately rushed in to grab her by the scruff and drag her away. Meanwhile, Will and Tommy pinned her mate between them and Bryce began to move in for the kill.

Nothing had ever sounded so good to Renny's ears as the shrill wailing of sirens in the distance. She dug her claws into the earth and pulled back against Eric's grip, wincing when his teeth bit through fur to the skin and muscle underneath. Damn it, she was sick and tired of bleeding already. She hoped the deputies were playing hell with the damned speed limit.

A series of vicious snarls had her head snapping around and drove the coyote's teeth deeper into her neck. She couldn't have cared less, because she caught a glimpse of Mick rearing back on his hind legs, jaws locked in combat with Bryce while the Molinas attempted to bring him down with swift, diving attacks from either side.

That was just fucking cheating.

With a low huff of anger, she twisted sharply, dropping her shoulder and flipping herself onto her back. The move surprised Eric and weakened his hold on her enough that she was able to jerk free and scramble back to her feet before he recovered. She didn't pause to take advantage of the moment, instead spinning on her heels and throwing herself at the closest coyote attacking her mate.

She sank her teeth into Will's back, tearing him away just before he went for Mick's exposed side. She used every ounce of her body weight to flip him to the ground, then shifted to get a better angle on his spine. She'd snap it in two before she'd let him harm her mate.

Will twisted himself almost in half and snapped back to his feet, his yellow eyes glowing wild and manic in the darkness. For a moment, they stared each other down, then the sound of rubber on pavement rose above the fighting and the glow of red and blue emergency lights began to emerge in the distance.

About damned time.

The coyotes scattered. Eric and Will spared her matching glares before bounding into the trees, and Tommy left off his attack on Mick's flank to follow. Bryce didn't give up so easily. He wrapped his forelegs around Mick's shoulders and attempted to drag the larger canine off balance, using his teeth and jaws for leverage.

Mick shook him off and dropped to all fours, fangs flashing as he went in fast and low, looking to open up the coyote's belly. Bryce might be smaller, but he was nearly as fast, and he managed to leap out of the way before Mick could grab hold. He spun in midair, offered one last bark of frustrated rage, and disappeared into the forest.

Renny dropped to her haunches and struggled to

catch her breath. Damn, forget Zumba; mortal combat was apparently the true path to physical fitness. She felt like she'd just had the hardest workout of her life. If she'd been in her skin, it would be drenched with sweat.

Giving a good shake, she resettled her fur and turned to face her mate. He responded by pouncing on her and forcing her onto her back, pinning her to the rough surface of the asphalt. She felt his jaws close around her throat and the intensity of his growl against her skin and made the decision to keep very, very still. It sounded like someone was not very happy with her at the moment.

He held her pinned there, belly up and whining for mercy, while two squad cars screeched to a halt a few yards down the road. She heard doors fly open and voices shouting and felt a surge of relief that the cavalry had finally arrived. Only now, she wondered if she was the one they were going to have to rescue.

Chapter Twelve

Mick held Renny pinned to the pavement and struggled to control his temper. Damn it, he would die before he did anything to hurt his mate, but in that moment, he really, really wanted to strangle her. What the hell had she been thinking?

His heart had stopped the minute he'd heard her jump out of his truck, but when he'd seen that coyote dragging her away from him, he'd wanted to tear the world apart with his bare claws. He'd told her to stay in the fucking truck, and what had she done? She'd completely ignored him and leapt into the middle of a battle where she was outnumbered, outclassed, and very nearly out of luck.

He'd had the situation under control. Yeah, he'd been one wolf against four coyotes, but he hadn't been in any real danger. He was bigger and stronger than any of his opponents, and he had an advantage they couldn't hope to achieve—he was fighting to defend his mate.

He could have handled them. Sure, he might have

gotten a cut or two, and if they got lucky, he might even be limping afterward, but Mick had no doubt that he'd be the one walking away from the confrontation. These fucking vermin had spent months stalking and terrorizing *his* female, one of them had dared to lay tooth and claw on her, and they thought they could take him down just because they had him outnumbered?

Like. Fucking. Hell.

They should be the ones relieved to hear the approaching sheriff's deputies, because Mick would have torn out every one of their throats and then sent up a howl to celebrate. He had been out for blood, and his mate had denied him.

He growled again and tightened his jaws around her throat. Not enough to hurt her, just enough so that she could feel the noise and the heat and the sharpness of his teeth and think for one Goddess-damned second about what kind of danger she had just put herself in.

Damn it, he wanted her to shift back to her skin, so he could turn it bright red with the flat of his hand. If any female had ever earned a spanking, it was this one.

"Mick. You okay, buddy?"

Zeke's voice reached him, as deep and steady as his steps as he approached them. Mick could hear the caution in the slow movements and wondered if the coyotes had circled back toward them.

"Dispatch said someone called in a coyote attack on the road out to your place, so I got the posse together and we came running. Only that doesn't look like a coyote to me, and she sure doesn't appear to be attacking anyone."

Mick snarled, but he didn't release his mate. He kept his eyes on his friend's heavy black boots as the man inched closer.

"Uh, Mick, I don't think Renny's planning on going anywhere anytime soon. How about you let her go so I can make sure neither of you is hurt?"

His mate whined as if seconding the motion. He felt her quivering beneath him and abruptly realized he might be scaring her. Reluctantly, he released his grip and stepped back, waiting for her to spring to her feet and confront him. Instead, she just turned her head and licked the underside of his chin. She was reassuring him.

Mick retreated another step and reached for his humanity, drawing it forward until the wolf was swallowed up and he stood in his skin in the middle of the road, bathed in two sets of headlights. He had to struggle to control his anger, though control came easier than it had in his fur. He still had the urge to shake his mate and demand to know what the hell she had been thinking when she'd let herself out of the safety of his truck, but the violence behind the emotion was beginning to subside.

He took several deep breaths and ran a gaze over his mate. He saw a couple of tiny red stains in the fur around her ruff, but she didn't appear to be seriously injured. The reassurance helped take him down another notch, and that was when he remembered he was standing in the middle of the road, bare-assed naked with four armed deputies watching him warily.

He glared down at his mate. "Don't even think about shifting back."

She wagged her tail and batted at the air with one paw like a puppy. Damn, she was cute.

Zeke relaxed a bit, holstering his weapon and giving his friend a quick once-over. "You don't look dead, so I guess the emergency wasn't quite so urgent. Care to tell me what happened?"

"Pants," Mick growled, and stalked back to his truck to grab his jeans. He also snagged his shirt. Eventually, Renny would want to shift, and he'd be damned if she stood around naked in front of this bunch of perverts. His shirt would be big enough to make a minidress for her. It wasn't a nice, thick pair of baggy flannel pajamas, but it would do.

He pulled on his jeans and rejoined Zeke in the glow of the red and blue emergency lights. Renny had rolled onto her belly but remained lying in the same spot where he'd left her.

For a change.

"It was an ambush," he said, and gave Zeke a brief summary of the situation, beginning with the injured deer being driven out in front of their truck and following through to the moment when the sheriff's department had arrived on the scene.

"You know, I'm getting damned sick of all the coyote stink around town," Zeke said, his eyes glinting dangerously. "I think it might be just about time to open up hunting season. How about you?"

Mick let himself smile. "You gonna make me carry a permit?"

Once again, Renny found herself clad in nothing more than one of her mate's shirts, struggling to make sure her ass and pussy both stayed covered at the same time. It was harder than it looked, especially when she had to climb into Zeke's patrol car while gripping her purse and phone in her hands. And damn, but that nighttime breeze was chilly.

Mick had finally let her shift (behind the truck, while every other man present kept his back turned and his eyes shut, thank you very much) and immediately covered her up, while Zeke set his deputies to examining the scene and looking for evidence. She didn't know what they expected to find, since she doubted any of their attackers had been carrying a map with the coordinates to their supersecret gang hideout. None of them had exactly had pockets when they attacked. But the deputy said knowing how they'd planned this attack could be useful, so Renny had just waited until someone escorted her to Zeke's car and helped her inside.

She still didn't know why she'd had to sit in the back, though. Mick got to ride up front, on the right side of the protective mesh barrier.

He and Zeke spoke in low voices, which seemed kind of insulting. She'd, you know, *been there* during the ambush, so it wasn't like they needed to shield her from what had happened. Plus, since she was the target of all the trouble that had descended on Alpha, it seemed only courteous to include her in any discussions about it.

She opened her mouth, prepared to make her feelings known, just as Zeke rounded the curve in Mick's long drive. The house came into view, and immediately, Renny knew that something wasn't right. It just took a minute for her brain to catch up to what her eyes were taking in.

Forest litter extended from the tree line toward the front porch, bits of mud and twigs and pine needles decorating the grass and gravel. A distinct trail formed from the debris, showing where something limp and heavy had been dragged across the ground.

She followed the path and spotted it, draped with mocking contempt over the stairs leading up to Mick's front door. The injured deer they had almost hit, now dead, had been left bloodied and vacant-eyed on the threshold, like a cat's gifted rodent.

"Fuck!"

Zeke slammed on the brakes, but Mick didn't wait for the car to stop before he shoved open his door and bolted toward the carcass. The deputy followed as soon as he'd shifted into park, leaving Renny trapped in the back with wide eyes and a sick feeling in her stomach.

"Don't touch it."

"Wasn't planning to."

Renny's sharp lupine sense could pick up their words, a bit muffled, from where she sat. It didn't hurt that they hadn't bothered to close the car doors when they'd leapt out.

"It's the same one they drove out in front of the car. You can see the injuries on the hindquarters where they harassed it to make it move."

Zeke hunkered down at the side of the steps and leaned in to sniff the dead animal. "Something doesn't smell right, here."

Mick bent in closer. The porch light caught the way he exposed his fangs in a snarl. "Poisoned."

"The damned thing's had its throat ripped out. Why the hell bother with poison?"

"Wasn't to kill it. Take a whiff. The poison's on the meat, not in the blood. The deer wasn't poisoned. Someone put something on it when they left it here to poison anyone who decided on a snack."

Zeke stood, his expression troubled. "That's . . . kind of insane. And I mean that literally. What did the coyotes think? That you'd find a dead deer on your porch and just chow down without wondering where the fuck it came from? Who would do that?"

Geoffrey.

Or Will, Renny supposed. There was no shortage of mental imbalances among the coyote pack. But she knew this was Geoffrey's work. Something inside just told her.

She lifted a fist to pound on the car window. They needed to let her out of here.

They didn't.

The men continued to talk, lowering their voices until she could make out their tones but not the actual words being spoken. That, Renny concluded, was unacceptable.

Her first instinct urged her to break the glass on the rear window and let herself out that way, but she knew from pounding on it how sturdy the stuff was. She had a feeling that even a well-placed mule kick wouldn't shatter the glass. A town full of shifters had apparently done some planning in the design of their police vehicles and had taken into account shifter strength. The grating separating the front and rear compartments of the vehicle appeared equally tamper resistant.

Renny considered her options and looked down at the phone in her hand. An idea formed.

Within seconds, she found what she needed, used the house's Wi-Fi to download the correct file, then pressed her phone's speaker up against the mesh and hit "play."

An earsplitting shriek ripped through the air. With the volume set to maximum, the front doors of the patrol car open, and the device aimed away from her, even Renny wanted to cry at the pain the noise invoked, but it had the desired effect. Both men turned toward the car and shouted at her.

Well, she assumed they shouted. Their lips were moving, but she couldn't hear a damned thing over the assaultive din of the siren she'd triggered on her phone. It took only seconds before Mick marched back to the car and wrenched her door open. He reached for the phone and she shoved it at him, darting past him straight to the front door.

She recognized the scent immediately and noticed it didn't stop at the top of the stairs. She reached for the door.

"What do you think you're doing?" Mick grabbed her wrist before she could turn the knob. He glowered down at her even more fiercely than he had right before he ran the truck off the road.

"He's here. I can smell Geoff on the deer. The others might have used the deer to waylay us on the road, but Geoffrey Hilliard made the kill, and I can smell him all over the door. What if he went inside?"

"Fuck! What if he's *still* inside?" Mick demanded. "You plan to march in and hand yourself over?"

Renny scowled. "Of course not."

"Then get your butt back in the car while Zeke and I check it out."

"Really? You want me to wait out here in the dark, all alone, where we have evidence my stalker has recently been? With an unlocked police car still running for a convenient getaway?"

She folded her arms over her chest and raised an eyebrow. Her mate looked ready to strangle her.

Zeke cleared his throat. "How about you both stay here, and I check things out inside. I seem to recall that being part of my job." He flipped open the latch on his weapon holster and waved the others back. "You two wait in the yard. Stay away from the door and windows. I'll be back in a minute."

Mick hauled her back down the steps and around to the other side of the squad car, as if he expected gunfire to erupt and wanted to make sure she was behind something solid when the bullets started flying. He didn't bother to speak a word, though, and she couldn't decide whether that scared her or pissed her off. She hadn't forgotten the subject she'd brought up just before they were attacked, and she definitely hadn't forgotten that he'd never given her an answer.

"Mick—"

"Quiet." He didn't bother to look at her, just stared at the open doorway through which Zeke had disappeared as if he could monitor the deputy's progress through the unlit house.

"Um, excuse me?"

He spared her a glance full of temper. "We can fight this out later, once we know no one else is going to try to kidnap or kill you tonight. Right now, we've got bigger things to worry about than your sense of independence and the foundations of our relationship. All right?"

No. No, it wasn't.

She took a deep breath and tried to get a handle on her anger before she did something irreversible, like castrating her mate with her bare hands. He might be acting like an asshole now, but later maybe he'd regain his senses and she'd consider letting those parts near her again.

"Look," she bit out. "I get that you're pissed off and outraged and worried and overprotective and drowning in alpha instincts right now. That's fine. You get to feel how you feel, but you don't get to dismiss me and my opinions and my concerns because of it. We need—"

Zeke appeared in the door with his police radio in his hand and a grim look on his face. Renny almost forgot what she'd been saying.

The deputy murmured something into his radio, then clipped it back on his belt and motioned them forward. "House is empty, but someone left you a present."

She scurried to keep up with Mick's ground-eating strides as he joined his friend on the porch and then followed the lion into the house.

It looked like a tornado had passed through—a very small, localized tornado that followed a direct and un-varying path from the front door of the house back to the bedroom she and Mick had been sharing. The path was easy to follow because of the destruction that lit-tered it. Everything within arm's reach of the center had been smashed, shattered, torn, broken, or crum-bled in angry fists. Pictures had been yanked from the walls and ground beneath a heavy foot. A chair now looked more like kindling mixed with random shreds of fabric and upholstery batting.

Dirt, glass, wood, ceramic, plastic, and paper crushed underfoot as the trio made their way through the space to the master bedroom. The contrast between the chaos along the path and the untouched area at the edges of the rooms seemed almost surreal. It looked as if whoever had done this had been on a mission or a deadline, so they hadn't spared the time to trash the whole house but simply grabbed and ruined everything within easy reach.

Renny could smell Geoffrey everywhere, but she noticed that the odor increased the closer they came to the bedroom door. When they reached it, Zeke stepped in front of them, blocking them from entering or even looking very far into the chamber.

He met Mick's gaze and held it. "I want you to remember that things are just things, okay? They're not important, but your reaction here is. I think this is Hilliard's way of sending you a message, and that he's deliberately taunting you. If you fly off the handle in reaction, you won't be thinking straight and you'll make mistakes. Hold it together. Understand?"

Mick nodded sharply, and Zeke reluctantly slid to the side, allowing the wolf to pass. Renny stayed hot on his heels.

Okay, she thought, trying to take everything in at once and winding up dazed by the attempt. This was where Geoffrey had decided to take his time. Obviously.

The room stank of coyote and looked like the site

of a bomb blast. Every window, mirror, and glass in the place had been shattered, shards glistening all over the floor and making Renny wish she'd at least grabbed her shoes before she'd let the men haul her away from Mick's wrecked car. No way could she get a closer look in her bare feet.

Every drawer had been yanked from the dresser and smashed. The closet had been emptied, bottles, glasses, lamps, and candleholders broken. The curtains and shades were torn from the walls, one of the rods dangling crookedly from a single nail still in the molding. Renny's favorite shade of lipstick—a brand-new tube she'd bought on her shopping trip with Molly—had been used to scrawl a message across the wall behind the bed.

MINE

But it was what had been done to the bed that freaked Renny out.

The frame was broken, the side rails torn away from the headboard and the footboard cracked in two down the middle. The violence used to damage it had moved the entire piece of furniture away from the wall and angled it into the center of the room. The bedding had been torn away and tossed to the side. The mattress had slid off one side and flopped half onto the floor, its surface stained with that smelled—overwhelmingly—of coyote urine. Geoffrey Hilliard had destroyed the bed she and Mick shared and then marked it with piss for good measure.

Her stomach churned a little. Coyotes, like many canine species, used scent marking to establish territory, but coyotes in particular were also known to urinate on the remains of their prey in an effort to warn off other predators.

The message was clear. Geoffrey had not given up on catching her, and he wanted her to know that he wouldn't let Mick or their mating stop him from taking what he wanted.

He really was out of his mind.

It looked like he'd driven Mick there, too.

Her mate took one look at the ruined mess, grabbed her around the waist, and physically hauled her back through the house. Renny couldn't decide if she was too shocked to protest or if she really didn't mind. She felt contaminated just by seeing Geoffrey's message to them. It's not like she wanted to stick around the scene.

Zeke followed them back to the front of the house. By the time they returned to the porch, they could hear sirens in the distance and see the first strobes of more emergency vehicles speeding down the drive. Mick didn't even acknowledge them. He set Renny on her feet and climbed down three steps until their eyes were level.

"I don't want to fight you on this, Renny." His blue gaze seared into her, all heat and determination. "I *won't* fight you. I need to get you someplace safe, and I need you to stay there while I find Hilliard and deal with him. Understand?"

Oh, she understood, all right. She understood that Mick was in a killing rage and that at this point, nothing would satisfy him but bloodshed. She had a harder time understanding why that didn't really bother her.

She took a deep breath. "What did you have in mind?"

"Yeah, I'm interested to hear that, too." Zeke stood

just a few feet away, outwardly calm and stoic as he always was on duty. Renny could see the tells in his posture, though. He had his weight balanced on the balls of his feet, ready to move, and his arms hung relaxed at his sides, hands visibly clear of anything that might encumber a quick reaction. "I hope you don't think you're going off alone after this son of a bitch. Because that's not happening."

Mick turned cold eyes on his friend, his body all but vibrating with the tension of suppressed fury. "You saw what he did, Zeke. You saw the threat he implied against my mate, and this time he didn't do it through a proxy or from a few hundred miles away. Hilliard is here, in Alpha, and I will go *through* anyone who tries to stop me from finding him."

"I'm not trying to stop you. I'm just saying you aren't doing it alone, you aren't going off half-cocked, and you aren't going anywhere until we can make sure that Renny will be safe till you get back. Or did you forget we're still dealing with Hilliard's pack, too? They're still out there, and while you're chasing after their boss, they could circle back after your mate."

"She won't be here. I don't care if we have to lock her in a jail cell and post the entire sheriff's department outside until this is over. Renny stays safe."

"Yeah, well, I care about that." Renny held up a hand and eased back a little. "I'm not down with the incarceration idea. I don't want to get hurt any more than anyone wants to see me get hurt, but locking me up sounds a little extreme."

Mick's hand came up to grasp her chin. He leaned in close, tugging her forward to meet him, and his thumb traced the line of her jaw. "Don't you get it, little red? Extreme is just the tip of the iceberg when it comes to what I'll do to protect you. I'd burn down this whole forest if I thought that's what it took to keep you safe. And I wouldn't think twice at who got caught up in the flames."

Renny felt her breath stutter to a stop. Her whole world seemed to freeze as she read the truth in his eyes. He meant every single word he said, and even the most dubious, insecure parts of her couldn't put that kind of vow down to lupine possessive instincts. Any wolf would die to protect its mate, but her mate was promising to take the world down with him.

That had to mean something, right?

Her heart leapt at the thought. What had Marjory said to her about the way men didn't always express their feelings with words? Maybe this was one of those demonstrations she needed to pay attention to.

She leaned into his touch. "I get it, Mick. That's how I feel, too. You think I can just sit and twiddle my thumbs while you go hunt down a lunatic? A lunatic with four best friends still out there? I need you to stay safe just as much as you need me to."

His expression hardened. "I'm not the one in danger. Don't forget, I've done this kind of thing before. Geoffrey won't be my first hunt, or my first kill. And trust me, he's not going to be half the challenge of my grandfather."

It felt like he'd just erected a wall between them, and Renny wasn't putting up with it. If he'd burn down forests for her sake, she'd buy herself a wrecking ball for his.

"You think I don't know?" She reached up and grabbed his wrist, holding his hand in place when he would have pulled it away. "You think I don't know exactly what you've been through? You've done everything you could not to talk to me about anything important, Mick Fischer, but don't for one minute assume I don't know your whole story. I thought we got this out of the way that first morning. I know about you and Beth Hilliard, about Abraham Garry, about how you dealt with everyone responsible for your first mate's death. I've always known."

"Then you should know that I'll take care of this, too."

"You think I care?" Goddess, sometimes she wanted to smack him upside the head to see if any sense would shake loose. "You still think I'm expecting you to solve my problems? To save me? Michael Kennedy Fisher, I would strip naked and offer myself to Geoff Hilliard on a silver platter if that's what I needed to do to keep *you* safe. I don't need you to kill for me, and I sure as hell don't need you to die for me. You may have survived losing a mate, but that doesn't mean I would."

"I wouldn't this time, red. I know it, even if you're too blind to see it."

His soft admission deflated her like a pin in a helium balloon. First, her heart melted, but then her outrage flickered to life.

Really? This was how he was going to admit that he cared about her? He'd spent two weeks basically shut up alone with her, fucking her brains out at every opportunity, with few interruptions and even fewer distractions, and he thought he'd use the threat of death to demonstrate his feelings for her?

Her free hand rose and cracked against the side of his head.

"Ow. What was that for?"

"It was to make sure you're paying attention." She narrowed her eyes at him and stuck out her chin. "Listen up, Mr. Alpha Wolf. You're bigger than me and stronger than me and tougher than me, but you are not indestructible. I can't stop you from going after Geoffrey, but I can damned well make sure that you don't go running off unprepared and alone. You want to find Geoff? Fine. You want to stop him? Terrific. But you're not dropping me off like a piece of mail and going hunting in the heat of the moment."

Zeke shifted and cleared his throat as if he knew they'd nearly forgotten he was still there. "Your mate is right, you know. No one will argue that Hilliard has crossed the line and that he needs to be stopped. Hell, we all agreed on that even before tonight. But you won't find him like this, hopped up on rage and adrenaline. We need to think this through and come up with a plan." He stepped forward and laid a cautious hand on the other man's shoulder. He made certain to keep the maximum possible distance from Renny while he did it. "We'll get him, Mick. You have my word."

Renny watched while anger, frustration, and denial raced across Mick's features, then she saw when reason finally made its breakthrough. He clenched his jaw so tight, she expected to hear something snap, but then he took a deep breath and jerked his head in a brief nod.

"Fine." His hand dropped from her face and hooked around her waist, dragged her against his side. "We'll plan. But Hilliard is going down, and I'm the one who's going to take him. I claim the rights to the kill." He stared at Zeke until the lion inclined his head. "And we'll need a ride into town. I'll send someone out to clean up after that fucking dog, but there's no way I'm letting my mate sleep in that house until his stench is gone."

Renny snuggled into his side. "Sounds good to me." Then she remembered something and she stiffened, turning a glare on both men. "But this time, I'm riding up front."

Chapter Thirteen

"I still feel like we should have a code word or something. Maybe a secret knock everyone has to give before entering. Or we could have a Marine stationed outside the door, like on *The West Wing*."

"Molly, it's Jaeger's office, not the White House Situation Room."

"So? They're still planning a precision military strike against an unsuspecting enemy."

"On a handful of coyotes, not the nation of Afghanistan."

Molly shrugged. "Whatever."

"Ladies, if we could please focus for a few minutes?"

John Jaeger sounded more amused than annoyed. He sat perched on the edge of his desk beside the huge bulletin board on which all of Renny's problems had been tacked in blown-up prints of living color. Yeah, seeing that was fun, and it was even more fun knowing an identical board graced the office of Alpha's sheriff just down the road.

If this was her fifteen minutes of fame, Renny wanted to go back to peaceful anonymity.

"We're focused. Focused on kicking ass." Molly grinned.

"We can't kick until we can find." Zeke stretched his legs out in front of his chair and scowled at the large map of the town and its outlying areas. "I'm having trouble believing that five coyotes unfamiliar with this area are managing to stay so successfully hidden. Our patrols haven't found a thing anywhere aside from where we already know they've been. It's frustrating as hell."

"Tell me about it. Vonnie is refusing to field any more calls asking why we haven't taken care of this already. She's putting our concerned citizen callers straight through to me now."

Oh, good, because Renny hadn't been feeling bad enough about bringing her troubles down on Alpha. She'd never wanted anyone else involved in her mess, and she couldn't expect the residents of town to put up with it for much longer.

"You know, there's still the option of me leaving," she offered. "I'm the reason Geoff and the others are here, so if I go, I'm sure they'll follow."

"Yup, right over my dead body," Mick growled. He glared at her, clearly unhappy at her for bringing up a possibility he'd already vetoed.

"That's not an option." Jaeger dismissed the idea for at least the fifth time. "We're not letting a bunch of psychotic coyotes drive *anyone* out of Alpha. This is your home now, just as much as it is for the rest of us."

"It's not like I want to leave, but it would make things a lot easier for everyone else."

"Except me," Molly protested. "I finally have a pedicure buddy, and you want to take that away from me? How could you be so cruel?"

"No one is going anywhere."

"Except Hilliard and his little boy band," Zeke said. "The men at the scene last night confirmed that the coyotes had vehicles concealed nearby to both the ambush site and Mick's property. Their scent trails end there, so no luck tracing them back to wherever they're holed up."

"So, what do we do next? Just sit on our hands and wait until they stage another attack?" Jaeger shook his head. "I'm not happy with that option."

"Because it isn't one," Mick grumbled. "I want this done and my mate safe."

"That's what we all want."

"What if we're ready for his next attack?" Renny had spent all night thinking about this, barely sleeping despite the comfortable room they'd stayed in at the Stag's Rest Inn, Alpha's best bed-and-breakfast. She'd kept the thoughts to herself, of course, because her mate had been lying right next to her and she didn't want his head to explode on the crisp, white sheets. "We could set a trap for him. Lure him out at a place and time when we're ready for him."

Mick fastened that intense blue glare on her. "You mean use you as bait. Not happening."

Huh, no brain matter on the upholstery. Renny decided to consider that an encouraging sign.

"Why not?" she asked. "I'm the cause of all the trouble. Why can't I be part of the solution?"

"Hilliard is the cause, not you."

"Semantics. It doesn't alter the fact that I'm the reason the coyotes are in Alpha, and that they've shown us they're not leaving until they get me. It seems to me that it makes more sense for us to control the next time they attack instead of waiting for them to catch us unprepared."

Jaeger pursed his lips. "What did you have in mind?"

Mick turned on the mayor, fangs showing. "Nothing. It's not happening. Drop it."

Renny squeezed his hand. "Let's not have this fight again, Cujo. No one is going to get hurt. That's the whole point of us being prepared and in control of the situation."

"I still haven't heard what situation we're talking about."

"I figured you guys could work out the details." More like, they would demand to. "Luring Geoffrey out shouldn't be that hard. I mean, he's proven how badly he wants to get his paws on me. We just have to offer him the opportunity, or at least make it look like that's what we're doing."

"Brilliant plan," Zeke observed. "Expect for the one pesky detail about there being no actual plan there."

"She's going to be the bait, does she have to be the strategist, too?" Molly demanded.

Jaeger held up his hands. "Children, calm down. Before we start fighting over who's responsible for what may or may not be an actual plan, I think we need to consider a few hard truths. The attacks on Renny so far haven't exactly been predictable. I'm not convinced it would be so easy to lay a trap for these coyotes."

"John's right," Zeke said. "The first night, one of them chased Renny right onto Mick's front lawn, so clearly they weren't worried about stealth. Then they went after her in broad daylight, when she wasn't even alone, in the middle of a public shopping area. And last night's ambush might have been set up on a back road, but it was still early enough that they couldn't have predicted no one else would happen by to derail the operation. I'm not convinced that even the best plan we could come up with would end up going the way we expect it to. Hilliard's pack seems too unstable for that."

He looked like he was about to say more, but a buzzing sound made him reach for the phone in his pocket. The deputy frowned down at the display and rose.

"Excuse me," he said. "It's Sheriff Lahern. I have to take this outside." He had the phone to his ear before he was out the door.

"I agree with Zeke." Jaeger shook his head. "You can't lay a trap for an animal unless you know how it thinks, and I'm not crazy enough to figure out how Hilliard and his pals think. If they even do."

Renny bit back a growl of frustration. "Then what are we supposed to do? I can't just go about my business waiting for the other shoe to drop. My nerves couldn't take it. I already feel ready to crawl out of my skin."

"I get that this isn't easy, Renny, but keeping you safe is everyone's top priority. Catching Hilliard runs a close second, but it's still second."

She gave the mayor a sour look. "Speak for yourself."

Renny could see her mate gearing up to give her another lecture, but Zeke's return saved her bacon. Or at least her eardrums. He had an odd look on his face as he tucked his phone back into his pocket.

"Well, that was unexpected," he drawled. "The sheriff was calling to tell me that one of our fugitive coyotes has been located."

Mick stiffened. "Hilliard?"

"No, Bryce Landeskog. He's at the sheriff's office."

Renny frowned. "He turned himself in? I don't believe that."

Zeke shook his head. "No, he's dead. Someone left his body in the Dumpster behind the building."

The room went silent. They all stared at the deputy, as if waiting for a punch line.

"What the fuck?" Jaeger finally managed.

"That's exactly what the sheriff wanted to know."

A tone sounded from the corner of the mayor's desk. "John?"

"We're a little busy, Vonnie. Hold my calls," Jaeger instructed over the intercom.

The badger's voice came back clearly. "This call isn't for you. It's for Ms. Landry. The man said it was urgent."

"Put it through." Still frowning, Jaeger reached over to activate his phone's speaker function. The line clicked open.

"Hello, Renny, my sweet. Have you missed me?"

Mick wasn't sure whether the people in the room with him looked more surprised or confused. Renny just looked grim. She recognized the voice as well as he did.

"Hello, Geoffrey."

Molly's eyes went wide and she slapped a hand over her own mouth, as if to stifle any potential noise. Zeke and Jaeger both narrowed their eyes and focused on the speaker. Zeke crossed to the bulletin board and picked up a marker, then tacked up a blank sheet of paper where everyone could see it.

"I hope the snack I left last night didn't leave you feeling unwell this morning." The coyote's voice sounded falsely sweet in a way that made Mick's hair stand on end. "I regretted the decision almost immediately—it was the heat of the moment, you understand—but by then it was too late to reverse it."

Getting dept to trace call.

Need few mins.

Pump for info.

Location?

Zeke used one hand to scrawl his instructions on the board while the other typed text into his phone with surprising dexterity. The deputy was a man of hidden talents.

"The decision to poison me with tainted deer meat, you mean? Oddly enough, I wasn't all that hungry last night. Something about being attacked on the way home from work just killed my appetite."

Renny spoke to the telephone, but her eyes had locked on Mick's. Her hand squeezed his in reassurance.

"That was an unfortunate incident." Geoffrey's voice cooled and hardened. "I'm afraid my employees chose to ignore the limits I had placed on their actions. You were never to be put in such danger."

"It sounds to me like your 'employees' had a habit

of ignoring that kind of instruction, Geoffrey. Or didn't Bryce bother to tell you that he tore my side open trying to catch me a couple of weeks ago?"

"Bryce has been dealt with," the coyote snapped. "He disobeyed and disappointed me one too many times. You won't need to worry about him any further."

"No? So, I just need to worry about Eric, Will, Tommy, and you, then. Is that what you're saying?"

"You wouldn't have to worry about me if you had just cooperated from the beginning, Renny. But I'm afraid you've earned your punishment. Don't worry, though. I have too many plans for you to kill you. You'll live a good long while yet."

Mick watched the look of disgust cross his mate's face and stroked her arm. When she looked at him, he shook his head. No way was he letting Geoffrey Hilliard get his hands on *his* mate. He'd rip them off first.

"Really? Don't I get a vote there? Because if the choice is between death and submitting to your 'plans,' I saw this really pretty burial shroud on Pintcrest."

The coyote growled at that, then issued a soft, low-pitched woof all the more threatening for its lack of volume. "Don't make things worse for yourself, Renny. I only have so much restraint, especially where you're concerned. I could still decide to make you suffer."

And that was when Mick's wolf had enough.

The animal surged forward in his mind, not bothering with warning growls or posturing theatrics. It simply seized control of Mick's impulses and threw him in front of his mate.

"You'll die before you get within ten feet of my

mate." His voice sounded barely human, even to his ears, but no one in the room seemed to misunderstand. Zeke's eyes went wide, and Jaeger's mouth tightened. Renny cast him a worried glance.

There was a pause on the line. "Michael?" Hilliard sounded surprised for a moment, but he quickly masked the note. "You again? I don't understand why you're so determined to shove your snout into this situation, brother-in-law. I already told you, the little bitch is mine."

"She bears my mark," Mick snarled. "And I hers. You have no claim."

"You marked her? That's impossible." Uncertainty, shock, and then rage spilled out of the coyote's end of the connection. "You already had your mate, *remember*? Or did sweet little Elizabeth mean nothing to you in the end? Because you certainly went to a lot of trouble to avenge her. Don't tell me you slaughtered your own pack for nothing."

The taunt landed on the occupants of the room, and Mick glanced among them, trying to gauge the response. He knew that Renny knew his story, that she'd worked it out from the time she spent in his hometown after he'd left it. He'd suspected that Jaeger knew as well, because the mayor of Alpha made it a point to check out the histories of all the town's newcomers as a way to ensure they posed no threat to the other residents. But he'd never discussed his past with Zeke, despite their friendship, and he'd never talked about anything much with Molly.

He figured everyone in town knew or suspected that he'd had a mate before and that something had happened to her, but it wasn't something he talked about, and Alpha had certain rules. Most of the residents had wound up here because of problems that made it impossible for them to live among their own packs and clans and prides and families. It was considered only polite not to pry into those problems, but to let the individual decide what to share and when.

So much for that philosophy. Mick felt like his life story had just made the front page of the Alpha *Town Cryer* newspaper.

He pulled his gaze from the others and focused on the telephone speaker. "Don't try to turn this into another of your games, Geoffrey. I can still add you to the 'slaughter.'"

"You have to find me first, wolf. Let's see if you can manage it before I take back my little bitch. I can't wait to see if she tastes different now that you sank your teeth into her."

The line clicked and went dead.

Mick spit out a curse. Beside him, Renny leaned closer and stroked his arm. "It's okay. I'm okay. I'm right here," she assured him.

Fury rode him too hard to let him be easily soothed. He looked at Zeke. "Did you trace the call?"

Zeke stared down at his cell phone. "Hold on. They're pulling it up. . . . Fuck." He raised his eyes and his expression was grim. "He used a burner phone. The location of the tower he bounced from tells us he's here locally, but we won't be able to trace him by the phone. Especially if he's smart enough to have dropped it and moved on immediately."

"He doesn't sound stupid," Jaeger said, bracing his hands on his desk and leaning forward. "Dumb as a lump of shit for going after another man's mate, but not stupid. Send someone to check out the spot the signal originated from, but if they find more than that phone, I'll eat my shorts."

"I'll *feed* you your shorts if you let anything happen to Renny." Molly stood to glare fiercely at the mayor. "If the son of a bitch isn't going to stick around in the spot where he called from, then what the hell are you wasting time for going there? Shouldn't you be . . . oh, I don't know, out searching for this asshole?"

Mick's wolf approved wholeheartedly of the lioness's show of loyalty, and so did Mick himself. He was just too busy trying to control his urge to go kill someone to unclench his jaw and tell her so.

Jaeger's expression lightened with amusement. "Sheathe your claws, kitten. We're not going to let anything happen to your friend. We've already got the search under way. See those colored areas?" He gestured toward the bulletin board and its highlighted, marked-up map. "Those are the sections of the search grid we established yesterday. We had men out there all afternoon, and they hit the ground running this morning. No one is wasting any time here. We will find this coyote, and we will deal with him."

"Can the dealing include the introduction of his balls to a peavey hook, in true Pacific Northwestern style?"

Mick took in Molly's evil expression. Then he remembered what a peavey was and pictured her wielding the long-handled spike with its pivoting hook attachment. He reflexively crossed his legs and eased a little farther away. He caught Zeke and Jaeger doing something similar.

"At this point, I don't care about making him suffer

or pay or whatever." Renny sighed. "I just want him to go away and leave me alone. I'm ready to have a *life* for a change."

"We'll make it happen," Mick assured her. He tugged her close and nuzzled her hair. "Whatever it takes, even if it kills him."

"Duh, that would be the fun part." Molly looked as if she were still picturing what she could do with some uninterrupted Hilliard time and a few of her favorite logging tools.

Jaeger eyed her warily. "How about we concentrate on finding Hilliard for the moment, and worry about what's going to happen to him later? The quicker we locate the bastard, the quicker we can all have our turn to chat with him."

Mick bared his fangs. "Me first."

Oh, yeah. He had plans.

Chapter Fourteen

Having a boss who considered her the answer to a personal prayer and was desperate to ensure she didn't get away kind of rocked. Renny made certain to express her thanks to Marjory for giving her a couple of hours off this morning for the latest meeting in the mayor's office, but the older woman waved away her words.

"I have a vested interest in making sure you stay safe, young lady," she said. "I'm more likely to berate the mayor for not doing enough to protect you, especially after hearing about the latest stunt those coyotes pulled. I've been running this library on my own for forty years now. I can manage as many more mornings as it takes to get you safe and this sorry business dealt with."

"You are amazing," Renny said, meaning every word.

Marjory laughed. "What I am, my dear, is desperate. You're the first qualified librarian to come through this town in more than a decade. I would hunt this Hilliard fellow down myself before I let you get away. Now, let's take a look at last year's budget. You'll want to familiarize yourself, because we'll be starting on next year by the end of this month."

Honestly, Renny felt grateful to spend the rest of her day working. Not only had she been dying to return to a library for months now, but focusing on learning how to take over Marjory's role kept her too busy to worry about anything else. Such as when Geoffrey might strike again, and whether or not her mate was off doing something foolish, like going after the coyote all by himself.

He hadn't said that's what he had planned, but he'd been pretty evasive when he'd dropped her off at the library after they left the town hall. He had told her to have a good day, promised to pick her up at six, and tap-danced around her questions as to what he'd be doing all afternoon. Part of the time, she imagined, he'd have to spend arranging for someone to clean up the mess Geoffrey had left in their house and get the broken windows replaced, but she knew that wouldn't take him all day. She supposed that as long as he kept his promise to return by six, there was only so much trouble he could get into.

Or at least, that's what she kept telling herself.

He had arranged for a deputy to remain all day to guard her, which she thought was overkill and he insisted was the least paranoid plan he'd been able to come up with regarding her protection. When he'd started mumbling about cotton wool and how big a papoose it would take to hold someone her size, she'd let it drop. But her worry lingered until he pushed through the library's heavy old door right on the dot of six.

Her face lit up in a smile, and she heard Marjory

chuckle beside her. "Go on, now, young lady. We're done for today, but I'll expect you at nine o'clock tomorrow, barring any unforeseen emergencies."

Renny grimaced. "Yeah, let's hope we're done with those."

The women exchanged goodbyes, and Renny gathered up her things and followed her mate to the door. He kept a protective hand on her back and his gaze moving on the short walk to the curb where he had parked. His expression remained relaxed, but she could feel the tension in him and noticed that it didn't really ease up when they got moving.

"No news about Geoffrey, huh?"

He glanced at her briefly. "No. We covered another couple of sections of our grid, but so far no one has reported anything but old tracks."

"We?" She raised an eyebrow and fixed him with a stern gaze. "Which areas did you and *your partner* cover, my mate?"

"Relax, little red." His smile flashed as he navigated past the bed-and-breakfast where they had spent last night. "I heard you when you asked me not to go running off on my own."

Renny turned to look at the pretty blue house receding behind them, then back at her mate. "Um, did I miss the part of our day where you told me we weren't staying here in town again?"

"I had some folks out to the house this afternoon to get things cleaned up, and to upgrade the security system. I thought we'd both be more comfortable at home tonight."

She could definitely get behind that. It might have been only a little over two weeks, but Renny already thought of the small house in the woods as home. His den had become theirs, and she'd always feel most secure inside it.

It also didn't hurt that she'd rather not involve any innocent bystanders in her problems until they managed to catch Geoffrey. That included sweet, kindly innkeepers who made her pots of hot chocolate and left plates of cookies on the nightstand.

"As long as they got the stink out."

"Trust me, I gave them very specific instructions. And helped open all the damned windows myself."

His grumpy tone made her grin and also served to distract her as they drove past the spot where the truck had been ambushed last night. No evidence lingered to indicate what had happened. Morning rain showers had even washed away the clumps of mud kicked up by their tires when Mick had steered them off the road. The forest looked empty and peaceful, but Renny couldn't quite shake off her lingering tension.

It could be the natural wariness that came from knowing that someone who wanted to harm her was still out there somewhere, but she suspected that didn't explain all of it. In the chaos of dealing with being attacked, finding their home invaded, and making plans to find Geoffrey, she hadn't forgotten that she and Mick had never really finished the argument she had started about their relationship. The stubborn wolf still hadn't told her he loved her.

At least now she felt pretty confident that he did. He had shown her that and had even hinted at it with words, but a little voice inside Renny wanted to hear it from his lips in plain English. Not for her benefit as much as for his. He had vowed to protect her, indicated that he wouldn't survive losing her the way he had his first mate, but he still hadn't come out and said, "Renny, I love you." Until he did, she would be stuck wondering if he still resented having their mating thrust upon him or if he was ready to move forward and build their future together.

Mick tried to shove down the nerves boiling in his belly, but the things turned out to move faster and slipperier than a litter of baby otters. Last night, Renny had told him that she loved him, but she hadn't exactly offered the words as a tender vow of devotion. She'd pretty much thrown them down like a gauntlet and dared him to say them back to her. As if three little words could encompass the way he felt about his redheaded she-wolf.

Love didn't begin to describe it. He needed Renny, the same way he needed his heart to beat or his lungs to fill up with air. In fact, he wasn't entirely sure she hadn't wormed her way so far inside of him that she hadn't *become* his heart, taking over the very act of pumping the blood through his veins. Damn it, but he could swear he felt her fingers there inside his chest, squeezing and releasing in steady rhythm.

Even before last night's attack, he had known he was in love, and not because he recognized the feeling from his first mating. He'd actually been dealing with a profound sense of shame over the realization that what he felt for Renny eclipsed anything he'd ever had with Beth. He had loved Beth with his whole heart, but he'd never felt for her the things he did for Renny. He had killed for his first mate, but he hadn't died for her. For Renny, he knew he wouldn't even have the choice.

There had been no conscious choice with Beth. He

had believed for a long time that it had only been the need for vengeance that had kept him from following her into the beyond. Eventually, he'd thought the bitterness of losing her would dry up, and he would go ahead and join her in death. In fact, you could say that for more than eight years now, he'd been sitting around waiting to die. Only now, because of Renny, he was living in painful, vibrant Technicolor.

His new mate had brought him back to life, but she seemed oblivious to that fact. Hell, he was an artist, wasn't he? Maybe he could just draw her a damned picture.

Mick pulled his truck to a stop in front of the house and raced around the hood to help Renny down before she could just jump for it. Something in him compelled him to physically lead her in to her surprise, so he folded his fingers around hers and tugged her up the porch steps.

She looked down at the freshly restained boards. "Wow, remind me to make a Yelp recommendation for whoever you used to clean this place up. You can't even tell there was ever any deer blood here. They did a fantastic job."

Rolling his eyes, Mick pulled her to the front door and fished out his keys. He was trying to set a romantic mood here, and his mate was talking about bloodstains and deer carcasses.

"Wait till you see how they did the inside."

Renny lifted her face and sniffed. "So far, I can't smell a thing. I mean, I can't smell anything out of place. No Geoffrey on the porch, at least."

"Coyotes have been permanently banished," he grumbled, and led the way inside. Immediately, he closed and locked the door and turned to the new and more elaborate security pad beside the entry. "The security company did a total upgrade," he explained as he gave her the new access code. "The mayor authorized it, so now anytime the alarm activates here, it immediately notifies the Alpha Sheriff's Department. You can call to give them a safe word in case of a false alarm, but they can be here in less than ten minutes from the time they get the signal."

Renny wrinkled her nose. "Okay, so I know that's a good thing from a safety standpoint, but it's going to make me paranoid to open the door. I'll be afraid of setting it off every darned time. One too many false alarms and the deputies will hate me."

He looked down at her. "Deal. I don't care if every single resident of the state of Washington hates you, as long as you're safe. Understand?"

She sighed and patted his chest. "Okay, Cujo. Maybe I'll just bake them preemptive cookies, or something."

With the alarm activated, Mick hung up their coats and led her through the living room. Everything looked neat and orderly, just the way it had before Geoffrey had been there. A few knickknacks might be missing, but the furniture had been repaired, the pictures rehung, and the debris vacuumed up as if it had never happened.

Renny made approving noises as she looked around, and he could see her taking deep breaths to scent the air. Carpet steamers, open windows, furniture polish, and a lot of elbow grease had dispelled the coyote miasma. Her smile told him she had noticed.

"Come on." He nudged her toward the bedroom. "Come and make sure the cleaners didn't toss away anything you wanted to try to salvage."

She dragged her feet a little on their way down the hall. "What was there to salvage? If Geoffrey touched it, I sure as hell don't want it anywhere near me anymore. And as for the things he pissed on? Ugh, don't make me gag. There's not enough Tide on earth to make that okay."

"Just take a look," he urged, positioning her in the doorway and then swinging the door open in front of her.

He heard her gasp and glanced down to make sure it wasn't for any of the wrong reasons. Her lips had parted and her eyes had gone wide, and he thought he saw a shimmer of tears glaze over them.

Panic threatened.

Renny stepped forward, staring at the changes to their den's inner sanctum. The bedroom had been completely transformed, from new flooring and rugs to new paint and curtains. It looked like the "after" picture from one of those guerrilla home makeover shows, and it smelled of vanilla and spice and home, not a trace of coyote to be found.

The walls, once deep blue and cavelike, had been lightened to a pale, smoky slate color that managed to be both light and cozy. Navy curtains had disappeared, leaving the windows looking larger and brighter with their frames of filmy white. All of the trim in the room had been repainted white as well, giving it a cleaner, more open look that softened its formerly masculine edges. The old carpet had disappeared, replaced by dark walnut planks and accented by a subtly pattered rug in shades of gray. Its placement drew attention to the room's new centerpiece.

Gone was the bed the coyote had broken and defiled. In its place, Mick had chosen to decorate their shared space with the bed she had bought on her shopping trip with Molly, only it, too, had been transformed. The battered, functional tester she remembered with its scratched finish and two missing top rails now stood as a graceful four-poster. She couldn't even see where the remains of the canopy frame had been removed, because the tops of the posts had been decorated with classic acorn-style finials. The entire piece had been painted a rich ebony to match the espresso color of the dresser and nightstand Mick had already owned. The dark finish contrasted beautifully with the thick, fluffy duvet, which sported a silver-on-white, leafing branch design. A spray of pillows in shades of blue, gray, and deep burgundy added a pop of color and made Renny want to fling herself into the pile and roll around like a puppy.

Her mate had done this for her. He had transformed what had been *his* bedroom—a masculine bachelor's quarters—into something for both of them, a combination of the bed she had chosen and the pieces he had owned for years. He'd made the room softer and more inviting without adding frills or girly bits that didn't suit him, and he'd clearly looked at the items she had planned to use in her bedroom at Molly's apartment to get an idea of her taste in colors and textures. He'd done it all in one day, and he had done it to make her happy.

Renny's eyes welled up and she started to turn around, gratitude and praise on her lips, but something else caught her eye. She tried to remember what had been there before—nothing? a clothes hamper? a pile of muddy boots?—but her mind had gone blank.

All she could see was her vanity table, looking regal and elegant and as perfect as if it had just left the cabinetmaker's workroom, sitting in pride of place on the wall beside the bathroom door.

Gone was the peeling, discolored paint. The mirror gleamed, reflecting the light from the bedside lamps, and the surface of the table looked so smooth and shiny, she thought she could trace every single grain of the wood through the dark, polished finish. It was perfect, exactly the way she'd pictured it in her head when she'd rescued it from the bargain section of the dusty antiques shop.

The tears started in earnest, and when she finally turned to face Mick, her mate took one look at her wet cheeks and red eyes and went whiter than the new curtains.

"What is it? Baby, what's wrong?" he demanded. He reached out to grasp her shoulder, hands rubbing soothingly up and down her arms. "Whatever you don't like, we can change it. I can get rid of it right now. Tell me what should go. The rug? I'll toss it. You don't like the colors? You can pick out new paint first thing in the morning, I swear. Just don't cry, little red. You're killing me."

"I'm killing you?" She half laughed and half sobbed, the sound catching in her throat. "You just destroyed me, Michael Kennedy Fischer, and I will love you forever for it."

His mate threw herself into his arms and kissed him as if he were a soldier who had just returned from war, thus rendering him utterly and hopelessly confused. He wasn't dumb, though. He returned the kiss with interest.

It tasted salty and sweet and absolutely perfect, just like her.

He got to savor it for only a moment before she pulled away and began peppering his face with equally enthusiastic but much less intimate kisses. He had to close his eyes to keep from taking lips to the eyeball. Huh. Maybe he hadn't actually done anything wrong?

"Thank you, thank you, thank you," she chanted in between pecks, and he finally had to pull her away for a moment in order to get a look at her and figure out what was going on.

"Can I take it this means I did something right?"

She wriggled until she could reach to give him one more smacking kiss. "You did amazing. I can't believe this. How on earth did you get this all done so quickly? It hasn't even been twenty-four hours since this place looked like a disaster area."

Mick didn't need the reminder. The sight of the destruction Geoffrey Hilliard had left in his home was seared into his memory. "I called in a few favors."

And threw money around as if it were confetti, he admitted to himself. But, so what? His mate deserved it, and he deserved to see her looking happy and excited instead of tense and worried. The history of their mating so far looked like the design schematics for a theme park thrill ride, and redecorating their bedroom was his way of trying for something more along the lines of a romantic chick flick.

Or, you know, a late-night erotic feature. He wasn't picky.

"Okay, write down their names in the morning," Renny said. "I'll add them to the cookie list."

"You want me to wait till morning?" He slid his

arms around her waist and tugged until her soft curves
nestled against him. "I could jot it all down now, if
you'd rather. Get it done tonight."

"Oh, no." She stretched up on her toes and looped
her arms around his neck, pulling herself up until their
lips met. "I have plans for tonight."

Mick let himself sink into the kiss and reconsidered.
A little thrill ride never hurt anyone.

Renny wasn't the kind of girl who believed in trading
sexual favors for the things she wanted. She didn't use
it to get her way, and she didn't think of it as a bar-
gaining chip. Good sex had enough to recommend it
that she'd never felt it needed any other justification.

Of course, with all that said, she saw nothing wrong
with using it as a well-earned reward, especially when
that reward was so easily and satisfyingly shared.

She pulled away just long enough to take Mick's
hand and tug him toward their new, magazine-ready
bed. "Come on. This bed was a little rickety when I
picked it up. Let's test out the repairs."

Her mate chuckled and scooped her up, taking two
long strides and then tossing her through the air to land
in the middle of the mattress. The duvet billowed up
around her and pillows scattered to the floor. Renny
snuggled into the pristine softness and giggled.

"So far, so good."

Mick leaned over her, bracing his palms beside her
shoulders. "Good? Let's try for spectacular."

He took her mouth with greedy hunger. She could
feel him looming above her, his weight carefully
balanced so as not to crush her. Even so, she could
feel his presence like a roof over her head, sheltering

and protecting her, and that's when she knew herself to be a dirty, rotten liar.

Renny was not "most of the way" in love with him like she'd told him in his truck the night before. She was head under water, fully submerged, soaked to the skin, and drowning in love with him. It no longer mattered whether he said the words to her, because there was no going back and nothing she could change. This was it. Her story was written.

She believed now that he loved her back. What else could he have been trying to tell her with this surprise, with all the time and effort and thought he had put in to not just repairing their den, but changing it to suit her and the new life they could build together? Actions, as Marjory had tried to tell her, really did speak louder than words.

But she still wanted to say them to him. They really had been important to her when she had confronted Mick about his feelings. Even though she now realized that she could hear them with her heart instead of her ears, she would feel like a coward if she didn't speak them. It would be as if she held something back, and she wanted nothing of that between them.

She nipped at his lips, hard enough to get his attention. When he raised his head, she looked straight into his beautiful blue eyes and bared her soul. "I love you, my mate. Completely."

His eyes blazed and his features took on a look of fierce satisfaction. "Good, because you're mine, little red. And I love you, too."

His mate stared up at him in silence just long enough to make him kick himself for being an idiot. The world's biggest idiot. For Renny to react to his declaration of love with such shock meant that she hadn't expected to hear it. So, either she still doubted his feelings for her or she doubted he had the stomach or the balls to man up and express them to her.

Either way, it meant he had some serious work to do. Before this night was over, his mate would have no doubt in her mind that he loved and cherished her above everything else in this world. He'd show her with both actions and words, but first he needed her naked.

He knelt on the bed, straddling her legs, and reached for the buttons of her prim, striped shirt. The tailored fit and conservative neckline had been driving him crazy all day.

She probably thought of it and of her trim, gray suit as professional and conservative, but to him they served as nothing more than a constant reminder of all the luscious things they concealed. Renny might think she dressed as a librarian should, but it only made him want to chase her behind a stack of books and ravish her. He could picture how she would look when he was finished, all soft and rumpled, her hair untidy and her eyes drowsy with satisfaction.

Oh, yeah. He'd like to see that look on her face again. Right about now.

She watched him while he undressed her, and he had a hard time choosing between staring into those sweet pools of green and staring at every inch of pale skin he uncovered. She watched him with such hunger and trust and love that it made his hands shake, and by the time he got to the button of her trousers, he lost all control. He ripped the fabric from her and tossed the pieces carelessly behind him.

She grinned. "You realize I don't have many clothes left to spare, don't you?"

He stripped off her panties, leaving her bare and beautiful on the rumpled new duvet. "Good. I like you naked. I think I'll keep you that way."

"Only if you join me." She flipped open the button on his jeans, then lay back with a smug expression while he shed his own clothes at record-breaking speed.

When he eased back down on top of her, she arched and rubbed skin to skin, as if she were a cat instead of a wolf. Not that Mick minded. The feel of her bare curves and sweet softness beneath him made him harder than tempered steel. "My pleasure."

It felt like a punishment to have to move, because he wanted to stay right where he was forever, pinning his mate to the mattress beneath him and savoring the inviting warmth of her. But then it became a punishment not to move, because the hunger inside him demanded more.

Mick slid down her body, unwilling to break contact long enough to shift with any real efficiency. She moaned and undulated a little beneath him, which turned out to be its own reward. He trailed kisses over her skin, along the arch of her neck, the dip of her shoulder, the firm smoothness of her breastbone.

When he reached her breasts, he stopped and lingered. He couldn't help himself.

He nuzzled against the soft inner curve, drawing her scent in deeply. It lingered here in the sweet, dark space underneath, tangy lemon, dried tea leaves the color of her eyes, and hints of piquant nutmeg. He lapped at her skin, trying to draw in the taste, but that only increased his craving.

Her nipple beckoned to him, the stiff, pink berry drawn hard and tight. He closed his lips around it and felt as well as heard her low moan of pleasure. Her legs shifted restlessly, or tried to, since his lower body held her pinned in place, and he slid his hand between them.

He found her hot and wet and ready for him, and as his fingers glided through her plump folds, he felt the way her body reacted every time he drew hard at her breast. His little red mate liked the heavy pressure. He could give her that.

Part of him wanted to draw out the moment, to tease and torment and savor the tight drawing of need in his belly. His wolf clawed at him, but even that became part of the pleasure, the tension of struggling against his own base needs even while the means to sate them melted under his touch.

As it turned out, that part of him wasn't quite as strong as the other. The second part was all need and urgency and it was damned tired of waiting. It wanted their mate *now*.

Abruptly, he pulled away from her, ignoring her whimper of confusion. Her hands reached for him, but he brushed them away and seized her at hip and shoulder, rolling her onto her stomach. She didn't need further prompting but immediately pulled her knees forward and raised her hips, offering herself to her mate.

By the Goddess, she looked gorgeous. Her back slim and straight, her ass round and firm and curving down toward his glimpse of heaven. Her sex glistened with her arousal, puffy, pink, and inviting. The sight made his mouth water.

His dick could wait a second, he decided, and leaned

forward to drag his tongue across her center. Renny shuddered and turned her face into the duvet, muffling her urgent little whimpers.

Oh, no. She didn't get to do that. His mate didn't get to deny him the sounds of her pleasure, not when every one of them made his chest swell with pride. And his cock swell with need.

He tangled a hand in her hair and used the grip to turn her head until her cheek pressed against the smooth cotton and her breathless little cries echoed around the room. That was more like it. He continued to tease her for another minute, savoring both the music of her noises and the salty, sweet flavor that was her essence. He didn't believe he would ever have enough of this woman.

Mate.

Mine.

Love.

Need.

Take.

Mick reared up behind her and gripped her hips with both hands. His fingers dug in with bruising pressure as he fit the head of his cock to her entrance and began to ease inside.

He intended to plunge. Dear, sweet Lady of the Moon, how he wanted to plunge, but as his mate's body closed around him, he felt how tight and snug the position had made her, and his instincts compelled him to relish every second of sensation.

She closed around him like a fist, her body milking him with tiny little contractions he knew she couldn't control. She wasn't trying to drive him out of his mind; she just couldn't help herself.

"Mate. Please." She panted the words, quiet and high-pitched with desperation. "More."

Mick eased forward, sinking deeper, and had to grit his teeth against the impulse to let go, to spill himself then and there and damn anything but his own pleasure. His wolf snarled at that idea, grabbing him by the balls and demanding that he satisfy their mate, that he pleasure her so thoroughly, she would never have sufficient energy to think about other males.

"Please."

He thrust forward with a muffled shout, burying himself to the hilt in her tight, hot passage. She felt like paradise, slick and soft and snug, and he was moving before he could think, setting a hard, driving rhythm that had their new bed shaking beneath them.

Renny met him thrust for thrust, throwing her weight backward to drive him deeper inside her. Her hands braced against the mattress, fingers curling into fists as he continued to ride her toward climax. He heard the hissing tear of fabric and saw her claws emerge, puncturing through the duvet to the sheets and probably the mattress beneath. The sight didn't bother him. It only made him hotter.

His head fell back and he struggled not to unleash his own claws, unwilling to break his mate's pale, smooth skin. His hips snapped in a primitive beat, keeping time with the fierce pounding of his heart.

Nothing this perfect could possibly last. He felt the climax rushing toward him with the speed and power of a locomotive, but he'd be damned if he'd go over without taking his mate with him.

He released his grip on her hips, shifting one hand to the mattress beside her head and draping himself across her back like a heavy, living blanket. The other hand he slid around to cup her sex, fingers finding the place where they joined and tracing a firm path up to her clit. He circled it and drew a sharp, keening wail from her lips.

That was all it took. Her pussy clenched around him, orgasm tightening every muscle in her body until she quivered like a bowstring. It made it hard for him to move, but Goddess, he needed to *move,* so he threw all his power into it and hammered into her until his own body seized up. He felt like he'd been struck by lightning, or maybe just stuck his dick in a wall outlet. But he wouldn't have been surprised to see the room light up around them as he poured himself helplessly and endlessly into his mate's welcoming body.

By the time he was spent, gravity had taken over, and he collapsed on top of Renny like so many pounds of dead meat. She grunted but offered no protest. Instead, she snuggled deeper into the mattress and slid her arms across the cool cotton surrounding their overheated bodies. When her hands found his, she twined their fingers together and brought one pair to her lips. He felt her press a kiss to his palm and slipped into sleep thinking no moment in his life had ever felt this good.

He couldn't wait until they managed to top it.

Chapter Fifteen

Had Renny really thought of what she shared with Mick as "good" sex? Because if she had, she needed to check her dictionary for the definition of good. She didn't think it stretched to the kind of sex that could render her deaf, dumb, and blind for the better part of a night. That kind of sex crossed over into the realms of spectacular, possibly even earthshaking.

Life-changing?

Oh hell, yeah, she decided, grinning into her pillow. She felt like a new woman, after all. A new, slightly sore, and thoroughly mated woman, with a man who possessed an unfortunate tendency not to hog the covers, but to kick them off the bed entirely during the middle of the night.

The chilly air had her shivering, and she fumbled around on the floor for the missing duvet. It had turned out her nails hadn't damaged it too badly, and only a few feathers had spilled out to stick in her hair.

It had been totally worth it.

She kept smiling even when she realized the blanket

hadn't landed on her side of the bed. If she wanted it, she'd have to get up and find it, or make Mick do it for her. Rolling over, she found the space beside her empty and blinked into the fading darkness. Judging by the sky outside the windows, it had to be the last hour or so before dawn.

"Mick?"

A squeak of a floorboard and the low murmur of his voice told her that her mate had gone into the living room to have some kind of conversation. Really? In the middle of the night? After they had wrecked each other like that?

Now *that* was stamina.

She climbed out of bed and shrugged into one of his shirts but didn't bother with the buttons. With luck, she wouldn't be wearing it long, but it was too chilly to walk around naked without her fur.

Her bare feet padded silently down the hall. She found her mate pacing across the living room with his cell phone pressed to his ear. He looked concerned, but not murderous, and his movements spoke more of restlessness than suppressed fury. No immediate danger, then. It still left her with questions. Who was he talking to in the middle of the night, and about what?

She stepped in closer, lifting her hand to cover a yawn.

". . . expected to hear from you before now. What the hell happened?"

Eavesdropping really wasn't her style, and damn it, it *was* chilly out here. The cold front the forecasters had mentioned must have moved back into the area. She entered the room, seeking her mate's warmth.

Mick scented her and turned. She watched as he

initially stiffened, then adopted a resigned expression and relaxed. He beckoned her forward. Renny settled into his side underneath his arm and snuggled close. The male gave off more heat than an old-fashioned radiator.

He pulled the phone away from his ear and pressed a button, then held it a few inches in front of them both. "Wait, what was that again?"

"I said that we expected to call before now." Zeke's voice came over the speaker clearly. He sounded tired. And cranky. "The fuckers played us. We had the decoys in place in the room you used last night, surveillance was active but covert, and everyone involved maintained strict radio silence, but they still made it as a setup."

"Are you sure? Maybe they just decided tonight wasn't the night to make a move."

"Oh, no, they moved." Zeke's tone filled with disgust. "One of the fuckers managed to sneak in close and mark the damned wall under 'your' bedroom window. The coyotes knew you weren't at the B and B, and they wanted us to know they knew. The sting flopped."

Renny pursed her lips and peered up at her mate. He didn't have the grace to look ashamed of himself, but he at least looked like he knew he should pretend to look ashamed. He failed.

Mick sighed. "All right, then. Back to the drawing board. If they know we tried to set them up, it would be stupid to try the same thing again. We'll have to come up with another way to lure them out of hiding."

"Yeah, but later."

"Yeah. I'll call you in the morning."

"Oh, no, you won't. I'll be asleep. You can call the department. They might actually answer."

The line clicked off, and the phone screen went dark. Renny raised an eyebrow. "Let me guess," she said dryly. "The menfolk came up with a plan to lure Geoffrey and his pals out without putting poor, vulnerable little me in danger. What did it involve? Dressing one of the deputies up like a woman and sending him and his partner to the B and B to pretend to be us for the night?"

"Don't be sexist. This is the twenty-first century. We have deputies who actually are women."

"Riiight. How'd that work out for you?"

Mick made a face. "You heard Zee. It didn't."

"Did Jaeger not mention that Geoffrey isn't stupid?" she asked. "He's been stalking me for months, Mick. He's not going to be fooled by any other stand-in with breasts. He would have known right away that wasn't me at the inn. Hello, coyote, remember? He'd be able to scent that it wasn't me."

"I gave them some of our clothes, and they used some hunter's tricks to mask their own scents. We're not idiots, no matter how badly our master plan flopped."

She patted his bare chest, trying not to let the feel of it distract her. "Sorry, baby. I didn't mean to underestimate your intelligence, but you just underestimated Geoffrey's, big-time. He's no genius, but the man is a coyote, and an alpha at that. He's clever, and he's sneaky. Since tricks and cheating constitute his normal set of tactics, he's going to expect them from others and be on guard for it. You're more likely to catch him by breaking down his door and dragging him out by the ears."

"By the balls, sweetheart." He stroked her hair and cuddled her close. "I'd drag him out by the balls. It would be the last use he ever got out of them."

Renny snorted. "Yeah, anyway, if someone had bothered to ask me, I could have saved a bunch of Alpha's finest a really late night. A decoy was never going to work."

"You blame us for trying?"

"Of course not."

He held her in silence for a moment, then blew out a breath and chuckled. "Go ahead. Lay it on me."

She tilted her head back to meet his gaze, blinking innocently. "Why, whatever do you mean, darling mate?"

He pulled away and took her hand, leading her back down the hall to the bedroom. "I mean, we may not have known each other long, but I didn't need much time to figure out that my independent, opinionated, and intelligent mate was going to have a few things to say about our planning this sting behind her back."

Renny discarded the shirt and smoothed the duvet back over the bed. She climbed onto the mattress and tucked the fabric neatly around her. "In that case, I'm sure you've also figured out exactly what I might have to say."

He slid into bed beside her. "Yeah, but you deserve the chance to say it."

She nodded. "Good. At least you've learned that much." She turned to face him. "Why the secrecy?"

"Would you believe because I didn't want you to worry?"

"I know you don't want me to worry. I also know that you're smart enough to realize you can't stop me.

Did you think I'd try to interfere somehow? That I'd insist on being part of the sting myself, instead of letting you send a deputy in my place?"

He eyed her warily. "Maybe."

"Mick, we just got done acknowledging that no one around here is an idiot, and that includes me. How many times do I have to tell you that I have no desire to put myself at risk? I'm not a hero. I'm not even particularly brave. And I'm certainly not trained in self-defense, police procedure, and criminal apprehension the way a deputy is."

"Are you trying to tell me you wouldn't have put the kibosh on our plan just because we replaced you with a decoy? I'm not sure I'm buying that. You were the one who suggested trying to lure Geoffrey out, and you initially suggested yourself as bait."

"True, but I dropped that idea once you guys vetoed it. I thought we'd moved on. If I'd known you still planned to pursue it, I could have told you exactly why it wouldn't work. It would have saved everyone a lot of time and effort. And you wouldn't have had to hide it from me."

"But you're not mad at me because I did hide it?"

She settled back against her pillow. "No. I thought about it. Mind you, I still think I have a *right* to be mad. Not at the operation itself, but at not being consulted on the change in plans. This does all affect my life, after all." She speared him with a glare, but only a half-hearted one. "But then I realized that even if I'd warned you, you might still have wanted to give it a try, and what could I have done if I did know ahead of time? You wouldn't have let me participate, and I'd only have been waiting around here for news the same way you were. What would that accomplish?"

He shook his head on a laugh. "I'm not sure, but I can tell you what you're accomplishing right now."

"That's not exactly a challenge." She glanced dismissively at his erection tenting the covers.

"I meant besides that." He tugged her closer and stroked her hair back from her face. "You're making me feel pretty damned guilty without hardly trying."

"I don't want you to feel guilty—"

Mick cut her off. "I know, but your reasonable, mature, and rational response is nonetheless pointing out to me that hiding things from you wasn't any of those things. It was . . . well, I guess it was stupid. And I'm sorry."

"Thank you. I don't want you to hide things from me, Mick, and I *really* don't want you to lie to me." She brushed a kiss across his lips. "Just tell me stuff, okay? Even the stuff I don't like is better off out in the open where we can deal with it together."

"Agreed. Now will you let me apologize to you?"

She frowned, confused. "I thought you just did."

He grinned and slid a hand down over her hips. "I want to be certain you know how much I mean it."

The look in his eyes lit the familiar spark in her belly and sent arousal sneaking through her. "Oh. Well, in that case . . ."

She leaned up into his kiss and prepared herself to be convinced.

"Isn't the library open on Saturdays?"

"It is, but the librarian only works one Saturday a

month, usually the first one. The rest of the time it's a Monday through Friday gig."

"Ah, I've heard about those." Molly sipped her coffee and reached for another of the cookies cooling on the kitchen table. She took a bite and moaned in pleasure. "Are you sure you want to give these to a bunch of ungrateful idiots like my brother and his colleagues? I'm telling you, double chocolate is wasted on them. You should give them to me."

Renny grinned and shook her head. "I've already set off the alarm once this week and had to call in to cancel it. By the time I found the number and the code word and dialed, the patrol car was halfway here. Believe me, before I get used to that stupid security system, I'll be baking the sheriff's department individual soufflés in their choice of flavors. The cookies are a stalling tactic at best."

"You know it's their job to monitor alarms for high-risk citizens, right? As in, it's part of what they get paid for."

"But they don't get paid for the fact that I am an idiot who can't remember to check the alarm before I open the window to let the steam out of the bathroom."

"Let me tell you how happy Deputy Draper was that he got the all-clear on that call before he actually got here," Zeke drawled from the kitchen doorway. "He would not have wanted to explain to your mate why he was breaking down the front door while you ran around the house wearing nothing but a towel."

Renny pulled a fresh rack of cookies from the oven and smiled in greeting. "Hey, Zee. Want a cookie?"

"Do dogs have fleas?"

She snatched the tray out of his reach and glowered at him.

He coughed and tried out a charming grin. "I mean, do bears shit in the woods?"

"I don't know. Maybe I should ask Jonas Browning. Over a nice big plate of cookies." She narrowed her eyes as she teased him.

"There you go trying to get me in trouble again." Mick appeared behind Zeke and strolled to his mate's side to steal a kiss. And a cookie. "You really want me to have to wrestle a grizzly bear because you were flirting with him over baked goods?"

"Who said I was planning to flirt with him?"

Mick shot her a deadpan expression. "You were feeding him cookies."

Her eyebrow shot up. "And the way to a man's heart is through his stomach?"

"No, it isn't," Molly chimed in. "It's hanging between his—"

"Mary Margaret Finula Buchanan!" Zeke roared, looking horrified.

"What?" She blinked wide, innocent eyes.

Renny laughed so hard she almost dropped the cookies. She had to set the baking sheet down on the stove top until she could stand up straight again. Mick just watched the show with a smile.

Zeke continued to gape at his sister, seemingly paralyzed into speechlessness. Taking mercy on him, Renny swallowed another laugh. "I think your brother would prefer not to think about your hypothetical familiarity with the male anatomy, Moll."

Molly blew a raspberry. "Hypothetical, my ass. I'll have you know—"

In a gesture of desperation, the big lion shifter stuck his forefingers in his ears and began to sing the theme song to the classic *Dukes of Hazzard* television show at the top of his lungs. He even managed to put a fairly decent twang into his voice.

"Have a heart, Molly, and stop torturing your brother so that he can stop torturing us."

Renny had never said he could hit any of the actual notes.

"Fine." Molly rolled her eyes but changed the subject. "In that case, why don't you inform us little ladies what you're both doing here? Is there news?"

Renny looked at the two men with renewed interest. She hadn't even stopped to wonder why they had wandered into the kitchen during Molly's visit. Zeke had become such a fixture around the house while they remained on guard against Geoffrey that she'd forgotten today wasn't his shift patrolling the area around their property. The infamous Deputy Draper was working today. And Mick was supposed to be working, though she suspected he was just trying to give his mate some alone time with her girlfriend, aka staying out of the estrogen atmosphere.

"Maybe." Zeke pulled out a chair and straddled it, reaching for a cookie. "I checked in with the office this morning. It looks like our teams have covered about half of the search area we laid out with no luck. No one has spotted where the coyotes are hiding out."

Renny grimaced and began transferring cookies from baking sheet to cooling rack. "That's not news. It's the same thing you've been telling us for days."

"No, before I was telling you we'd covered less than half of the search area."

"Har-har."

"Wow, tough crowd. Give a man a chance to elaborate, would you?" He brushed crumbs off his shirt and snagged his sister's coffee, stealing a slug. "The important part of today's update is that the sections we've cleared include all of the private and urban areas on our map."

Mick stiffened where he'd been leaning up against the counter. "They've got to be in the Forest, then."

Renny shot him a look like he'd lost his mind. "Um, hello? What else is there around here? This place is all forest. It's the Pacific Northwest."

"Not the forest, the Forest. Capital F. The Wenatchee National Forest," Mick explained. "And if they're in there, we have a lead."

"We do? Why? How big is the forest?"

"About four million acres." Zeke held a hand up when she would have laughed. "Obviously, we're not searching all that, but knowing they're in there gives us a bunch of new options."

"Have you called the NFS?"

Renny might have grown up in a more suburban part of California, but she'd lived in Sawmill long enough for "NFS" to enter her vernacular. The National Forest Service still had a visible presence in Trinity County, and apparently, they did here as well.

"Sheriff's doing that now. Even for shifters, roughing it gets old after a while. They could pull up permits for hunting cabins, alert us to any public structures, even have their rangers keep an eye out for us. They probably wouldn't join the formal search, but they're out there every day, right where we need to be looking."

Zeke grinned fiercely. "It's like you read my mind, brother. We should have a preliminary list of sites to check in the next few hours. We'll have to divide them up among the teams according to their assigned areas of the grid, but they'll be flagged as top priority. I want most of them checked out by the end of the day tomorrow. I'm getting damned tired of twiddling my thumbs and waiting for this asshole to make his next move."

Weren't they all? Renny felt a surge of excitement and renewed optimism. Maybe the end of her nightmare really was coming into view. Wouldn't that be a relief? No more endlessly looking over her shoulder, no more constantly being under guard and worrying about where she could go or what windows she could open. It would mean living like a normal person again. Did she even remember how that worked?

Mick reached out and gently pulled the spatula from her grip. "You okay, little red?"

She blushed, realizing she'd stood there frozen and staring into space for a good couple of minutes. What could she say? She been fantasizing about this whole nightmare ending for what felt like forever now. She could be forgiven a little daydream.

"Sorry. Just thinking."

Her mate smiled and wrapped his arms around her. "About this finally being over? It will be, red. Soon. I promise."

She shivered with happiness and felt her stomach growl. Suddenly, her cookies smelled damned good. If she wouldn't need them to bribe deputies for much longer, maybe she could help herself to a couple, along with a nice, tall glass of milk.

Yes, she felt like celebrating.

Chapter Sixteen

When the phone call finally came, it felt almost anti-climactic, and it didn't happen by Sunday night. Instead, almost a full week passed before the searchers struck gold.

"It's an illegal build," Zeke explained while Renny listened in on the call. It was Thursday night, and she and Mick were cleaning up after dinner.

"That's why we didn't find it when we got the initial list from the NFS. No permit." Mick cursed.

"Right. But one of the rangers thought he remembered seeing it during one of his last trips through that area. He made a note to check to see if it was still there this week, and he says it was. He also said he's certain someone's been using it, even though it was empty when he checked it out."

"What if it's just human hunters?" Renny wondered, almost afraid to get her hopes up again.

"We thought of that, and we sent one of our deputies to check it out before we brought it to you guys. He's a lynx, so he's pretty good at slipping in and out of places unnoticed, even by other shifters. He saw definite coyote sign and he scented all four of them. Hilliard and the three flunkies he hasn't killed yet."

Okay, hopes flew skyward. She reached automatically for Mick's hand. His fingers twined with hers.

"When do we move?" he demanded. "I can meet you at your office in ten minutes."

"Hold your horses, Liam Neeson. This isn't an action flick. We need to have a plan, and we need to hit at the right time. That means practicing a little patience."

"It's been almost a month, Zee. How much more patient do you want me to be?"

Renny felt a shock when she did the math and realized it really had been close to four weeks since she'd first arrived in Alpha. Four weeks since she'd abandoned her car on the side of the road, run panicked through the woods, and then collapsed, bloodied and exhausted, at the feet of the man who had become her mate. Part of her insisted it couldn't have been so long, that all that had happened just yesterday, but the other half felt so at home, so right and content here, that if seemed as if she'd lived here forever.

"You need to get through tonight, my friend. Meeting tomorrow at oh eight hundred. Sheriff's office this time. We'll hash out the strategy there and plan to move around dusk. We think that's when we'll most likely catch them either coming back to the cabin or getting ready to leave it. We're not going to take any chances that these fuckers could slip past us, so we'll be moving en masse and loaded for bear."

"You mean coyote."

"No, I mean bear. Who said there wasn't room for a little overkill?"

Mick's lips parted in a feral grin. "Buddy, I like the way you think."

"Good. Make sure you get plenty of rest tonight, because tomorrow could turn out to be a long day."

The call ended and Renny found her hands shaking in her lap. Mick scooped her out of her chair and transferred her into his lap. "Don't worry, little red. We've almost got him. By this time tomorrow, this could all be over."

She laughed and twisted her fingers together to still them. "I don't know why I'm shaking. I'm not scared, really. I mean, of course I'll worry that someone could get hurt tomorrow. Geoffrey and his bully boys won't give up without a fight. But that's not it. I just feel . . ." She searched for the right word and failed to find it. "I don't know. Anxious, I guess is closest, but even that's not really it." She made a face. "And now you're going to think I sound like a basket case. Are there mental health services available in Alpha? I've been meaning to ask."

Mick chuckled. "Are you kidding? This is where other shifters *send* their basket cases. We have two therapists, a licensed social worker, and a psychiatrist on full-time staff at the medical center."

"Good. If I can't figure this out or calm myself down, I might need one."

"It's adrenaline." He laid his big hand over hers to still the fidgeting. "That ants-in-your-pants feeling. We got the call that Hilliard's been found, and those glands on top of your kidneys wanted you to be ready *right now*. They don't care about strategies and advanced planning and choosing the perfect time to strike. They're more here-and-now kind of guys."

She laughed and tried to relax. "Is that what it is? Does that mean I'm going to feel like this until tomorrow? Zeke told us to try to get some rest."

"I think I could come up with a way to tire us out," he said, stroking a finger along the back of her hand. "If I really put my mind to it."

"Sex isn't the answer to everything, you know," she said, feigning exasperation.

"Oh, yeah? Prove it."

Renny couldn't. She was laughing too hard, hanging upside down over her mate's shoulder as he strode quickly for the bedroom. And after that, she forgot what side of the argument she'd started on.

She knew perfectly well where she ended.

Renny looked around her and sighed. "If we were in Jaeger's office right now, I'd be having the worst sense of déjà vu."

Mick guided her to a chair at the front of the small conference room and urged her to sit. "Don't worry, babe. This should be the last one of these meetings we have to sit through."

Goddess willing, he added silently.

"I just don't know why I have to be *here*. I mean, it's not like you're going to let me get within ten city blocks of the actual raid, so I don't know why I need to sit through the planning. You know I'll make you update me once you figure out what we're doing, but now that I'm gainfully employed again, I'd rather be at work, where I can keep myself busy and think about other things."

And where Mick would have a heart attack every five minutes worrying that something could happen to her. "I told you, today I'm keeping you where I can see you. After tonight, you can even work overtime if you want to." He paused and frowned. "Did Marjory give you grief about taking today off?"

Renny rolled her eyes. "Of course not. As far as Marjory is concerned, I could stage a burlesque show on the circulation desk during the children's story hour, and she wouldn't give me grief. The woman wasn't kidding when she said she's ready to retire. She told me to take all the time I needed, but made me promise that I wasn't planning to quit. In fact, I think she made me sign a contract when I filled out my personnel file. I remember her asking me to prick my finger. . . ."

He shook his head at his mate's antics. He'd already noticed that she tended to ramble on when she was nervous about something. Her stories became longer and more convoluted with every wave of anxiety. "Good. She's your boss, so listen to her. Take today as a favor to me. I need to know you're safe until we have Hilliard and all his puppets in custody."

Or until they're dead, he thought, but he didn't share that with his mate. He wanted to keep her mind off the possibility of violence.

"Good morning, everyone." Sheriff Ewan Lahern strode up the aisle between the rows of chairs, a cup of coffee in one hand and a thick stack of papers in the other. He set everything down on a table next to a lectern and looked out at the assembly. Two dozen men and women filled the seats or leaned up against the walls, all of them either deputies, junior officers, or carefully chosen volunteers from the community. Anyone with law enforcement or military experience had been recruited over the past few weeks to help find and bring in Geoffrey Hilliard. Really, the coyote should be proud of all the trouble he'd caused.

Lahern was a big, barrel-chested man with dark gray hair, piercing eyes, and an impressive brush of a mustache. He was in his late sixties, by Mick's estimate, but he still moved and acted like a much younger man. One of the benefits of being a shifter. The black bear had been elected sheriff in the nineties, after twenty years of work in law enforcement, and had filled the position ever since. He was steady, competent, and a mean son of a bitch in a fight. Mick liked him.

"Glad you all could join us," Lahern continued, "because we've got a situation on our hands that's going to take strategy, teamwork, and manpower to bring to its proper conclusion. I take it you've all been informed of the events surrounding Renny Landry's arrival in Alpha, and the trouble that's being caused by the pack of coyotes who followed her here. Am I right?"

Nods and murmurs of assent filled the room. Beside Mick, Renny turned pink and slumped down in her chair as if she wanted to hide. He squeezed her hand. No matter how often he told her that she wasn't responsible for the actions of the bastards who'd chosen to torment and threaten her, he knew she still struggled with a sense of guilt. His mate hated that she had caused trouble for the people around her, even the ones who had volunteered to take it.

"All right, then." Lahern turned to Zeke and gestured for the lion to join him in the front of the room. "Deputy Buchanan here has been in charge of coordinating this investigation, and he's going to be the point man on the ground during the operation. I'm going to let him bring us all up to speed."

Zeke stepped in front of a familiar map, a near twin of the one in Jaeger's office. Only the last time Mick had seen the map in the mayor's office, it had lacked two important features: the big red pin stuck straight into an empty patch of green that represented the Wenatchee National Forest and a detailed enlargement of the area represented by the pin.

He felt a surge of excitement. Almost time.

"We finally tracked our subjects to this spot here." Zeke indicated the pin. "East of Cle Elum Lake and south of Mount Stuart."

Linus Russu frowned. "That must be fifteen miles from here. It's on the other side of the Teanaway. You really think they're based out that far?"

"We're sure of it. We focused our initial searches closer in and came up with nothing. This is probably why. Remember, regular coyotes can travel ten miles a day just in the course of patrolling their territory. Fifteen miles for a shifter is nothing given the proper motivation."

"And we all know these assholes are motivated." Deputy Draper spoke from the center of the room and blushed rhubarb red when Renny turned to look at him. "Pardon my language, ma'am."

She leaned close to whisper to Mick, "Am I really a ma'am now? I thought I was too young for that. Is it because I'm mated now? Or because I'm a librarian?"

Personally, Mick guessed it was because Chris Draper's mother wielded a mean wooden spoon, but he didn't mention that.

"Niemenen did most of our scouting on the location, so I'm going to ask him to describe it firsthand."

A deputy with short, ash-blond hair and ruthlessly high cheekbones came forward to address the room. "The target location is a semiconcealed structure of rough timber with a shake roof and limited access points. I counted two windows and one door. That's it. It's built at the base of an escarpment about half a mile from a small creek that flows roughly east–west right here." He pointed to a line on the enlarged map area. "The coyotes chose it fairly well. The escarpment provides protection from the rear, and the door and window allow a full view of the other three sides. The area around it has been cleared to about thirty feet, and judging by the young growth at that boundary, I think it used to extend more like fifty or sixty, which limits the options for good cover. We're going to have to plan carefully and be absolutely certain of our timing if we want to keep the potential for casualties to a minimum."

Mick examined the detail map. Whoever had drawn it had been thorough. The prominent natural features had been clearly marked, including the stream and the short cliff that rose behind the cabin. It sat in the center of the sketch facing southwest. Even the larger trees and denser thickets had been marked in the surrounding area.

He considered the options, letting his wolf surge forward to help. Of course, he had to remind the animal that this time, they were going to use their heads as much as their teeth to solve the problem. This wasn't going to be like eight years ago, when he had burst in to avenge his mate with claws bared and fangs flashing. He'd been stupid back then, and although he hadn't cared at the time, he was lucky he had survived. This time, he wouldn't be taking those kinds of chances. He had too much to live for now.

Renny only half listened to the discussion around her. Like she'd told Mick, she wasn't certain why she needed to be here. She understood his need to keep her safe and even got that his tension right now would be particularly high because they all had their ultimate goal firmly in sight. But her mate didn't seem to understand that sitting in this room listening to recon reports and watching people she now knew and cared about assessing angles of attack and discussing the minimization of casualties kind of made her want to vomit.

She squeezed his leg and leaned in to whisper, "I need to use the restroom. I'll be back in a minute."

Mick grabbed her hand and held on. "Wait five minutes. I'll call a recess and take you."

It took some effort, but Renny resisted the urge to scoff. "Really?" she hissed. "We are inside the Alpha Public Safety Building, sitting in the middle of the sheriff's office, in a facility full of armed officers of the law. You really think I'm going to get kidnapped walking from this room to the second door down the hall, which is still inside the secured area of the department? *Really?*"

He frowned and she saw him fighting with his instinct to shove her into a bulletproof bubble so he could just sit on her and keep her where he put her. To be fair, he'd done his best not to smother her while still keeping her safe over the past few weeks, but she couldn't stay in this room another minute.

"This is important," she whispered, softening her tone. "You need to be here to plan this, because I know you aren't going to be sitting at home with me while the rest of these guys go find Geoffrey. I want you informed, because it's the best way to keep you from getting hurt. I'll only be a minute."

She saw him wavering and pressed her advantage. "The restrooms are visible from the bullpen down the hall. The officers there will be able to see me walk to and from the door. I'm pretty sure they'd stop an attacker before he got within ten feet of me. Please." She held up her cell phone. "I'll keep my finger on speed dial."

He growled under his breath, but he released her hand. "Five minutes. I'm timing you."

She kissed him quickly. "Thanks."

It surprised her not to see smoke rising from her heels as she made her escape. Maybe she'd watched too many *Looney Tunes* as a kid.

The minute she cleared the doorway, she dragged in a deep breath. Her stomach would need a few minutes to unknot, but at least now it had the opportunity. In there, watching all those people ready to risk their safety for her, listening to them planning a military-style tactical assault on what she knew to be a group of vicious, unfeeling monsters, she'd felt herself turning into one giant Gordian knot of anxiety.

She needed to hear a voice of reason.

She hurried down the hall and slipped into the

ladies' room, then made use of that speed-dial function. Her call was answered with a sleepy yawn.

"H'lo?"

Renny winced. "I'm sorry. Did I wake you? Were you on duty last night?"

"Nah, I had second shift. I got off at midnight. I'd have been up soon anyway." Molly yawned again. "What's up? I thought you'd be at the big powwow about now."

"I was. I mean, I am. I just had to get out of that room for a minute."

"Tell me about it. The testosterone cloud in there is toxic, especially when they're in serious prep mode."

"No, it wasn't that." Renny leaned against a sink. "I think I might have been having a little panic attack."

"About what, sweetie?"

"About this whole Operation Coyote thing. I want Geoffrey handled worse than anyone, but not if it means someone is going to get hurt. I don't want that on my conscience."

"It won't be." The lioness's voice firmed, the sleep draining from it. "They're grown men and women, Renny, and apprehending rogues and criminals is what they're trained to do. They'll be fine. And if anyone does get injured, I'll be there to patch them up. We'll be on call for the whole thing."

"Great, so I can worry about you, too."

"Stop it, Renny Louise."

Damn it. She never should have told Molly her middle name.

"None of what has happened to bring things to this point is on you," Molly said, her tone hard and certain. "None of what happens tonight will be on you. At

every step of the way, Geoffrey Hilliard and the ball-
sacs who work for him have made a choice to persist
in coming after you. At any point in the last however
many months, each and every one of them has had op-
portunities to stop and walk away. Many opportuni-
ties. The fact that they've persisted is on them, not
on you."

Renny had been trying to tell herself that without
much success. "I know, but—"

"But, butt, behind. Listen to me. Not. On. You.
Tonight, when the sheriff's department and half the
macho alphas in town descend on the coyotes' hiding spot, they will *still* have the opportunity to make
a choice. If they *choose* to give themselves up, no one
will get hurt. If they *choose* to fight back . . . well,
that's on them, isn't it?"

Molly was right. Renny took a deep breath and focused on that knowledge. "Yeah, I guess it is. Thanks,
Moll."

"You're welcome. And let me give you another piece
of advice while I'm at it. Guilt about people risking
their lives for you is not what's got your panties in a
knot, my friend. The truth is, you're scared for your
mate, and you don't have any reason to be."

"Um, hello? Life risking? He is going to be on that
raid tonight. You know it, and I know it."

"Of course he is. But he's going to have a dozen or
more trained law enforcement and ex-military types at
his back, and they're going to outnumber those coyotes at least four to one. Trust me, my brother does not
believe in being outgunned."

Molly was right, and Renny knew it. In the end, the
only thing that really scared her was the possibility of

losing her mate. Dear Goddess, but she wondered how Mick had gotten through it.

"Yeah. Thanks, Molly," she repeated.

"Ain't no thing, chicken wing. Now get back to your mate before he goes all Hulk Smash because you've been away from his side for ten seconds too long. Oh, and if the vultures have left any doughnuts in the conference room, be sure to grab me one. I'll see you later."

Renny ended the call and slipped her phone into her pocket. Her anxiety hadn't disappeared, but she at least felt like she could breathe again, and the urge to vomit had faded. She took a second to use the restroom for its intended purpose, washed her hands, and splashed a little water on her face. One more deep breath, and she was ready to return to the fray.

She stepped out into the hall and spotted her mate opening the conference room door. Shit. She must have taken more than five minutes. She hurried forward.

"Sorry. I'm sorry I took so long. Is everything okay?"

Mick gave her a quick once-over and nodded, a little of his tension easing. "It's fine. We decided on a break so Zee can get everyone copies of the map to make notes on."

A break. There went her fantasies about the ordeal of planning being over. She had to force a smile. "Oh, okay. I was hoping maybe this wouldn't take too much longer."

"Another hour, maybe. The sheriff already has in mind how he wants to run things. The rest is just tweaking the details and making sure everyone's on the same page. We're going to want to give them all a chance to get home and rest up for a few hours. They need to be fresh for the zero hour."

Well, she could probably survive another hour. She hoped. "When is the 'zero hour'?"

"Sun sets at six. We'll meet up at our rendezvous point at five thirty." He brushed a finger over her cheek. "With luck, we'll be home in bed by eight."

"You won't want to celebrate your victory?" she teased, praying to the Moon that a celebration would be called for.

Mick grinned. "Like I said, we'll be in bed by eight."

"Hm, so I only have two or three hours of lonely terror to get through while I wait for you at home, then?"

"Oh, you are *not* going to be alone," he proclaimed. "I don't care how good our intelligence is or what our scouts tell us when we get the signal to go. I am not taking any chances that one of those fuckers could slip past us and get to you while I'm off launching this attack. There will be an armed deputy with you at all times. At least one. Half a dozen, if Lahern can spare them."

She sighed and patted his chest. "Yes, dear."

Just one more night, she told herself. She just had to make it through tonight, and this long, depressing nightmare would finally be over. She could survive one more night.

Just as long as her mate did.

Chapter Seventeen

Mick crouched down behind a fallen log with a handful of other shifters. Less than a hundred yards away, the small, rough cabin crouched in the fading light, a thin tendril of smoke rising from the chimney tube and quickly disappearing in the quickening wind.

The weather wasn't offering them what you'd call ideal conditions for the evening's operation. The cold front that had hit a few nights ago had finally passed, but in its place a storm seemed to be blowing in from the south. The sheriff had warned them that with the predictions of heavy winds beginning within a couple of hours after sunset, they wanted to keep this shindig on schedule. No one wanted to be stuck out in the woods when trees started shaking and branches started falling. Get in, get the targets, and get home—those were their instructions.

Other clusters of deputies and volunteers had taken up positions in the surrounding brush and even up on the top of the ridge behind the cabin. The sheriff was taking no chances that any coyotes would be able to make a run for it, sheer rock face or no sheer rock face.

Zeke shifted minutely beside him. He knew that his friend, still in human form and clad in black tactical gear, had one of the small in-ear radio communicators that allowed him to coordinate movements with the other team leaders in the operation. It was how they knew that four figures had been confirmed inside the structure and how they would coordinate the timing on their assault.

Mick wished they'd start it already. He could practically taste the blood of one particularly doomed coyote.

Geoffrey Hilliard would fall under his fangs, and woe betide anyone who tried to interfere with his kill. The rest of the men had been warned.

He had to work hard to control his wolf, a particular challenge given that he currently wore his fur. When in his animal shape, instinct always had more power and reason tended to fall by the wayside. Not that he became some sort of mindless beast or anything. He retained his identity and even his personality as a wolf, but the world always looked a little more black and white through wolf's eyes. Predator or prey, friend or enemy, kill or be killed.

The growing charge in the atmosphere wasn't helping. The approaching storm was messing with the barometric pressure and electrostatic energy in the area, making his sharp canine senses go on high alert. He thought his ears even caught a rolling rumble in the distance. Given the rarity of thunderstorms in the area, he figured this meant tonight could get wild in more ways than one.

He shoved back an impatient whine and kept his gaze focused on the cabin. He could smell the coyotes even at this distance, even over the thickening ozone. Hell, they might as well have put up a neon sign and mailed out invitations for all the good their hiding spot did now. He scented the motor-oil aroma of Ayala, as well as the sweetly rotten and decaying fungus fragrances of the Molina boys. And there was no way in hell he would ever mistake the thick, sulfurous odor of Geoffrey Hilliard, especially not after he'd had to spend so much money purging the noxious stuff from his home.

All four scents were fresh and strong, offering proof positive that the coyotes were indeed holed up inside the ramshackle cabin. They carried easily on the stiff breeze, making him hope the troops on the upwind side of the cabin had taken the scent-dampening precautions the sheriff recommended seriously. No one wanted to give away the element of surprise. Now that the presence of the targets had been confirmed, they just had to go in and drag the fuckers out.

He felt Zeke shift again, felt the sudden rise in tension overtake his friend, and knew this was it. The time had come.

Now.

Zeke gave the order, sweeping his hand forward and releasing the members of his team like the surge of a tide. Mick bounded from cover, soaring over the log and eating up the distance to the target with long, galloping strides. The wind seemed to surge with him, carrying him forward and whipping through his fur with primal energy.

The attack began in eerie silence. No one howled

or roared or wasted breath on warning the enemy they were coming. They simply moved forward, fast and quiet and deadly.

Mick didn't waste time looking around, but he could still sense the rest of their force converging on the cabin. He caught glimpses of bears and wolves and big cats of all kinds joining the attack while the team leaders in their human forms made use of weapons other than tooth and nail. Two of them moved into position and hurled flashbang grenades through the windows, shattering glass and formally announcing their presence.

Immediately, the cabin door swung open and a disheveled and disoriented shifter appeared, hands raised in a sign of surrender. Mick skidded to a halt at the base of the steps and wondered what the fuck was going on. A second man followed on his heels, this one looking less confused and more smug.

"Welcome to our humble abode," the second one said, his scent and appearance identifying him as Tommy Molina. He had to shout to be heard over the commotion of the attack and the steadily increasing wind. "We've been expecting you, wolf. You and your friends."

Mick shifted back to human, stretching to his full height and stalking slowly toward the coyotes. "Send out Hilliard," he snarled, lips curling to bare gleaming fangs. "He's who I came for. Tell him to face me like a man."

His wolf whined, urging him to shift again or, better yet, to assume his wereform. After all, this was a battle, and he intended to win it.

"We'd love to, but I'm afraid Geoffrey's not at home right now." Tommy grinned. "May I take a message?"

Mick cursed and leapt up the steps, shoving the coyotes aside and forcing his way inside the cabin. His gaze swept around the single room and landed on the sofa in the small living area. On it, two life-size mannequins had been dressed in the clothes of Geoffrey Hilliard and Will Molina and propped up in conversational style.

His heart dropped to his stomach and he spun back toward the door.

Renny.

Fuck. The coyote bastard had taken a page out of their book and set up his own decoy operation. While the Alpha Sheriff's Department had deployed its forces on the supposed coyote hideout, Geoffrey Hilliard was nowhere to be found.

Double fuck.

His mate was in danger.

Renny gave up trying to relax about three seconds after Mick walked out the door that evening. Yeah, playing it casual just wasn't going to happen. Until her mate came back safe and sound, she was just going to have to live with an unbearable sense of trepidation. Woohoo.

She tried pacing, reading, watching television, yoga, and deep breathing exercises, but nothing managed to keep her mind off of her worry for more than a minute at a time. It was enough to drive a wolf crazy.

The worsening weather wasn't helping things, either. Her tension rose as the barometer dropped. The restlessness many shifters felt during a coming storm only increased her tension, giving her yet another variable to worry about. Would the storm just bring wind, the way the forecasters had predicted? Or would her mate and the others find themselves trapped out in heavy rains, or even one of the area's rare thunderstorms? Geoffrey and his minions were dangerous enough; she didn't need to add the possibility of lightning strikes to her list of irrational fears.

"Ma'am, I've told you not to worry." Renny turned to scowl at the junior deputy who had pulled babysitting duty during the most exciting operation his department had launched in years. He was trying to be a good sport about it, but it didn't take a mind reader to see he really, really wished he were in on the action instead. "Everything is going to go like clockwork. I've never seen a team more prepared."

Obviously, the kid had never heard about Landry's Law. He didn't seem to have checked the weather forecast, either. "Deputy, what did I tell you earlier about calling me ma'am?"

"Sorry, m—er, I mean, miss." Deputy Draper turned pink once more. She was starting to think it had something to do with her.

"Forget it." Renny waved a hand and resumed pacing. This was her third bout of it, and Mick hadn't been gone even an hour. The operation wasn't due to start for another twenty minutes. She'd be ready for a padded room by then. "I'm a little cranky this evening."

"I understand, but you really shouldn't be. Sheriff Lahern has this planned out to the last detail. Nothing bad is going to happen to your mate. Mr. Fischer will be just fine."

Good Goddess, but this cub was making her feel old with all the "ma'ams" and "misses" and "misters." What was he, five years younger than her? He couldn't be much beyond that. What age did you have to be to go to police academy, anyway?

She decided to ignore him.

It had been Mick's idea to station him inside with her in the first place. She had insisted that she was fine with having him stay outside and patrol around the house and yard the way the guards had been doing before now, but her mate had disagreed. Strongly. If he'd had his way, there would have been more guards doing the outdoor patrol thing as well, but Sheriff Lahern had preferred to use his manpower resources to take on Geoffrey and his pals with an overwhelming show of force. One deputy with solid training, a reliable sidearm, and a good eye would have no trouble protecting a single she-wolf. After hearing that scouts had confirmed all four coyotes had been sighted in the cabin and would remain under constant surveillance until go time, Mick had reluctantly agreed.

She supposed, given the turn the weather was taking, it was rude to wish she'd won that argument. She might feel a lot less itchy if she didn't have someone staring at her while she did her nervous twitching.

When all this was over, she and Mick were really going to have to work on this overprotective streak of his. She'd like to be able to get some time to herself in the future, maybe even shower alone from time to time.

Well, okay. She'd like that once in a while, anyway.

Deputy Draper cleared his throat until she looked in his direction. "Uh, is there anything I can do to help make this evening less stressful for you, Ms. Landry? I'd be happy to try and distract you. You play poker?"

Oh, she'd like to play poker, all right, but her version of the game didn't involve playing cards. It had more to do with her taking the iron implement usually reserved for stirring the fire logs and bashing it over his annoying head.

Whoa, Nelly, her inner voice chided. *And Renny. Get a grip, girlfriend. The kid hasn't done anything wrong. He doesn't deserve blunt-force head trauma. He's just trying to do his job.*

But his job should be joining the group of men and women protecting her mate, Renny thought. If everyone was so damned sure that Geoff and the boys were in that damned cabin, why did anyone need to stay behind with her?

Renny struggled to muster up a smile. "No, thanks, Deputy. I'm fine."

He looked skeptical. "Are you sure?"

Her fangs threatened to erupt. She fought them back. "Positive."

And back to pacing.

Things went on like that for another fifteen minutes, while the wind began to howl around the edges of the house. Finally, Renny just stopped in front of the fireplace and watched the second hand of the mantel clock tick slowly toward six P.M. For an instant, she thought she saw the damned thing move backward.

Draper rose from his armchair and joined her in front of the hearth. "They'll be moving in right about now. Just a few more minutes, and I'm sure the phone will ring to let us know everything went off without a hitch. Trust me."

Trust had nothing to do with it, or rather not the way he meant. The problem with this whole scenario was that Geoffrey was the one she didn't trust.

A particularly wicked gust of wind rattled the windows, making Renny jump. She turned instinctively in that direction, only to gasp as the sound of cracking wood ripped through the air.

"What was that?"

Draper looked toward the front of the house and frowned. "Sounded like a branch coming down to me. Right out next to the driveway, from the ruckus." He pointed toward the sofa. "Sit there. I'm just going to take a look out the window. We need to make sure nothing is blocking our road access in case of emergency."

Right. Like Renny had plans to go anywhere until her mate got home. She huffed to herself. You couldn't get her to step foot out the door with a bulldozer, not until Mick returned safe and sound.

She watched through the doorway as Draper stepped into the front hall and approached the glass. He twitched back the curtains to peer out into the twilight dimness, then appeared to jerk. She heard a sharp tinkling sound and saw a crack in the windowpane even as he folded into a boneless heap on the floor. The front of his shirt looked suddenly darker.

It took a second to process the information. When the metallic scent of blood hit her, she knew. Draper had been shot. Someone had fired through the front window.

Another echoing crack sounded, this one much louder and more forceful than the presumed falling branch. Renny jumped to her feet as she heard the thump of the front door banging into the wall. Someone had just broken it down.

She had enough time to blink before the alarm sounded, but not enough time to run. Her feet remained stubbornly planted on the floor as a menacing figure filled the doorway.

Geoffrey Hilliard smiled at her. "Hello, Renny, my sweet."

Chapter Eighteen

Renny tried to run, but it was already too late. Geoffrey sprang forward, pouncing on her before she made it around the coffee table. He knocked her to the floor, slamming her cheek on the corner of the wooden board on the way down. She felt the sting of the impact and a trickle of blood on her skin. Damn, that was going to leave a mark.

Her head spun with temporary dizziness, then ached violently when he grabbed her by the hair and hauled her to her knees.

"You should never have run from me, Renny," he snarled in her ear. "I could have been so much nicer to you."

"Fuck off and die," she hissed, clawing at his hand, trying to loosen his grip. He responded by backhanding her across the formerly uninjured side of her face.

"How about I just fuck you, and you just die afterward?"

Heavy booted feet stomped into the foyer. "Time to go, boss." Renny recognized Will's distinctive voice immediately. It always managed to carry an edge of mania, in spite of the deep timbre. "Cops were out the door the minute that alarm sounded. We gotta move before they manage to cut us off."

She glanced up and saw the crazy coyote framed in the doorway, his clothing woodland camouflage and his favorite rifle clutched in one hand. Of course. If anyone could have shot Draper from a distance through a reflective surface, it was Will Molina. The shifter was even deadlier with a gun than he was with fangs and claws.

"Fine," Geoffrey snapped, "but you're driving. I've been waiting too long to put this little reunion off another minute."

Renny fought like a wildcat, or rather like a cornered she-wolf. She dug her heels into the floor and abandoned her clawing attacks at Geoffrey's grip on her hair in favor of simply attacking him. She twisted and slammed a fist into his side, low and sneaky over his kidney. He howled and responded by throwing her to the floor. Immediately his weight came down on top of her, pinning her in place.

"Give me that rope," he barked. "I don't have time for this shit."

She heard Will grunt, then the sound of something exchanging hands. She bucked fiercely, trying to throw Geoffrey off of her, but he dug his knee into her spine until she shrieked at the pain.

Curses spat from her lips, but two against one weren't even odds, and the pair of coyotes overpowered her. Two sets of hands grabbed her wrists and ankles, yanking them together into a brutal improvised hog-tie.

She screamed her frustration and cursed herself for not shifting faster. She might have managed it while Geoffrey had her pinned, but if she tried now with arms and ankles tied behind her back, she'd end up dislocating both hips and shoulders in the attempt. That wouldn't exactly leave her in fighting shape. She felt certain it was why her captors had chosen this particular tie.

Renny might have been restrained, but she wasn't gagged, and she screamed at the top of her lungs while she was hauled off the floor and carted outside to a waiting van. The coyotes tossed her in the back, Geoffrey climbing in beside her while Will slipped behind the wheel and stowed his rifle against the passenger seat.

"Hold on," he warned his employer. "I want to get as much distance as I can between us and these crazy shifters before they pick up our trail. Plus, I want to get to the highway ASAP. The roads out here suck."

"Whatever. Just drive," Geoffrey snarled, and reached for her shirt.

Zeke managed to catch up with Mick just before he reached the rendezvous point where the teams had left their vehicles. The lion had to dig claws into his shoulder to stop him, because he wasn't wearing any clothes to grab on to. He hadn't wasted the time or energy for another shift before he took off after his mate. He'd run through the damned woods naked, and he'd do the same down the streets of Seattle if it would help him save his mate.

The pain didn't stop Mick, so Zeke exerted enough

force to spin him around. "Wait a fucking minute!" the lion snarled. "You can't—"

"Back the fuck off, cat! My mate is in danger. That coyote's already got her. I can sense it."

"Not arguing." Zeke wrenched open the door of a burly SUV emblazoned with the sheriff's seal. "Just let me drive. I don't trust you behind the wheel right now. Besides, there were two coyotes missing from the cabin. You might need backup."

"Exactly." Linus Russu climbed into the vehicle behind Mick and slapped the back of his seat. "So, let's get moving already. We've got fifteen miles to cover and a woman to rescue."

Zeke slammed down the gas pedal and took off in a shower of gravel. The rear end skidded a little during the sharp turn onto the logging road that would take them back to the highway, but the tires quickly found their grip.

The police scanner chirped and a voice came over the loudspeaker.

"All available units, please respond. Code three alert. OOS not responding. Alarm triggered at high-priority location on Dry Creek Road. Possible 41–40. Proceed immediately."

Mick had the only house on Dry Creek Road, and there was only one reason he could think of for the alarm to go off while the officer on scene was not responding. He braced his hands on the dashboard, feeling his claws gouging holes into the vinyl.

Zeke cursed and flipped on the lights and sirens. He sent the truck flying across the rough terrain, barely bothering to slow down when they hit the pavement. In fact, he sped up.

"Don't worry," he said, mouth grim and eyes focused on the road. "We'll find her."

Mick didn't bother to reply. He couldn't. His mouth was too misshapen and he realized he had unconsciously shifted into his wereform in the front seat of the SUV. Apparently, his wolf thought he needed to be ready for war.

Linus leaned forward. "We won't find her at that house. The coyote would be an idiot not to grab her and run like the devil's on his heels."

"Great deduction, Sherlock. You want to tell me which pedal makes this thing go faster now?"

The tiger ignored the sarcasm. "You said he's from California, right? He headed for his den as soon as he got her. He'll want to get back to his own territory where he feels safe and in control."

"No shit. Do you see me heading west? Sunset was behind us. I'll be able to pick up 97 in another four miles."

"No, head straight south. Cut over to 903 as soon as you can. We want to pick up 90 before they get too far ahead of us."

Zeke jerked and shot the tiger a dubious glance. "Ninety-seven would take them more directly south. That's the road they're going to be taking."

"Yeah, and 90 is a hell of a lot bigger and faster. You take 97, you'll be chasing their heels for hours. Take 90 and really make this bucket move, and we might get across 970 in time to cut them off."

The deputy hesitated only an instant. "I hope to hell you're right, Shere Khan, because our buddy over here is going to kill something real soon, and I'd rather not be the only thing available when he does."

Tires squealed as he changed direction and tested what an official emergency vehicle could be capable of.

Renny fought and squirmed for everything she was worth, but it was hard to fight off an incipient rape with both hands *and* feet tied behind your back. Of course, it would also be damned hard for Geoffrey to consummate the act without untying at least her legs, and when he did, she would not be holding back.

The van lurched over a particularly rough patch of ground, temporarily interrupting her attacker. Geoffrey slammed his shoulder against the side of the vehicle and swore.

"Watch the fucking road, asshole," he growled. "What the hell is going on? Shouldn't we be on the highway by now?"

"We are, but the things these yokels around here call roads are nothing more than fucking goat tracks," Will snapped. "This is a major fucking interstate artery, and the goddamned thing's barely two lanes wide. Shit, if this is what they call a highway, you can forget all about a smooth ride. You want one of those, you'll have to get it from the bitch."

He sneered over his shoulder, his gaze raking across Renny's half-naked form. Geoffrey had already managed to tear off her shirt and slice through her bra with a wickedly sharp pocketknife. Scraps of fabric dangled from her elbows, because once he had her breasts exposed, he seemed uninterested in finishing the job.

The alpha coyote chuckled evilly. "I don't care if it's smooth or rough, but she might." He leered down at her, pressing the tip of the blade against her bare chest. "Or maybe you like it rough, sweetheart. What do you say? You get hot when your 'mate' slaps you around a little?"

She spit in his face. "Unlike you, Mick doesn't have to kidnap and rape a girl to get her to touch him. I wanted him from the first time I set eyes on him. You? You made me throw up in my mouth a little."

Renny half expected him to backhand her again, but instead he drove a solid fist to her belly, knocking the wind right out of her. She choked and gasped for air.

"You might want to watch your mouth, bitch, before I find a way to silence it," he bit out, looming over her. "No one said I have to fuck your cunt first."

She actually whimpered and immediately hated herself for it. She was not some stupid fucking damsel in distress who would swoon and beg for mercy while her virtue was brutally stolen from her. This was not a 1970s bodice-ripper romance. This was her *life,* and she would damned well survive anything this mother-fucker could dish out.

Pride and determination had her baring her teeth and letting her fangs descend. "Go ahead," she hissed. "Try shoving your dick in my mouth, you asshole. I double-dog dare you."

He woofed and attacked the fastening on her jeans.

"Oh, shit!"

The shout was the only warning they got before the van made a sharp, unplanned ninety-degree turn.

"What the fuck!" Geoffrey shouted.

The good news was that he shouted it from the other side of the van. The sudden motion had thrown him off of her before he got her jeans much past her hips and hurled him against the back of the driver's seat.

The knife skittered out of his hand and across the floor. Renny immediately threw herself toward it.

It didn't have quite the effect she would have gotten had she been able to actually use her arms and legs to launch herself. Instead, it wound up less like a surge of motion and more like a desperate, semi-humiliating wiggle. She probably looked more like a beached whale than a graceful, lethal wolf, but she could care less. She needed that knife.

"Incoming!"

Will shrieked the warning too late.

The rear doors of the van practically exploded outward, wrenched open by the most terrifyingly gorgeous thing Renny had ever laid eyes on. Her mate loomed in the opening, seven solid feet of hard-packed muscle. She had never seen a lupine in wereform up close, had never tried to assume the shape herself, and it took her breath away.

Thick, dark fur covered his body from head to toes, longer on his head, neck, and shoulders, almost like a wolf's ruff, plush and short on his chest and belly. His features appeared not remotely human, his face elongated into a wolfish snout with a full set of predator's gleaming fangs. Only his eyes remained vaguely human, still blue and piercing and filled with so much rage and violence, she almost backed away from him herself.

"Motherfucker!"

Out of the corner of her eye, Renny saw Will in the front seat diving for his rifle, but he never touched it. Instead of moving forward, his body flew backward out the driver's door and his scream was cut off by the bloodcurdling roar of an adult tiger.

Mick leaned his monstrous upper body into the cargo area and growled a low warning, gaze fixed and staring at Geoffrey. At his prey. He didn't climb in, though, and she had to guess it was because in his current form, the van was too small a space to allow him to move around freely. He'd want the coyote to come outside where he could kill it properly.

Renny could see the fear in the coyote's eyes, but Geoffrey quickly masked it with a sneer. "Well, Michael, long time no see," he taunted. "I have to say you're really not looking your best. I have to wonder what my dear sister would have said if she could see the way you've . . . let yourself go."

Okay, Renny rapidly revised her opinion of her stalker's native intelligence. Only a fucking moron would taunt an animal as close to losing control as her mate appeared to be. It was like voicing a death wish.

She eased herself a little farther to the side of the van, trying to get as far out of the line of fire as possible. She did not want to get in the way of what Mick obviously had planned for his target. Ever heard the term "collateral damage"?

Something low and menacing rumbled out of the werewolf's mouth, and even though it bore almost no resemblance to actual English, Renny didn't need a translator to work out the hidden message. Something along the lines of, "Die, coyote scum," would be her guess.

"What's the matter, wolf?" Geoffrey asked. "I thought you wanted to kill me. Are you afraid to come in and get me?"

Mick fell back, still growling long and low, and beckoned the coyote forward with deadly claws.

The coward laughed. "Yeah, I don't think so, Michael. I think I'm pretty comfortable inside here and out of the wind. You want me, you're going to have to drag me out."

"You sure about that?"

Zeke joined the conversation by sliding into the recently vacated driver's seat and pressing the muzzle of his pistol against the back of Geoffrey's head. Renny saw the coyote go pale, his eyes widening.

"I think that you have two choices at this point, coyote," the deputy purred. "You can stay where you are and let me shoot you in the head like the bullying fucking coward you are, or you can go out those rear doors and fight my friend there like a real alpha. Now, I'm pretty certain both those options end up with you bleeding out and begging for mercy. The question is whether your friends get the deposit back on this shiny new rental van. So, what's it going to be?"

Mick watched his friend hold a gun to the asshole coyote's head and prayed like hell he wouldn't pull the trigger. A bullet to the head would bring too easy a death for Geoffrey Hilliard. Mick wanted to rip him into tiny little pieces, just to ensure he suffered.

In other circumstances, his own thoughts would have disgusted him, but this was a special situation. This man had spent months and months stalking and tormenting Mick's mate. He had driven her from her home, destroyed her belongings, sent his lackeys chasing after her, and now kidnapped and attempted to rape her. As far as he was concerned, the coyote's suffering would only begin to balance the scales.

"So, what's it going to be?" Zeke asked.

Geoffrey's Adam's apple bobbed, then his features hardened and he yanked his shirt off over his head. "Fine," he spat. "We'll do this the old-fashioned way. I'm not afraid of your fucking mutant beast form, Michael. It might make you bigger and stronger, but let's see how fast you can move."

The man finished stripping, shifted into his fur, and dove at his enemy.

Mick's tongue lolled out in a canine grin. It was about fucking time.

Chapter Nineteen

Renny couldn't hold back her gasp when Geoffrey the coyote launched himself out the back of the van and straight at her mate's ridiculously larger form. For an instant, she expected to see him bounce off the werewolf's chest before being torn apart by those five-inch claws. But Geoffrey hadn't completely lost his mind. Instead of attacking Mick, the coyote copied the move Renny had used to outmaneuver Bryce her first night in Alpha: He threw himself past his opponent to land untouched and ready behind the wolf's back.

Before Mick could spin to face him, Geoffrey darted forward, fangs slashing at the back of the larger animal's leg. He was trying to hamstring the enemy.

Renny recognized the merit of the tactic. The coyote didn't have a prayer of matching the werewolf when it came to size or strength. Even had Mick worn his fully animal form, he still would have outclassed Geoffrey in both areas, so the smaller man had to rely on his one real advantage—speed.

He danced out from under the werewolf's swiping

claws, spinning around to launch another attack at the other leg. This time he scored a more solid hit, and Mick howled as the tendon in his leg tore and weakened.

He went down to one knee, and Geoffrey pulled another unexpected move. Instead of leaping immediately for the werewolf's throat, the coyote gathered itself and threw its full weight against its opponent's weakened legs, attacking its unstable balance and sending Mick sprawling to his back in the dirt.

Shit, shit, shit. She should have known there was no way Geoffrey was going to play fair. She had to get out there and help her mate.

Renny squirmed to the left and froze when her hip rolled over a long, narrow, cold metal object. The knife. She had just rolled onto Geoffrey's knife, only it was currently pressed to her belly, and she needed it behind her back where her hands and feet remained tied. Shit, now she knew why her mother had always encouraged her to take up gymnastics. Maybe her occasional forays into yoga would prove to be enough.

Rocking her weight to the side, Renny slowly and carefully worked to reverse her position without sending the knife sliding away across the slick floor. It took some doing, but she finally managed to get herself flipped onto one side with her back facing the blade. At the moment, back equaled hands, and her fingers itched to close around the sharp object. If she could even manage to free just her feet, she'd be able to run to her mate's side, and then she could—

"Damn it, hold still, you little hellion." Zeke cursed, reaching around her to grab the knife and saw through the rope binding her wrists to her ankles.

Her body immediately unbowed, and she gave a whimper of relief. Her hands and feet remained tied, but at least they weren't being yanked to the small of her back and turning her into a lupine pretzel anymore. The relief was staggering.

"I said hold still," the lion ordered, grabbing and shaking her arms to emphasize his point. "You want me to accidentally cut your wrist instead of this rope? Your mate would finish up with that coyote and have my liver for dessert."

Renny didn't bother to respond. She was too busy gritting her teeth against the pain of the newly restored circulation in her limbs and calculating the time it would take her to shake off the rope, leap out of the van, and rip a certain coyote's heart out once Zeke got her fully untied. She was estimating about 4.7 seconds. Give or take.

Unfortunately, things didn't work out that way. If she thought coming out of the hog-tie had been bad, it was nothing compared with the searing agony of her contorted limbs finally relaxing from the bonds into which they'd been tied. When the last of the rope slipped away, instead of jumping into battle at her mate's side, Renny found herself involuntarily curling into a fetal position, as if her muscles were rubber bands that had stretched too far in one direction and now had to overcompensate by collapsing in the other.

Her eyes watered the same way they had done when Geoffrey was dragging her around by the hair. Shit, it hurt!

She fought to control her breathing and to beat down the red tide of pain that obscured her vision. Okay, she decided semi-hysterically, crossing bondage off the list of kinks she might be willing to try. Really not her thing.

"Oh, shit. Come on, buddy," Zeke muttered, and Renny's eyes popped open immediately. She followed the lion's gaze to where her mate knelt once more in the dirt. He might not be lying on his back anymore, but he clearly hadn't managed to regain his feet, and she could see by the blood on his fur and the oddly limp appearance of his right leg that Geoffrey had gotten in a fortunate swipe and severed the Achilles' tendon. Mick would be lucky if he could stand, let alone walk.

What a pair the two of them made at that moment, she thought, choking back a laugh. Him crippled and on his knees, her so stiff and in such pain, she could barely move. Talk about matches made in heaven.

Mick's fur whipped around in the heavy wind while the coyote faced him uninjured. She saw the smaller animal shift its weight back and felt time slow down.

She knew with perfect clarity what was about to happen. Geoffrey was coiling himself into a position to spring at her mate. One leap would close the distance between them and have his fangs around Mick's throat. The unusual thickness of the muscles in his current form might spare him from the worst possible injury, but all the coyote had to do was get one fang deep enough to nick the carotid artery, and the werewolf would bleed out in seconds.

Her mate would die, and not even the hope of vengeance would be enough to keep Renny from following.

Her body moved on pure instinct.

She didn't plan out her actions. In fact, later when

someone asked her about it, she couldn't remember when the idea had occurred to her, because it didn't really. There was no idea, there was just reflex.

Ignoring the pain and stiffness, ignoring the small chance of success and the impossibly long odds, Renny rolled to the side and in one smooth move, she snatched Zeke's weapon from the holster where he'd replaced it, flicked off the safety, pointed it at the coyote's head, and pulled the trigger.

Of course, this wasn't a movie and Renny wasn't either a stuntwoman or a sharpshooter. She missed. Her bullet went wide of Geoffrey's head and instead struck him in the side, in the vulnerable spot where hip and side and belly all converged. He collapsed to the ground at Mick's feet with a shrill howl.

The werewolf immediately took advantage. Instead of Geoffrey sinking his teeth into the wolf's throat, Mick hurtled forward, never rising off his knees, and closed his powerful jaws around the coyote. He crushed the windpipe and severed the arteries with one vicious tug.

And then, *Holy shit,* Renny thought as the gun slipped from her hands. It was really over.

Chapter Twenty

Renny could barely express her gratitude when the ambulance braked to a stop in the center of the highway and blocked both lanes of traffic. She would owe Molly for the rest of her life for the way her friend quickly assessed and treated her mate, staunching his bleeding, stabilizing his wound, and ensuring that he got loaded quickly and efficiently into the back of the emergency vehicle.

But she would never admit—not under pain of torture—that she didn't breathe easily until her mate arrived at the Alpha Medical Center emergency room, had his tendon stitched back together by Dr. Kirby, and was pronounced in excellent condition. All things considered.

You couldn't drag that admission out of her if you channeled the spirit of Tomás de Torquemada himself. She preferred for her hair to remain *in* her scalp, thank you very much.

Mick had insisted, predictably, that she undergo her own examination, even if he hovered over her and growled low in his throat the entire time. She honestly wasn't sure if in the end, Dr. Kirby didn't pronounce her healthy just out of fear for his own life. Still, his diagnosis of muscle strain, minor lacerations, and a slight sprain to her left shoulder seemed to fit with the way she felt. She'd be back to normal in a few days.

Better than normal, because in a few days her wounds would be healed and she would still be free of Geoffrey Hilliard. The coyote was out of her life forever.

"He's out of everyone's lives, including his own," Zeke observed when she said as much.

A small crowd had gathered in Mick and Renny's living room. A few had made up their escort home from the hospital, such as Zeke and Molly, while others had met them there to offer help, congratulations, and hear the whole story. Already, Jaeger had someone replacing the busted front door, and the broken windowpane was just a distant memory. Deputy Draper would remain in the hospital for another day or two to monitor his serious, but not life-threatening injuries, but at the cabin things looked almost as if nothing dramatic had ever happened.

Well, as long as she ignored the way her mate had his heavily bandaged leg propped up on a pillow atop the coffee table. Just looking at the wound got her hackles up every time.

"I don't think anyone's going to miss him," Jaeger observed.

"Not even the rest of his pack?" Jonas Browning asked. He had tagged along with the mayor, ostensibly to offer his family's aid if there was anything Mick and Renny needed. In reality, Renny suspected it was so he could check her out and decide if she was good enough to meet his precious lupine mate.

"I doubt it," she answered. "Most of them will be just as happy he's gone. He wasn't what you'd call a man of the people."

Mick snuggled her closer. "I just hope for their sake that someone will step up to keep things running. I don't want the town to have to go through a repeat of the mess I caused, especially since this one would be pretty much my fault, too."

"Nope, this one is on me as much as you," she told him. "Besides, those were completely different circumstances. Eight years ago, Sawmill lost a multigenerational pack hierarchy. This time all they're missing is one egomaniac and a handful of his demented friends. I think the town will be able to go back to the way it was before Geoffrey took over, just a regular small town with an interesting mix of humans and independently minded shifters."

"That sounds a little like us." Molly grinned. "Except for the human parts."

"Yeah, I think 'independently minded' is one way to describe the folks around here," Jaeger drawled, then chuckled.

"And epic pains in the ass is another," Zeke grumbled. "I don't think I've had a day off or a night with more than five hours of sleep in a month. And all because of all the independent minds I'm sworn to serve and protect."

"Don't worry, Zee. The council is preparing to hear the proposal for Sheriff Lahern's new budget. I have it on good authority that there's a high probability he'll get approval to hire at least two more full-time deputies. Apparently, residents are concerned about rising crime in the area."

Renny winced. "Yeah, sorry about that. Do you happen to know if these residents in question have a favorite kind of cookie?"

"Not. Your. Fault," Mick growled. He squeezed her hand. "You need to stop taking responsibility for everything that goes wrong around here, little red, before you start trying to stop the rain in April."

Molly shook her head and gave an exaggerated sigh. "I've tried to knock that into her head, Mick, but the girl is stubborn. I hope you know what you signed up for with this one."

Mick turned his head to smile down at his mate. She couldn't see a single shadow left in his gorgeous blue eyes. They had each walked through the worst life had to offer, and now there was nothing left for them but each other, and was there any other definition of the best?

"Oh, I know," he purred, his attention all for Renny. "I know exactly what I'm going to get."

"Me, too." Renny laid her hand against his cheek and returned his smile. "We get each other."

"And the rest of our lives," Mick promised, and kissed her. "Let's get started on those."

Look for the next novel in
the Alphaville series
by Christine Warren

YOUR
LION
EYES

Available in May 2018

from St. Martin's Paperbacks

And don't miss these other paranormal romance novels
from bestselling author

Christine Warren

The Gargoyles series
HARD BREAKER
HARD TO HANDLE
HARD AS A ROCK
STONE COLD LOVER
HEART OF STONE

The Others series
HUNGRY LIKE A WOLF
DRIVE ME WILD
ON THE PROWL
NOT YOUR ORDINARY FAERIE TALE
BLACK MAGIC WOMAN
PRINCE CHARMING DOESN'T LIVE HERE
BORN TO BE WILD
BIG BAD WOLF
YOU'RE SO VEIN
ONE BITE WITH A STRANGER
WALK ON THE WILD SIDE
HOWL AT THE MOON
THE DEMON YOU KNOW
SHE'S NO FAERIE PRINCESS
WOLF AT THE DOOR

Anthologies
HUNTRESS
NO REST FOR THE WITCHES

From St. Martin's Paperbacks